THE LOST GUARD'S HEALER

Alexa Ashe

THE LOST GUARD'S HEALER

Copyright © 2024 by Alexa Ashe

All rights reserved.

No portion of this book may be reproduced, distributed, or transmitted in any form or by any means, including photocopying, recording, or other electronic or mechanical means, without the prior written permission from the publisher or author, except for the use of brief quotations in book reviews.

This book is a work of fiction. The characters and events in this book are fictitious. Any similarity to persons, living or dead, real or fictional, is purely coincidental and not intended by the author.

https://www.facebook.com/authoralexaashe

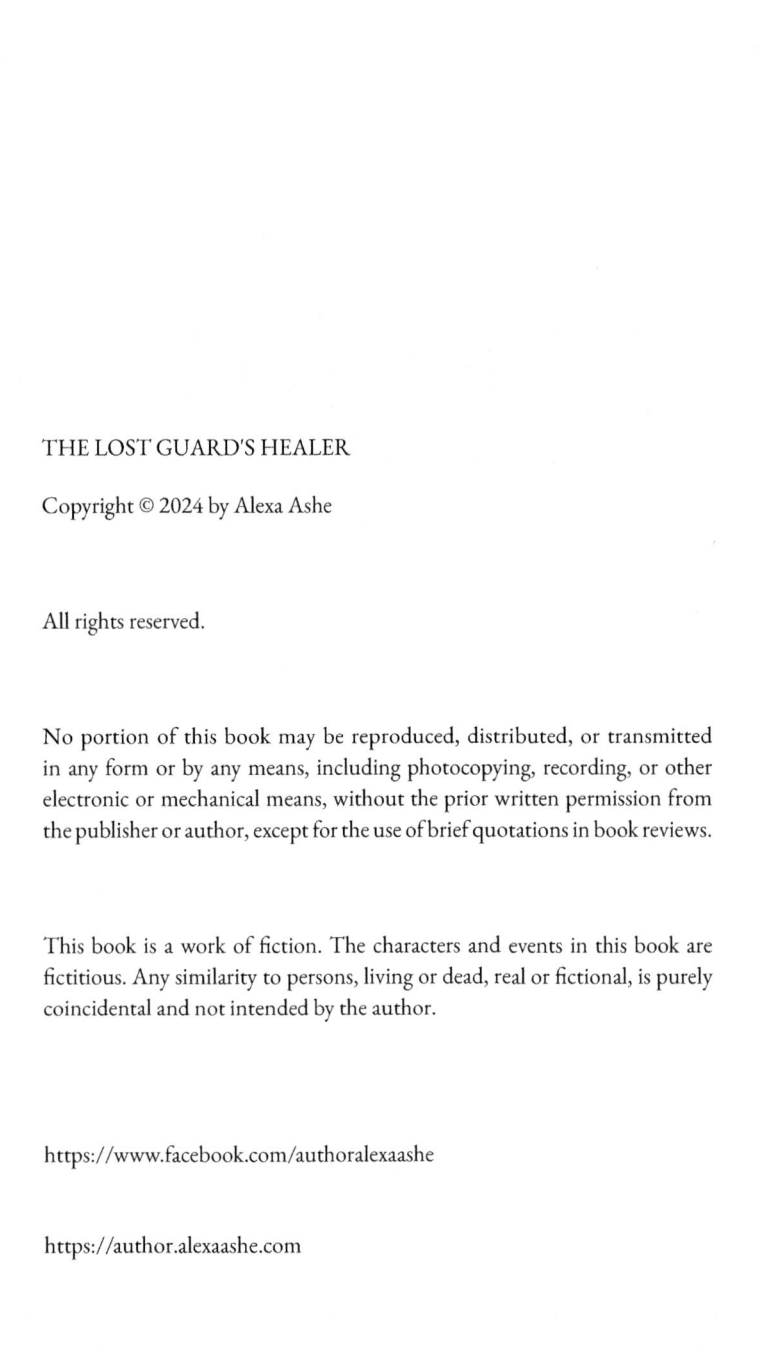

https://author.alexaashe.com

CONTENTS

Prologue	1
1. Rourk	3
2. Rourk	12
3. Rourk	21
4. Galene	33
5. Galene	39
6. Rourk	47
7. Rourk	59
8. Rourk	66
9. Rourk	73
10. Rourk	83
11. Galene	91
12. Galene	100
13. Galene	105

14.	Rourk	115
15.	Galene	121
16.	Rourk	133
17.	Rourk	139
18.	Galene	147
19.	Rourk	152
20.	Rourk	165
21.	Galene	168
22.	Rourk	176
23.	Rourk	186
24.	Rourk	201
25.	Galene	207
26.	Rourk	215
27.	Rourk	220
28.	Rourk	228
29.	Galene	234
30.	Rourk	240
31.	Rourk	245
32.	Galene	250
33.	Galene	260

34. Rourk	267
Epilogue	273
What's Next	275
Also by	278
About Author	280

PROLOGUE

Galene

The sight of him is a wretched thing.

He is Oathlander all over. From the precise shade of his skin down to the dark shade of his eyes that I've seen on the rare occasions they've been open.

I wish my father wasn't foolish enough to ask me to heal him. Even more, I wish he wasn't cruel enough to make it my Task.

Meaning I have no other option. If I ever want to be valued in this community—if I ever want to be someone or something beyond a whispered name and a stain of shame to my family, I have no choice.

Like clockwork, I rouse the bulky Oathlander from sleep with slow, gentle touches. Anything else and I fear I'll frighten him into a stupor of an attack. Not that I couldn't take him—especially with the rotten shape he's in—but I'd rather he not ruin all my hard work and force me to start over with him again. I've already spent far longer in the presence of an Oathlander than I ever intended to.

What would my mother think if she knew I was caring for one of them? What would she think if she knew my father had all but forced me to?

I toss the questions aside. The answers don't matter. It wouldn't change anything. I would still be here, mixing tonic into a bowl of soup to keep the Oathlander from starving, mixed with something that I give him to heal him—and to keep him asleep a little longer. I'm not quite ready to face him, as harmless as he may be in his current state.

Not quite ready to look a monster in the eyes.

Chapter One

ROURK

Falling. Darkness. And then nothing.

I jerk awake with a cry, my muscles tense and ready to fight for my life. It takes several long seconds for me to adjust to my surroundings, my vision coming back blurry and dull before eventually clearing.

I'm in a round hut with a campfire simmering in the center, faint wisps of smoke drifting out through a hole in the domed ceiling. At first I think I'm on the ground, but I see I'm lying on a straw bed with a thick, coarse blanket beneath me and a furred blanket over me. My shoulders heave and my heavy breaths sound loud in the quiet air. The strong earthy stench in the air, like mud and feces, makes me think of animal stables and almost makes me gag. But at least I'm alive. It smells like actual shit here, but I'm alive.

Where am I? This is like no place I've ever been. Or is it? Maybe I have and I just don't remember it. My mind feels blurred, like fragments are missing.

I know who I am, though, and that's something. Rourk Bearon, General Commander of the Oathland's Military. Second-in-Command to the Grandmaster General Darius Archaeus. I can remember all that, but not where I am or how I got here. I've yet to decide whether or not that's a good thing. Maybe I'm somewhere safe right now—or maybe I'd be better off dead.

I sit up to get a better look at the dimly lit surroundings and hiss out a breath when a flood of pain hits me. My arms give way and I drop back on the rough bedding. My first thought is that I'm injured. Or drugged. I'm too weary to think straight.

The heavy flaps of the hut entranceway shift aside as someone comes in. Bright sunlight streams in momentarily through the shifting flaps, almost blinding me. It's a woman; tall and slim with long dark hair falling about her broad shoulders. The sight of her heightens my confusion, which immediately shifts to alarm. The worn cream dress she wears has wide sleeves and the long, sleeveless cardigan flowing about her is frail and extremely weathered, with several holes. Her vibrantly bright blue eyes contrast against her tanned complexion. This is no Oathlander. That's clear enough.

Better off dead might not have been too far off.

I've been kidnapped and am being held prisoner.

The woman, who must be in her late twenties, seems vaguely surprised to see me awake. I can't help but stare into those eyes as I try to gauge her intentions. Friend or threat?

She watches me for a long, quiet moment. Then she turns sharply away. "You should rest," she says absently as she goes about the hut, no longer interested in me.

"Should I?" I've managed to prop myself on one elbow to get a better view of her. My other shoulder flares with pain if I try to move it, but I bite down on the groan that threatens to leave me and ignore it.

"Yes, you should," she says, her sharper tone brooking no argument. "If you want to get back on your feet."

"What's wrong with my feet?"

I can tell from the way she huffs out a breath that she won't be answering that question. While she collects a pot and pours water from a leather skin into it, I shift my legs under the blanket. Dark discomfort swells through me. I can barely move my legs. They feel like dead weight. I can *feel* them, though, and can shift them ever so slightly. They certainly won't support my weight, though.

"How did I get here?" I ask, figuring that bluntness is better than pretending I'm not confused and, honestly, fifteen seconds away from contributing to the smell of shit around me. Her back is to me as she prepares something on a table. The curve of the ceiling almost reaches her head.

"We found you on a riverbank in the East Garlands," she says with an almost bored air. "You're lucky to be alive." Stoicism emanates from every word and every movement. Something tells me she couldn't care less if I lived or died.

East Garlands. The name is vaguely familiar, but not familiar enough that I could point to it on a map. Someplace north of the Oathlands, perhaps?

The woman brushes her hands together and steps away from the table, then surveys the tent with a calculating eye before taking a few quick steps to the diminishing flames across the room. She squats by the dying fire and strikes two stones together. On the second strike, a spark flies out and ignites the twigs and clumps of weeds she just added. She expertly blows into the glowing embers until flames begin to lick and crack, slowly gathering in strength. I'm actually impressed at how effortless that was for her. I know less than a dozen people who could light a fire like that so easily.

"Who are you?" I ask.

"That is none of your concern," she says, ignoring me once again as she collects a pot from the table and sets it over the fire. Something dark swishes within the pot.

"I beg to differ," I say, in a challenging mood. "I should know my captor."

"I am not your captor," she snaps, and leaves it at that. She doesn't seem to be very talkative and I get the sense of annoyance every time she speaks. Although there is no outright hostility. Yet.

She kneels by the fire and crushes a few leaves and flowers into the pot. As she does so, the split of her skirt unfolds to reveal a shapely, smooth, toned thigh.

Has she intentionally revealed her thigh and is pretending not to have noticed? What game is she playing? I gaze over the room, not wanting to stare.

Every item in the tent looks worn and weathered. It's a simple way of living with the bare basics: a table with two stools as chairs, a large trunk with a pile of furred blankets on top, and a bucket containing some clutter that looks like hunting tools and weapons. Two rabbit hides are on hooks on the curved walls. A fishing pole is in the corner. A familiar dark blue jacket is hanging over a high-backed chair. My military jacket.

I'm no longer wearing my full uniform, I notice. My armor is missing, as are my shirt and vest. I'm in a dingy white vest that has several small holes and is far too big for me. They kept my military pants on, which is some comfort. My boots and socks must be somewhere in the hut as well. I guess it's too much to ask to have kept my sword nearby.

"Is where I am none of my concern also?" I ask.

She half-suppresses a sigh as she goes back to the table. "You're a long way from home, Oathlander. I suggest you rest and get your strength back if you want to return home."

While her voice is light and youthful, there is something dark in her tone. Something almost threatening, and she says Oathland as if it is an insult. I can't place her clipped accent. It's certainly not a local one.

I don't think I'm anywhere in the Kingdom either. Kingdom folk would not have called me an Oathlander. They have more colorful terms and curses for their sworn enemies. And no one in the Kingdom would keep me alive. Besides, Kingdom folk love nothing more than to tell people who they are and where they're from. So maybe I'm not as bad off as I originally thought.

One other thing makes me think I'm clearly not anywhere near the Kingdom, which some consider the beacon of civilization and say it is like coins flow through the streets, is that it would be nowhere as homely and simple as this hut. The air, despite its harsh earthy odors, feels fresh and open.

We found you on a riverbank in the East Garlands.

Her words spark a flash of a memory. Then a flood of vivid images hit me hard.

The Oathlands had been under attack from the Kingdom. I was on a bridge, and it had snapped. I'd fallen into the darkness below. I must have fallen into a river and washed up somewhere. Yes, I remember my last moments, thinking I was going to die as I fell.

I feel like I had just been dreaming of falling. Like I'd been having those flashes during my sleep. The thought of all that pain and fear makes me feel even weaker, and my head throbs.

"How long have I been here?" I ask.

The smell of mint and something like damp soil drifts through the hut, coming from the steaming pot over the fire.

The woman clears a few things from the table, stoppering vials and wrapping leaves in a parcel. The lack of responsiveness from her irks me.

"Two weeks," she finally says as she takes a mug and a ladle to the pot. "You've been in and out of consciousness. This isn't the first time you've been awake, but it's the first you've spoken since you arrived."

Two weeks? And I've been awake before? I don't remember any of it. The thought fills me with dread. I need to get back to May. To Arthur. I don't even know what state the Oathlands are in. Did Clio survive the attack? Are any of them still alive? My heart hammers in my chest as thoughts race through my brain. I shouldn't be here. I should be home.

I try to rise but don't get very far before I collapse back onto the straw bed, completely exhausted and gasping for breath.

It takes me a moment to realize the woman is standing beside me. She leans down to hand me a mug of the concoction that had been brewing in the pot. It smells like foul tea.

"Drink this for now," she says, her voice not entirely without care. "I will be back later."

I glance at the drink and curl my lips. "I'm not thirsty," I lie.

She gives me a flat look that tells me she wasn't asking. "It will help you get better."

I remain firm, intent on not backing down. I don't like how much she's insisting on me drinking it. I don't like being forced to do something. Especially when that something is a suspicious and unnamed drink from a suspicious and unnamed girl.

"You should drink it while it is hot," she says.

"Why? Because the poison is most potent when it's hot?" The words are out before I can stop them, before I can work through something smarter to say. An angle to work. Maybe I should have played dumb.

She gives me a small smile that softens her features. "No. Because berrybush tea tastes best when hot."

So that's what this is? Some kind of tea? I will not fall for that.

We remain there for a long moment, staring each other down. Her enormous eyes are so blue and captivating, but they are just the allure. The illusion. I see the real, calculating, haughty woman within.

I decide to try to appeal to that version of her. If I can get her angry, I can get her off balance. That's the way to play this. "I can't imagine it tastes good at all when it smells like a homeless man's bathwater."

She scowls at me, growing red with anger, and then throws the mug across the room. It crashes against a wooden trunk and shatters.

"If I wanted you dead, you foolish brute, I wouldn't have spent so long saving you." Her words come out like hisses. "Perhaps I shouldn't have. You don't seem like you were worth the time." She looks like she wants to strangle me, her hands clenched into tight fists as she glares at me. But she doesn't take another step toward me. No—she turns away and storms out in a huff, muttering words that sound foreign to me.

I try to see beyond the falling tent flaps but can't make out much beyond the sunlight. As I lay back on the straw bed, staring at the curved roof, I wonder what had angered her so much. I almost feel a little bad and have to wonder if she was genuinely hurt, or if it was some kind of act. I can't be certain about anything right now.

I have to stick with the facts. I almost died, and now I'm here. My legs don't work and I'm weak as hell.

Have they been slipping me that tea in my delirium? Is that what has made me so weak? Or would that genuinely have made me feel better?

I look around freely now, trying to see everything I can. The remains of the clay mug lay by the trunk. The tea has stained the hard earth. It's then that I notice another stain on the other side of the trunk, and my heart quickens.

The dark patch of old, dried blood is clear to me. But whose blood was that? Mine? If I've been here as long as she says... my throat thickens with fear.

Within a bundle of cloths nearby, a large bone is jutting out. It looks like a human bone. It's been picked clean and polished.

With a sickening drop of my stomach, I suddenly know where I am. I've been brought to the Wildlands. I must have been found by the Wildmen. That means it's a wonder I haven't been skinned and eaten yet.

The Wildmen are a mysterious nomadic people out in the wilderness, known to be uncivilized savages. And cannibals. That blue-eyed woman hadn't seemed like a savage and had appeared somewhat intelligent. But that must be a ruse.

I'm glad I didn't drink that tea. Who knows what it would've done to me?

I have to find a way to escape before they tear me apart and roast me over a fire.

Or worse.

Chapter Two

ROURK

It's not until I drift back into consciousness that I realize I'd fallen asleep. The pounding in my head has lessened, but the lack of movement in my legs is very disconcerting.

I don't know how long I've been out for, but it feels like some time has passed. A shaft of white-hot sunlight is streaming through a gap in the hut flaps, which are softly billowing in the breeze. I can hear muted voices beyond the hut but can't make out any of the words. Just indistinct chatter. And bird chirps, I think.

I should try to leave before that woman comes back, but it's soon clear that my legs will not be supporting my weight any time soon. And I still feel a lingering fatigue in my bones.

They must have drugged me. The broken shards of the mug are no longer there, and the tea stain has dried up. The old blood stain is still there, as is the bone in the cloths.

I pause at the sight of a knife hilt on top of a small chest across the hut. A sheathed knife is there. Waiting for me.

A hidden weapon would do me just fine. I need to get back home and check on May. I need to know if she survived the attack on the city. She probably thinks I'm dead. Everyone must think I'm dead.

I sigh as I heave myself off the bedding and begin crawling on my belly, pulling myself along with my hands and elbows. My useless legs drag behind me. My left shoulder burns with pain, but I ignore it and keep going. I pass the remains of the fire in the center of the hut and maneuver myself around the large trunk. The dark stain has the metallic stench of old blood.

Gods, I hate how weak I am, and how heavy my head feels. I've never felt so useless inside my own body before.

But I'm getting closer to the knife.

The hut flaps fly open and the woman enters to find my arm reaching out, inches away from the sheathed knife on the chest. With a huff, she springs into action and kicks the knife away to send it falling out of view.

"I told you to reserve your strength," she hisses. Her angry scowl tells me she means business. "I'm not dragging you around. You got yourself into this, you get yourself out of it. Now, *back* on your bed." She throws an arm out and points at the bedding like she's scolding a child.

"Just a minute," I say, rolling onto my back and catching my breath.

Her eyes flash with something dark and she looks like she's about to yell. I nod wearily and begin my long trek back to the bedding. I notice my legs shift as I twist around, but don't bring attention to them. Maybe I'm not so weak after all.

"Why do you want me... to get better?" I ask between heavy breaths as I climb onto the bedding. I feel like an animal crawling through the dirt. "You're just going to kill me, anyway." I don't mention the being eaten part.

She gives me a quizzical look, tilting her head. I hate how hard she is to read. I can usually guess what someone is thinking or feeling. But this woman is a rock.

"You are not a prisoner, and your life is not in danger. I promise you this," she says with mild annoyance, like the idea of me being murdered in the Wildlands is so obnoxiously far fetched.

"Then I demand to go outside. I want some air, and to see my surroundings. If I'm not a prisoner, you will permit me this."

She crosses her arms over her chest and eyes me, as if judging my character. "How will you go outside? I'm not carrying you." There's a childish stubbornness in her tone. Like she's used to being given everything she wants.

"So I am imprisoned here?" I say. Without waiting for a response, I add, "You have made a big mistake bringing me here. You will have the full might of the Oathlands on your backs, and they will rain down hellfire if you harm me." I do my best to sound fierce, despite my position laying on the bedding.

The woman almost looks like she's about to laugh, which irritates me. "You don't listen very well. I've told you. You are not a prisoner. You would be dead were it not for us." She begins preparing things on the table again. Another tea?

I allow myself a moment to master my breathing and collect my thoughts. "Who are you? What is your name?"

Beyond the hut, conversational voices become a little louder, although I still can't make out the words. I think I hear a burst of children's laughter, but then I wonder if that was a trick of the wind.

"What do you want from me?" I ask. After more silence, I add, "What's in that tea?"

All of my questions go ignored as she sparks another fire and sets the pot over it.

Gods, why is this woman so frustrating? "I don't know what your customs are," I say through my teeth, "but where I'm from, it's rude to ignore someone."

That gets no reaction from her. I broke her cool exterior before, but it seems she's honed it with steel now. I drop my head back and have no choice but to rest. Weariness is seeping into my bones and making my eyelids heavy.

The woman prepares the tea and places another clay mug beside my bedding. She leaves without another word. Steam wafts from the mug and dissipates in the air.

I consider searching for another weapon, but my thoughts drift away as exhaustion overwhelms me. Sleep embraces me. Sweet, sweet rest.

I snap awake at the sound of heavy boots approaching the hut. Judging by the sun still streaming in through the hut flaps, and the steam coming off the tea, I don't think I've been out for long.

A bearded man in a fur cloak enters. He appears middle-aged, though it's hard to be certain from his full beard and weathered look. A faded green tunic and dusty pants speak of a life mostly spent outdoors. His thick boots look made for cross-country travel and are caked in mud. His salt-and-pepper beard matches his heavy eyebrows and thick hair that's tied in a loose tail.

"How is our guest?" the man asks, his voice deep and softly booming. A corner of his mouth rises, shifting his beard.

"Where I'm from, we treat our guests a little differently," I say as I shift myself onto my elbows.

"I'm sure you do a great many things differently," the man says with humor. There is something familiar in his deep, dark-blue eyes. He steps further inside and checks the full mug of tea beside me. "I apologize for my daughter. She... has a temperament. Her mother was the same."

"Who are you?" I ask.

"My name is Aldus Tavaris. Some know me as a keeper of books. Others know me as a drinker of ale." He gives me a crooked, humor-filled smile and clears a few things from a stool and sits with a heavy sigh.

"You are a Wildman?" I ask.

He grins at me, his dark eyes gleaming with mischief. "There is a lot for you to learn, Oathlander. Now that we can talk, might I ask your name?"

I consider that for a moment. "Tarin." I give the name of one of my soldiers. I don't want them to know my status. "I had requested to go outside and see my surroundings, but your daughter was more interested in ignoring me."

Aldus rolls his eyes. "Yes. I apologize for that as well. Well, you going outside won't be easy. I'm not a young man anymore, and you don't seem the type to be comfortable being carried out like a babe. However, I believe I can make it work."

He stands up with a grunt and eyes the tea beside me. "I suggest you drink that while it's still warm. It has a nasty aftertaste once cooled. And if there's one thing my daughter knows how to do, it's make a good mug of tea."

As he makes his way to the exit, I ask, "Can you tell me where I am?"

He stops and gives me a sideways look. "I will show you. Allow me a moment."

I drop my head back and let out a weary sigh after he leaves. When I test my legs, I see they have a little more life in them. I can just about wiggle my toes and, with some effort, can slightly bend my knees. But the actions require a lot of effort and concentration.

The minty scent of the tea does smell good. *No, don't drink it*, I tell myself. *Not until you know more about your situation.* If these Wildmen truly want to kill me and devour my body, I will not make it easy for them.

I sit up with some effort. At least the throbbing in my head is gone.

Aldus soon returns, and he is carrying two long sticks. A handle lashed with twine to both sticks tells me they are crutches. The bearded man has a gentle touch to him as he helps me up and hands me the crutches to support my weight. On my feet, the sticks take almost my entire weight. Thankfully, the tops of the sticks are padded with cloth tied with string, so they don't dig into my armpits. That gesture alone is almost enough to have me relaxing, nevermind the fact that he gave me makeshift crutches at all. But I wonder if it's meant to ease me, to allay my suspicions.

I don't let myself fall for any of their tricks.

"How are they?" Aldus asks.

I take a tentative step forward. The right stick gets caught in a crack in the earth and throws me off balance. Aldus catches me before I fall.

"Easy. Easy," he says. "Take your time. Go slow. Here. Come on."

He stays close as he encourages me to take a few more steps. I manage to shift forward without falling, but I hate how weak my arms are. My whole body feels soft and frail. And I have to ignore the pain flaring in my left shoulder. I wonder if I've broken a collarbone or something in my shoulder. There are old scrapes on my arms, but no major signs of damage. I wonder how broken I was when they found me on the riverside.

Aldus has his arms out as though he's ready to catch me at any moment as he slowly backs out of the hut. I get the sense that he's a good man with a good heart, but I remind myself not to trust anyone.

I blink against the harsh daylight as I finally step out of the hut, the flaps falling away over my shoulders. It takes a moment for my eyes to adjust.

It's late morning or early afternoon. The sun is somewhere behind the clouds, mottling the blue sky. A vast field is before me, and many people are roaming about. Several smaller and larger huts are among enormous tent structures, rising over the huts like rooftops.

Everyone I see is in weathered clothing. Loose cardigans, baggy sweaters, open vests, flowing dresses. They seem to like browns, creams, and grays, as most are dressed in those colors. Some people gather by a circle of logs with a fire in the center. A stick frame suspends an enormous cauldron over the fire.

Children's laughter cuts through the air. There's a group of them playing by a muddy pond across the way. I look upon elderly women, young boys, and some women with babes in their arms. They are simply going about their lives. There are even clothes hanging on a line, billowing lazily in the warm breeze. Farther across the field, beyond a collection of trees, I see what looks like a river bank.

This is a town. A town of Wildmen. But not a town of feral savages. I never thought they'd be so organized. And so calm. I hadn't been expecting this at all.

I turn to Aldus, who has been watching me closely. "I may have gotten the Wildmen wrong," I admit. "I didn't know you lived this... harmoniously."

Aldus's grin shifts his beard. "We are not Wildmen."

I raise my eyebrows with surprise, and he seems to enjoy my confused look.

Then something crosses the sky and catches my eye. I straighten at the sight of a figure cutting through the air in the distance. It's a person, and they are... flying in the air. A trail of golden dust-like light disperses in their wake. It takes me several seconds to understand I really am seeing someone flying.

I feel my mouth hanging open when someone sitting by the cauldron reaches out, and a spark flies from their fingertip. The spark hits the fire and strengthens it in a rush of hot air. Before I can recover from this, a small dog runs by me, yapping near my legs. But it isn't a dog.

It's a fox-like animal with auburn fur. Three fluffy tails are wagging happily from its rear as it circles my feet. As it darts away, I'm even more stunned to notice its paws are not directly striking the ground. It's effortlessly gliding through the air, a few inches from the ground.

Aldus is chuckling at my slack-jawed, wide-eyed expression.

"Come," he says. "Allow me to show you around. We have a lot to explain."

Chapter Three
ROURK

I manage to move around the village with the crutches, though my steps are infuriatingly slow. I'm not used to feeling so helpless, but for now, I take each moment as it comes. I'm still getting used to my surroundings and I have a lot of questions about what I've seen.

The people around me have wide faces with flawless, smooth skin. Some have large foreheads or heavy brows, while others have powerful jawlines. Very few of the men have facial hair. They are mostly dressed in furs and woven clothing, looking very rugged and rural. A life spent in rough surroundings with meager possessions. What catches my attention is the vibrancy of their eyes, which are mostly vivid blue or emerald. Only a few have dark eyes, but even those have glints of bright color when they catch the light.

"And so, once the Fae Queen reconnected with her magic, she opened the rest of the world to the magic that was locked for so long," Aldus tells me. He has a similar heavy tone and clipped way of speaking to the woman who had made the tea for me. It's a slow, deliberate way of talking. While he speaks the Standard Tongue well, it's clear he has picked up his own inflections and way of saying certain words.

"I don't quite understand," I say, hobbling beside him as we walk around. "How does a long-lost Fae bring magic to the entire world?"

Aldus gives a bewildered smirk that shifts his beard. "You will have to ask her that."

"This Fae Queen," I say. "Her name is Clio? Clio De'Kalo?"

Aldus shrugs. "We don't know her name. People just call her the Fae Queen. They say she is with Arthur Bearon. That is a name we know well."

"Oh?" I ask, feigning ignorance.

"The Grandson of the old Queen of the Oathlands, yes. He and his brother... Ryon, I believe."

Well. That stings me a little.

"Anyway," Aldus goes on. "The Lord Bearon rules now with his Fae Queen. A lot has changed in these past two weeks."

"I can see that," I say as I almost stumble on a rock.

"Stay," Aldus says. "Rest here a moment." He has a gentle hand when he helps me to sit on a nearby tree stump.

It's a relief to know that Arthur and Clio still live. I have no way of knowing if my daughter May made it out of the attack alive, but I have to hold on to hope.

A glowing ball of golden light swoops through the air in the distance. A fairy? Like from the old stories? I shake my head and crack a smile. I had underestimated Clio, and I feel bad for having been so short with her for so long. It had only been near the end when I'd seen how good she was, and how strong of heart and mind. I hope I get the chance to apologize to her.

I ask more questions, and Aldus seems happy to entertain them.

"Those who had magic in their bloodline simply woke up one day to discover they could access their magical abilities," he tells me. "They could summon magic, or fly, or control the elements, and many other unique gifts."

"And that three-tailed fox I saw earlier?" I ask. "Where did he come from?"

Aldus raises a hand to encompass the field. "From all over. The fiorin have been revealing themselves these past two weeks."

"Fiorin?"

"That's what we call the magical creatures," Aldus says. "We believed they had gone into hibernation, or simply vanished from existence once they were cut off from the magic that gave them life. People are looking into where the creatures were and how they have come back, I believe."

I look up to see a short, older woman is approaching us. Her long auburn hair is tied back loosely, which emphasizes the round fullness of her face. Up close, I see she might be closer to Aldus's age, with thin lines around her eyes as she gives me a broad smile.

"I see our guest is awake," she says, coming to a stop before us and clasping her hands behind her. Her tanned complexion is a shade of maroon, more red than brown.

"Magdalena," Aldus says. "I was hoping we would see you." He turns to address me. "Tarin. This is Magdalena Othas, a village elder."

"Oh, shush," Magdalena says with a wave of her hand. "My mother is an elder. I am still a... youngster."

They share a quiet laugh.

Their deliberate, controlled speech has a formal air about it. It reminds me of the way people used to speak in the olden days. A way that some people make fun of these days on account of how stiff they sounded.

Magdalena says, "I hope you do not mind me saying. You are far thinner than when you were first brought in. Allow me to have a meal prepared for you. You must be starving."

"Galene has been tending to him," Aldus says with a defensive air. "Our guest is well cared for."

"Of course," Magdalena says with a polite smile. "I simply meant we have some sister wives preparing lunch, and that I can spare a plate for our Oathland guest."

"That is very kind of you. Thank you," I reply. "You're a... village elder, is it?"

"Some day," she says. "In training, you might say. Though some already see me as one. But, no, my mother is the elder. I'm sure you will meet them. They are nice."

"Everyone here seems very nice," I say, not counting Galene. "I'm embarrassed to say we have the Wildland folk wrong back home."

"But of course you do," Magdalena says diplomatically. "As do we, with you Oathlanders, I'm sure. It has been so long since our people have communicated."

"Old blood," I say. "Old ways. Change can be difficult."

She gives me a knowing look with a small smile. She seems like a smart one, with quiet intelligence and a calculating way about her. I've always thought I could read people well, and can see that same quality in others who share it.

"I agree," she says. "One thing you should know is that we are not Wildland folk. We are the Shanti People. Very different, I assure you. I believe many across the land think of us as savages, but that is because they do not know us. They confuse us with the real savages out there."

I'm getting used to the slow, controlled manner of speaking these people have. And Magdalena's low voice has a soothing quality. It feels odd to have them both standing over me while I'm sitting.

"Shanti People," I repeat. "I'm afraid we do not know of your people."

Aldus nods. "We prefer to keep it that way. Stay out of others' affairs and keep to our own."

"There is so much conflict in the world," Magdalena says with a frown that creases her brow. "Terrible wars. Many deaths. You've seen your fair share, I imagine. All know the warring between The Kingdom and the Oathlands."

"I'm relieved to hear there is still an Oathlands to return to," I say. I don't tell them the particular circumstances how I had left the Oathlands and ended up washed up by a riverbank, although I see the question in their eyes. It's not something I'm ready to think about, and especially not something I want to talk about. With strangers. Who may or may not be bad people.

I'm having a hard time deciding.

"And we will get you back there," Magdalena says. "I must go help the sister wives for now. Please, Tarin, if you need anything, please ask. I'm happy to help. I will return with some food that I'm sure will satisfy you." She pauses and adds, "You eat mucus and fish eyes, correct?"

My face freezes.

Magdalena and Aldus both break into laughter.

"I'm sorry," she says. "Just teasing. I couldn't help myself." She chuckles, holding a hand against her stomach.

What an interesting sense of humor.

I nod my thanks as she leaves us.

"Is there more to see?" I ask Aldus. "I have the strength to keep walking now."

Aldus seems to consider that. "I will continue the tour, yes. If you'll follow me."

I take a deep breath and sigh as I rise to my feet and begin walking with the crutches. Magdalena was right. I have lost some weight and muscle. My arms still have some shape to them but they've lost their fullness.

Children's laughter carries in the wind, mixing with the low hum of conversations and people mingling about. Many eyes are on me, I notice. They all want a good look at the foreigner in their midst. One small child whimpers when she sees me and hides behind the legs of her mother.

"What is a sister wife?" I ask Aldus.

"What you call a widow," he responds. "They devote their time to care for the village, as they would care for their husbands."

"Is that a common thing here? Losing husbands?"

"We have hostility toward no one, and none to call our enemy. But the Wildlands, as you call it, can be a dangerous place. There are few laws and rules out here, and no one to maintain order but ourselves. And I believe you'll find there are more diseases and ailments in these less civilized parts of the world."

"You seem very civilized to me."

Aldus nods. "And yet there are those who would look down upon us, and our way of living."

"That's The Kingdom folk you're thinking of. Us Oathlanders are far more welcoming and open to others. Well, compared to them, anyway."

He stops and eyes me firmly. "I used to think that was the right way of thinking. 'Us' and 'them'. Which folk are better, and which are worse? But, as I get older, I see how futile that way of thinking is. I'd like to see us all as one people. All living in the same world, with the same desires to live, to be warm and fed, and to find some semblance of peace in our lives."

"Well said." I'm impressed. "If only others had some of your wisdom."

We round a fence and head towards a collection of vegetable patches. The ground is more even here, and walking on the short grass is better than the rocky earth.

"You said you are a... keeper of books?" I remember what he'd told me earlier.

"I did say that. I am someone who cherishes the past dearly and holds on to it. I have a grand collection of books which I hope will educate the next generations, so they know the past and can use it to shape their future."

"If we do not know our past," I say, "we cannot learn from our mistakes."

Aldus raises an eyebrow, clearly just as impressed with me as I am with him. A small smile curves his mouth upward. "Exactly. Some tease me for my collection, and it has earned me the title Keeper of Books."

"We call it a historian," I say.

"Yes. We have that term, as well."

As we walk, Aldus points out notable people and places to me. He points to the tops of the larger tents over the huts where many families live. Up on a hill is where they pick flowers. I learn that flowers have many benefits and purposes here. They add them to their food, their tea, and their medicine.

We pass a group of elderly women who seem lost in their own worlds as they pick seeds from fruits and pop beans from their shells.

A young man with flowing long hair is coming out from a collection of trees. He is bare-chested and has a muscular physique, but a softness around the edges that makes him look more like a boy than a man. A wet sack is over his shoulder.

"Freddick," Aldus says. "How are the fish today?"

"Bountiful," Freddick says with a beaming grin. There is a bounce to his step, and he seems to brim with energy. The wet stench of fish is coming from the sack over his shoulder, and beads of water on his torso are glistening in the sunlight.

Freddick's eyes widen when he sees me. "Oh, it's you. I mean, you're... I didn't think you were..."

"Our guest, Tarin, is awake and moving about, yes," Aldus says. "I'm sure at this point you're the last to know." He gestures to the young man and says to me, "Freddick here is our newest hunter."

"What do you hunt around here?" I ask.

"Whatever the land provides," Aldus says. "Rabbit. Wild boar. Fish. Frogs. Birds. The occasional snake, when we find edible ones. We used to have chickens, but they died off."

"And crickets," Freddick says, scrunching his face. "The worst."

I figure he must barely be out of his teens. I can't imagine him taking down a wild boar. That must be why they are having him catch fish.

"I was just going back to hand the fish to the sister wives," Freddick says, "before I head back to the fishermen. But I can find a cup of water for you."

"Oh, that's okay, really," I say, but my words go unheeded.

"It's no trouble at all. It would be my pleasure. Here, I will be right back before you know it." He flashes an infectious grin.

Freddick rushes off before I can stop him. Some water does sound good, though. I'm regretting not drinking that tea Aldus's daughter had made for me.

"Freddick is untested, but eager to do well," Aldus says to me. "He is hungry to do as many Tasks as he can. He should make a formidable hunter when he's older."

I stretch my shoulders and my neck when my muscles cramp up. I'm still getting used to my arms doing most of the work while walking and my muscles have started to burn.

Aldus leads me to a small hut where an old lady is sitting outside. Beside her is a log that has a cushion draped over it. I sit on the cushion with a heavy breath, feeling sweat beading on my forehead. The woman is staring at me, but she seems unbothered. Her deeply tanned complexion has a strong red hue to it. I nod and smile at her and she goes back to knitting something that looks like clothing.

I'm still adjusting to how these Wildmen live. No, not Wildmen. I should stop thinking of them like that. The Shanti People. They seem so peaceful and cultured.

Aldus looks away when I catch him watching me closely.

"Why are you helping me?" I ask him, growing serious. "You could have left me for dead. You didn't have to bring me all the way out here to your village."

He takes a second to answer, as if he's wondering what to tell me. "It is our way. Our way of life means we will help others, if it does not endanger us."

"I could be a threat to you," I say.

"You were hurt and in need of medical attention. And you were close to our borders. Our ways say we should help you, whether or not there are negative consequences because of it."

I feel like there's more he isn't telling me, but I don't press the matter.

"Well, thank you, for saving my life," I say.

He nods slowly and presses a hand over his heart. I take that to mean a gesture of gratitude, or thanks.

Freddick soon returns with a clay cup of water. "Boiled and cooled, just as your people like." He passes it to me with gentle hands, patient as I readjust my weight on the crutches to be able to hold the cup. Freddick sneaks a look at Aldus, who gives him a kind smile and a nod of the hair.

"Good on you, Freddick," Aldus says.

Freddick dips his head in thanks and sharply turns and strides away, off toward the trees and a streaming river, before I can remember to thank him.

I turn back to speak to Aldus, but something catches my eye. Two women hang laundry together in the grassy fields across from us, opposite the river. They work quickly and gracefully, but there's something about one of them that feels at once familiar and unknown. It's the way she carries herself, the way she moves, that has me captivated. Stark blue eyes meet mine from across the distance, as if she felt my gaze. And that's when I recognize her.

There she is again. The woman with the dark hair and the strange hostility. It isn't the underlying annoyance that has me turning away from her and back to Aldus, but the reminder that those blue eyes bring. Aldus called her Galene. His Galene.

"That is your daughter?" I ask, trying to cover up that I was just staring at her right in front of him.

Aldus says, "That's my youngest. Galene." He's turned to face her now, and I can't help but do the same once more.

She notices us watching her, and she gives me a fiercely hot scowl, like she's trying to kill me with a look.

"She doesn't seem to like me very much," I say.

"She doesn't like foreigners."

I catch a hesitant note in this voice and think there's more he isn't telling me.

Galene flashes another glare my way before turning her back and deciding I don't exist. Fair enough. I don't need her to like me, anyway. It's easier for me if she doesn't, actually.

I look around and think about how far away from home I am. I'm at the mercy of these people. People I still don't really know. People I can't fully trust, if at all. I have to wonder if I'm truly safe here with them.

I continue to study my surroundings and start making plans to leave. Whether or not they'll let me leave is something I'll have to wait and see.

Chapter Four

GALENE

I feel his eyes burning in the back of my head, and it's all I can do to stop from shuddering.

"Galene," someone says beside me with concern in their voice.

I turn to Kris who is hanging a cardigan onto the clothesline. I focus on our task and collect another garment from the washed clothing basket and hang it on the line. The scents of fresh roses and creamy valandias drift in the surrounding air.

She's watching me, and it's clear she will not let this go. I've seen that concerned, questioning look on her for most of my life and know it well.

"You had a question?" I ask her innocently.

She pouts at me as she hangs another garment up, attaching the pegs while looking at me. "No question. Simply an observation. If you don't want to tell me why your face is so sour, you don't have to. I will simply speculate on my own."

"Feel free to speculate," I say dismissively, hoping to put an end to this conversation.

I notice her perk up in the corner of my eye.

"Oh, my," she says, drawing out the words breathlessly. "Is that the Oathlander? I never knew how handsome he was. I see why you've been keeping him to yourself all this time."

A frustrated sigh that escapes me. "I haven't been keeping him to myself. My father agreed with the elders that we wouldn't draw attention to him. I just had to make sure he didn't die." I shoot a look behind me, swallowing hard as I assess his features. I search for a flaw in them to use to my defense, but can only think of a lie to tell. "He is not handsome. His face is too long to be so. And you should not trust him. I mean it, Kris. Don't get too close."

Kris remains eyeing him with a hungry look in her eyes. "I wouldn't mind getting closer to him."

"Kris," I snap, turning on her. "He is an *Oathlander*."

She pauses, and a look of horror passes over her. Heat flushes her cheeks. "I'm sorry, Galene. I didn't mean... I was being insensitive."

I dismiss her with a headshake and return to my task. I hate how bad I've just made her feel, but I needed her to understand that the Oathlander is not someone to interact with. The thought of my mother tightens my throat.

The Oathlanders are all murderers, thieves, and liars. They may differ from Kingdom folk, but are just as untrustworthy. Every society thinks they are better than the others, but I know that we Shanti People are the only true good-hearted people in the world.

"Why do you think your father Tasked you with him?" Kris asks, breaking the silence while we work.

I spare a look back to where my father is conversing with the Oathlander. I have no answer to that, but I give it a try. "He wants to push me, to see what I would do. He wants me to prove I am grown and sensible and can handle any situation." I sigh and shake my head again when I catch her looking back in his direction. "Kris. I mean it. Do not get close to him."

She seems to have sobered a little and gives a shaky nod.

Before I focus back on the washed clothes, I catch the Oathlander staring at me from across the field. Our eyes lock for an instant, and I think I see something strained and conflicted in his dark eyes. But the sight of him makes my skin crawl and I turn away with a huff.

I can no longer be out here with him, looking at me like that. So I mumble an excuse to Kris and storm away without looking back.

With several huts and tents around me now, I feel like I can breathe a little better. Why had the Oathlander been staring at me? It must be some kind of trick of theirs. I won't fall for it.

For a second, I think about using my gift on him, but it's a terrifying thought. I still don't know how to use it correctly, and there's no telling if he can detect my intrusion. And I'd rather not get any closer to him than I have to.

Someone approaching from the woods gets my attention. The elderly Mortin is bare-chested and soaking wet as he trundles through the grass, carrying a heavy-looking sack over his shoulder. The path is on a slight incline and he is panting heavily, his spotted bald head gleaming in the sunlight.

I rush over and take the sack to ease his burden.

"Bless you, Galene," he says, wiping sweat from his brow.

The stench of fresh fish stings my nostrils and makes me wince. "You should have helpers with you," I tell him. "You're getting too... ah, handsome... to go fishing and carry these heavy sacks."

He flashes a smile that shows several missing teeth. "Is handsome what the kids are calling old these days?"

"I said nothing about being old." I give him a polite smile. "But I do know several young ones who would love the chance to prove themselves."

He waves a dismissive hand. "Never needed help my entire life."

"Times are changing, you know?"

"I'm still waiting for my gift to show itself. Any day now. I can feel it."

"I'm sure it will be wonderful," I say with a grin.

We both know that anyone with magical potential has developed their abilities already. Everything had changed within the first two days of magic coming back to the world.

When we reach his workstation hut, I swing the fish sack onto a table outside. It lands with a thud and shakes the table.

"Good catches today," I note. I also note how the area reeks of wet and rotting fish, and I fear it's going to stick to my clothing and hair.

"This is the end of the season for their migration," Mortin tells me. "It will be a while before we get another harvest like this."

He's fallen into thought and is watching me closely. I try to pretend I don't notice, but eventually I face him with a frown. I already know what he's going to ask.

"How is your light show practice?" he asks.

I suppress a sigh. I should be used to this question by now, but each time it irritates me. "I haven't tried using it for a while. It's not really... me."

"Oh, but it is," Mortin says seriously. "It's more you than you knew before. You have been given a gift and you and your family can now utilize those gifts. Yelena In'Tara has been lighting fires to help people every day since she discovered she could summon it from her hands."

"I am not Yelena In'Tara," I tell him. "And making a light show is of no use to anyone. I didn't ask for magic to enter my life. And, dear Mortin, I would appreciate it if people stayed out of my business."

His brows rise. "The Shanti Tribe? Staying out of each other's business?"

"Yes, I know," I say, rolling my eyes. "Impossible. Now, if you'll excuse me, I must be going. I wish you a long and bountiful hunting season." As I step away, I turn back and add, "And I'll see about finding you an apprentice hunter."

He waves another dismissive hand and tells me not to bother, but I can tell he would welcome the help.

A shiver rushes over me as I walk down the path between the tents. I should be used to people watching me closely, like Mortin had just done. Everyone wants to know how I'm going to change the world just because I'm one of the chosen few who can wield magic now. Everyone seems to be excited about their gifts, except for me. I never wanted to be different or feel like an 'other'. I just wanted to remain myself. But now, I feel like I'm some kind of jester, expected to entertain people and be a source of gossip.

I nod a hello to a few people I pass by and wonder what they're thinking about me. By the time I reach my family tent, I'm relieved to get away from everyone and find sanctuary in my home.

I step inside to see my father and sister are in the tent. And the Oathlander is with them.

Chapter Five

GALENE

"Galene, my dear," my father says, standing up as I enter. "Your hard work has paid off and our guest is finally on his feet."

I do everything I can to remain calm and not shake with anger. "Good for me," I mutter.

The tent is large enough to fit us all comfortably, and the lanterns have been lit to give us enough warm light to see by. They are sitting on one side with the chairs and dining table, leaving the utility and kitchen side empty. I glance at the divider across the tent and wonder if my nephews are here in their beds or if they're out.

"You have my thanks, Galene," the Oathlander says. My name passing his lips feels like daggers across my spine. I fight off the goosebumps that threaten to form at the back of my neck.

"I'm so happy you can be here, in our home," I say through my teeth, not caring to hide my sarcasm. My father gives me a hard look.

"Always the great host," Leila says as she stands and steps away from the dining table. She has that older sister look on her face that tells me I should watch my words and be nicer.

I'm still frozen by the entranceway. My home no longer feels safe and welcoming.

"I was just going to make us some juice," Leila says.

My father waves me over. "Come, sit with us."

I glower at Tarin as I take the furthest seat from him and shift it away from the table. Why is he bothering me so much? And why am I letting him?

The Oathlander shifts in his seat to better face me. I take some comfort in his slight wince, as it tells me he is not at full strength and won't be a threat to us. His dark hair is ragged and greasy, giving him a disheveled look that is emphasized by his heavy stubble. I try to imagine him cleaned up and in a fine suit, like he probably normally looks back home, but he seems unexpectedly comfortable in our humble dwelling.

"I owe you an apology," he says, "for insulting you earlier by not drinking the tea. I... didn't know where I was or who I could trust. But I see now that you are good people with good intentions."

"Isn't that nice?" Leila says. For some reason, she's still standing there.

"You were brought to our village," I tell the Oathlander, "because you wore the uniform of the Oathlands Military, and we wanted to heal you to gain favor with your people."

My father huffs uncomfortably. "Forgive my daughter. She is cursed to speak her mind. Like her mother."

Tarin seems more amused than surprised. His cool dark eyes have a hint of good humor in them, or so it seems. He is surprisingly calm and infuriatingly hard to read. Unless... I could try to read him.

Boisterous calls fill the air as two boys burst into the tent. They are in the middle of a competitive run of sorts, and both are out of breath. Milo pauses when he sees Tarin at the table. The younger one, Jonah, takes a few more seconds to calm and read the room.

"What did I tell you about yelling?" Leila says, going over to them and nudging them into the tent.

"To do it more?" Milo tries, mischief sparking in his eyes.

"Close. But the opposite." Leila places them in front of her and says to the Oathlander. "These are my two boys. Jonah and Milo."

They have both become shy and quiet in the presence of the Oathlander. Little Milo has pressed himself behind Leila's leg. The ten-year-old Jonah had gone through a growth spurt recently and is almost a foot taller than his six-year-old brother. He's been losing his baby fat too and is looking more like his father each day. Same curly auburn hair and narrow eyes.

"Don't get too close," I tell them. "He has an infectious disease."

Their eyes widen, but they seem more curious than scared.

Leila rolls her eyes. "Don't listen to your aunt. Tarin is safe. But he is new to our land and doesn't know our ways."

"Are you from the Kingdom?" Milo asks eagerly.

"I am from the Oathlands," Tarin says.

Milo's shoulders drop. He's been going through a Kingdom phase for a while now, and loves the idea of princesses and princes living there. Like something out of a fairytale book.

But the older Jonah has perked up. "Are you magical, too? Everyone at the Oathlands is magical, right?"

"Not quite," Tarin says with a smirk.

The boys look disappointed at that, and instantly I can see they've lost interest in the Oathlander.

"They might be boys," Aldus says, "but they'll tell you they are men fully grown. Ripe for the hunt already."

Jonah scrunches his face. "I am a man. But not him. He's still a baby."

Milo nudges him and it looks like they're about to have a shoving match until Leila pulls them apart.

"Come," she says as she nudges them onward. "Let's make some juice for our guest."

They happily hop alongside her.

"Can I press the orangeberries?" Milo asks eagerly.

I catch Tarin's eyes on me. Again. What does he want from me? I face him with my chin high, not backing down.

"You said 'not quite' when they asked about your magical heritage. Was that a yes or a no?" I ask.

"Why?" he says. "Are you magical?"

I pause, not wanting to answer that. I hate how he's shut me up. What's a witty retort?

"I just woke up recently," Tarin adds before I can respond. "But I'm sure I have no innate magical ability."

I spare a look at my father and am relieved when he doesn't reveal our new abilities. At least he has some sense not to over share with the foreigner.

"So, you are in the military?" my father asks conversationally. "I don't mean to pry, of course. Simply curious."

"I was," Tarin says, nodding. "Though I'm not sure what I'll be when I return home."

We stare at him.

After an awkward beat, he sighs and continues. "Forgive me, but it's still hard to talk about."

My father nods.

But I say, "Surely you could repay your life with a simple story, Oathlander."

"Galene," my father scolds.

But Tarin lifts a hand and says, "No, no. She's... Galene is right."

I cannot stop the goosebumps at the use of my name this time. I wish he would leave it out of his mouth.

"It's not a very delightful story," he says, "And I remember little of it. But... I was on a bridge when our lands were attacked, and it collapsed. I fell into the ravine below, and I must have washed up on your shores. Now I'm here." I don't believe a word of it. His arms are far too muscled for a simple soldier, and he's too old to hold a basic rank. Unless he's a simpleton. But I don't believe that either.

"We heard of the attack on your land," my father says. "Terrible business."

"You seem fairly cut off from the rest of the world," Tarin says. "How do you hear so much?"

"Our hunters sometimes see things from afar when they travel far enough. And we have a few traveling tradesmen from the north and south who enjoy sharing news."

"Tradesmen from the north and south?" Tarin asks.

"From Syraxia in the north and Koprus in the south."

"I didn't think the Wildmen... Sorry, the Shanti People, had dealings with others."

"Tradesmen have no borders, nor care for differences with others. A patron is a patron, and if you have coins to buy, or possessions to trade, then they are happy to deal with you."

"The Oathlands wouldn't know about that," I say. "We heard you've fallen out of favor with most of the lands." I can't help the taunting smile I give him.

Something dark passes behind Tarin's eyes. For a second, I think I've gone too far and have actually offended him. But he composes himself and is instantly back to his carefree self.

"I have a question," he says to my father. "Why was Galene given the duty to watch over my recovery? It seems to me she would have just as likely sliced my throat in my sleep."

Or perhaps not as carefree as I thought. I glare at him. "I would never." And then add sweetly, "I would simply poison your tea."

"Ignore her," my father says, not even bothering with a scolding look this time. "She wouldn't know where to find poison, anyway. The worst she'll do is over-spice the tea. My daughter is young and untested. She is twenty and six and should have been wed and with child long ago. But she is stubborn and outspoken, and for some reason has yet to find a partner."

He says this as if it is very, very clear why I haven't yet done so. And it is. Simply put, I do not want one, so I make it to where no one will want me. "And so I have been giving her difficult Tasks lately. In our society, we complete Tasks to prove our worth to our people. Galene was given the Task of being responsible for you. To aid in your recovery and ensure you are not a threat to us."

"Seems that you picked the right person for the Task," Tarin says. He's trying to get a rise out of me, but I won't fall for it.

From the kitchen area in the corner, the boys and Leila are making a ruckus as they prepare the juices.

"A person does not choose their Tasks," I say. "A Task chooses the person. Those who turn down their Tasks are not worthy of them, just as a person who does not complete a task isn't worthy. It didn't matter that I wished you were dead, Oathlander. I had something to prove."

"We Shanti People complete many Tasks as we grow and mature," my father adds. "To prove we are capable and useful members of our society."

"What constitutes a Task?" Tarin asks.

I watch him closely, trying to understand what he's thinking and what he is seeking with his questions. His dark eyes are very alert and show a keen, quiet intelligence.

"They can be anything from helping an elderly person, contributing to the building of a hut, harvesting crops, or even going on hunts," my father says. "We grow up wanting to prove our strength and intelligence to everyone, to strive to be a valuable member of the tribe."

"Admirable," Tarin says. "The younger generations should work hard to be useful and strong."

I'm not sure if I like the two of them getting along. My father must be more than ten years older than Tarin, but they have the same old man energy.

Leila and the boys come back with cups that smell of freshly pressed juice. They hand one to each of us as Milo and Jonah argue over who pressed the most juice.

Tarin raises his cup to us. "You have my thanks. Without you, I would not be here."

"You can thank us by leaving," I say. Seeing the way my father narrows his eyes at me, I add, "Once you are healed, and in your own time, of course."

"Galene," Father admonishes. "You're being rude."

I shake my head, hating how I have to pander to this foreigner. "You know what," I go on. "No. I'm not doing this." Sharing a drink with this man is beyond my capacity. "How can you all ignore the fact that this man is an Oathlander? Mother would be ashamed of you."

I get up and stride out of the hut, not looking back and ignoring their confused questions and murmurs.

As I walk away, I hear my father telling Tarin about my mother. That's enough for me to pick up my pace and wipe moisture from my eyes. He's going to be telling Tarin how my mother was killed by an Oathlander, over ten years ago. She was pregnant with my unborn brother at the time and was slaughtered by bandits from the Oathlands. Cut down like an animal.

And now we are treating this Oathlander like a beloved guest. I won't have it. I won't allow him to weasel his way in just to destroy everything I love.

There is no way I'm going to allow him to stay here.

Chapter Six
ROURK

Galene spends the next three days making my life a miserable hell.

She does everything she can to make me uncomfortable, but won't affect my health. It seems she's petty enough to, just as her father promised, overspice my tea, but never to go far enough to ensure I might have to stay a day longer than necessary. From tea to serving me cold dinners to wrapping my bandages extra tight to "accidentally" dumping an entire bottle of stinging antiseptic all over my wounds, Galene seems intent on torturing me.

Besides fending off as much of Galene's torment as possible, those days are mostly spent recovering and learning how to walk again. My strength is slowly returning and I've been able to get to know some people in the Shanti Tribe. I'm still getting used to not calling them Wildmen. Everyone has been nice and welcoming to me so far. Everyone but Galene, who seems intent on forcing me out with vicious glares and sighs. Although many others are either distantly mistrustful or forcibly polite, likely not wanting to anger the foreigner.

While I still sleep and rest in the small hut I'd awoken in, she no longer comes to check on me or make me a healing tea. Which suits me fine, as it's too exhausting to be around someone who hates me so much.

It was a shock to learn that an Oathlander had killed her mother and unborn brother. That was over ten years ago, just beyond the Oathlands border, but I don't recall ever hearing of such a thing happening. Aldus told me they had been dressed as bandits in weathered cloaks, like some of the feral savages known to traverse the Wildlands. The savages whom we Oathlanders had called Wildmen. We hadn't known there was also a large community out in the Wildlands. Good people who had villages all around the wilderness. I wonder if The Kingdom folk know of the Shanti People.

During one of my trips to bathe in the riverbank beyond the woods, I notice how heavy my stubble is when I look into the water's reflection. It's practically a full beard at this point, but I don't mind the look. I do mind how much weight I've lost, however, and how weak I still am. But I've been making progress and only need one crutch now, and can mostly walk unaided on even ground, if I take it slow and steady. I feel like a child learning to walk for the first time.

Aldus has proved to be a gracious host and has been happy to show me around and introduce me to more people, and share insights into the ways of his people. Now, knowing that an Oathlander had killed his wife and unborn child, I have to wonder if he is putting on a false front. There could be an ulterior motive for his hospitality.

But I don't sense any ill intention from him. I tell myself that isn't reason enough to fully trust anyone.

Leila finds me coming out of the woods after bathing. My shirt is in my hands and my baggy pants are partially wet from the water dripping off my bare torso. Her eyes roam my chest as she pauses, likely noting the history of scars on my upper body. She gives me a small wave.

She has a strong build for a woman of thirty years, with broad shoulders and strong-looking arms. Her dark hair is similar to Galene's but cut shorter to brush against her shoulders. Her vibrant blue eyes have some green in them, which is easier to see in the bright sunlight.

"I was just coming to look for you," she says. "We have a great amount of fruit that needs separating. Have you ever de-seeded an orangeberry?"

"Not professionally," I say. That earns me a smirk.

"How about picking green beans?" she says. "If you're available, I figure we'd put you to some work."

"Let me check my schedule." I stop before her and take a moment to look around. Birds chirp in a nearby tree. A warm breeze blows over us. "Would you look at that? I'm free right now."

She smiles and nods, and I follow her down a path. She walks slowly for me to keep up with her, using my crutch on the gravelly, uneven ground. We make small talk until a question comes to my mind.

"Your boys are wonderful," I begin. "Their father is away from the village? I don't think I've met him yet."

"My Geralt was struck by the crops disease," she tells me, so casually she could be speaking about the weather. "It's been... almost five years now."

"I'm sorry to hear that. I don't think I know about this crops disease."

"It has nothing to do with crops. They just thought it did back in the olden days, and the name stuck. It's an airborne sickness that some of us are susceptible to. A deficiency in our blood, or something we're simply born with. Anyway, it was a brief illness, mercifully."

"That must have been hard, raising the boys on your own."

She shrugs and nods. "I've had help from everyone. Here, we all look out for each other. We all want to better ourselves by bettering others. That's our way of life."

"I... lost my wife to an illness," I say.

She turns to me with raised brows. "I didn't know you were married."

"A lifetime ago. She caught the flu and couldn't recover. We did everything we could, but the illness worked through her swiftly." The memories still sting, but I'm no longer gutted by them. I can now remember her fondly instead of the heart shattering grief that swallowed me for years.

Leila is frowning. "I'm so sorry."

I leave out the part about me having a daughter. I wouldn't want them to trace me back to my real self, or risk May's safety by telling these people of her existence. I don't even know why I told Leila of my late wife.

"I applaud your way of helping each other," I say, breaking the silence. "That is the opposite way to those in the Kingdom. There, they are all out for themselves, stepping over each other to be in the highest tower. To have the most coin."

Leila gives me a sideways look. "Are you sure about that? I mean, you had your preconceptions about us. Maybe you just need to look closer at the Kingdom folk to see them better."

"They launched an attack on our land just a few weeks ago. We've been at war for centuries. We've come too far for any peace."

Leila's eyes flash with humor. "This is a new world. Full of magic and unknown wonder. Who knows? That's all I'm saying, anyway."

I nod. "You have a point."

She has is good height, not too short and not too tall. And I find myself drawn to her amiable air. In my experience, it's rare to find an easy conversationalist like Leila. But I don't tell her that.

"Your walking is getting better," she says, pointing with her chin.

It's then I realize I haven't been using my crutch. I don't know how long I've been walking without it, but the moment I see I'm not using it, my balance tilts and I sway. Leila catches me in her arms before I fully go off balance.

We pause in each other's arms for a moment, our faces close together. Her hair smells like flowers and freshly cut grass. She smiles and steps away as I regain the support of the crutch.

We keep going to the workbenches where a few people are busy preparing fruits and vegetables. I've heard that the fish recently caught is at risk of going bad, and so tonight they have decided to have a large feast for the entire village.

I get to work, happy to have something useful to do.

I'm finding that the Shanti People are a very hard-working bunch. They pride themselves on being productive members of their village. Speaking to some of the others preparing the fruits and vegetables, I learn that there is another tribe of Shanti People on the coastline of the northern continent, though the two have not communicated for years now.

"We are all Shanti," an elderly woman says. I think her age is close to a hundred.

"What does that mean?"

She studies me for a long moment, pondering. "It means that the Shanti are the oldest tribe, the oldest society in the world. The oldest that still remains, anyway."

"That's not what the history books say," I reply, confused.

"Do you know what is so fun about books?" She asks me. "Any old fool can write whatever they'd like, and in a few generations, everyone will think it is so." She gives me a sad smile. "Not everything we learn is truth."

"But I'm supposed to believe this is?"

"Think for a moment. What do I have to gain from lying to an Oathlander who will be gone in a few days? And what was to gain from an entire population of people believing otherwise?"

I don't know the answer, but her words settle into my bones, nevertheless.

Movement from the pathway between the tents catches my eye. Three young girls are peeking out from around a corner, watching me. They look to be barely out of their teens, if that. They giggle when I notice them and hurry away, shoving each other and laughing.

I shake my head.

That night, I sit by the campfire and enjoy a meal with a dozen or so of the villagers. They have prepared a rabbit and potato stew with green beans and fresh herbs. Their herbs also include some crushed flowers for flavor. They seem to eat flowers with almost every meal. I'm surprised at how flavorsome the simple ingredients of the stew are.

Aldus is sitting beside me and has been telling me about his day tending to the garden behind his tent. He had taken his grandsons out to a nearby field to catch firebugs earlier, so he's more than happy to be resting and eating now.

A bottle of wine is being passed around and we've been filling our clay cups as it reaches us. The first sip of the red wine hits me like a punch in the face, which makes a few of them laugh. I soon find that the homemade wine of the Shanti People is fragrant and considerably stronger than I am used to.

"I've never seen the stars like this before," I tell them.

It is a clear night and with little light beyond the campfire, the heavens are clear for us to witness. A sheet of glowing stars is overhead, more than I've ever seen. Some even have a shade of red, blue, or green to their light. The more I look, the more my eyes adjust and the more faint stars and clusters I can make out. I'm overwhelmed at how vast the star field is.

"Your buildings are too close together and block out much of the sky," a robust man around my age says from across the fire.

"Not as bad as in the Kingdom," I say, "but yes, we have enough to hide this expansive view each night."

Magdalena, the daughter of an elder, cocks her head. "You compare yourself favorably to the Kingdom many times. Are you aware of this?"

I think about that. "Old habits," I admit.

Gazing at the stars, I spot a familiar constellation. "Do you know the names of the constellations?" I ask, pointing up. "That one is the Shield."

Aldus nods. "We call it the Shovel."

"Ah, yes," I say. "It resembles the shape of a shovel, as well."

A woman with a blanket draped over her shoulders points up. "What do you call that one?"

I find the collection of stars she means. "That's the Warrior," I say. At their questioning looks, I add, "You see the shape of a man holding a sword."

It takes me a moment to explain what I'm seeing, having to point out the brightest of the stars sweeping across the sky. It turns out they know it as the Chair, as it takes the form of a high-backed chair, but they don't include two stars that make up the Warrior.

An older man with a bushy white mustache nods knowingly. "Interesting. Your take on the stars often involves war imagery."

I've never thought of it like that before. "We have one called the rabbit." I try to find it but can't see it. "It's by the one called..." I pause. "The dagger." I smile at them. "Perhaps you're right."

I take a spoonful of stew and savor its warmth and flavor. It feels like the first proper meal I've had in weeks. As the days have been passing, I've slowly begun to feel my strength returning, and my appetite has come back with it.

A red-haired woman points up. "I think that one looks like a flame. Maybe we should name a new constellation."

"You would think it looks like a flame," someone says.

Another adds, "You think we should name it after you, huh?"

Aldus leans closer to me. "Yelena has the ability to summon fire magic."

"That explains the hair," I say.

"Actually, the hair came first," the woman, Yelena, says. "It was just a coincidence, I think." She has more of a naturally spoken accent to my ears, and less of the thick, clipped way of speaking that many others in the village have.

I risk another sip of wine and ask, "Are there many here who discovered magical abilities?"

Yelena shrugs. "Only... ten, is it?"

"An even dozen," Aldus corrects. "We don't know how much of the overall population discovered new abilities, but it has been a small number within us.

I think that's around ten percent of the Shanti People's village, and I wonder if that percentage extends to the rest of the world.

They tell me of some of the abilities awakened. Someone could heighten their senses to see far into the distance, hear the lowest of sounds, and pick out specific smells in the air. Another could control the flow of an open body of water, which would account for how well their fishing had gone the other day. Someone could summon balls of lightning, although they were intent on not using that ability after they'd almost killed their parents. Someone was thought to communicate with animals, although they were still exploring and defining that ability. I'd already seen the one who could fly, although I don't think I've met them in person yet.

"Milly's son claims to have seen a dragon the other day," Aldus says. "Out across the Pellworts Fields."

They seem to believe that the boy must have been mistaken, as no one else had seen it. But it was true that many new creatures and animals had been showing up these past two weeks. I'd seen more variety in that short time alone than I have in my whole life.

The older man with the bushy mustache finishes a mouthful of stew and says, "There is a family of small fairies living in the woods around the back there."

I can't help but smile and shake my head. It's a lot to take in and I'm still adjusting to being in a world where magic exists, and is quickly becoming commonplace.

"How about yourself, Aldus?" Magdalena asks. "How's your magical training going?"

I raise my brows at Aldus.

He shrugs sheepishly and says to me, "I can only summon light from my hands. If I really try. It is nothing fancy."

"It's a hot light," Magdalena says.

"Not as impressive as fire," Yelena mutters.

"It's nothing fancy, and has no use," Aldus says. "Unless you're out at night with no light to see by. But even then, I can't summon it at will."

I look at him with new eyes. "You must have a magical lineage," I say.

He shrugs again and looks away dismissively. "As far back as I know with my family, we have been nothing but dull and ordinary. So I was as surprised as anyone else to learn of my ability."

The conversation shifts to the duties in the village tomorrow, and the current state of their community. It's almost like a town hall meeting. My head begins to feel hot and I think I've had too much of the wine. I'm surprised to see my cup is empty now.

Eventually, we decide to withdraw for the night. I have my bedding still in the hut in which I had awoken, which has become my temporary home. The hut that Galene has stayed clear from for days now.

The man with the bushy mustache, whom I learn is named Yovin, walks beside me as we leave the dwindling campfire. A chill has developed in the night air that makes me shiver.

"You are an interesting one, young man," Yovin says. He stands almost two feet shorter than me, though he has a large and commanding presence. I judge him to be around his seventieth year, but his bright eyes gleam with youthful mischief.

"I've been called many things in my day," I tell him. "Interesting is not near the top of the list."

"I can see that you are," the old man says with a knowing look. "I sense a grand purpose within you. You are destined for great things. I know it. And you were brought to us for a reason. I know that, also."

I'm not quite sure what he means, but I accept his words and thank him. I catch him stopping and watching me as I walk away to my hut. Every now and then, I get a feeling that I'm missing something, and that I should not be trusting these people as much as I have been. A feeling that tells me I should plan to leave as soon as my legs can carry me enough away. And this evening, that feeling is very strong.

It takes me a long while to fall asleep, and it isn't until nearby sounds stir me awake that I realize I have drifted to sleep. A woman screams in the night. Heavy footsteps and grunts mix with the growing panic spreading through the village.

I know the sounds, and my heart pumps with adrenaline. I rush out to see my fears are real. Dark figures in heavy coats are rushing through the village, waving clubs and spears and chasing people down. A fire has begun to burn through a tent.

The Shanti Tribe is under attack.

Chapter Seven
ROURK

I run out into the night in my loose vest, with no time to find my crutches. Adrenaline is shooting through me and my fight senses are up enough to push me along. The village is in absolute chaos as the attackers throw lanterns that crash into the tents and huts. A fierce wall of fire has spread on one side. People run about in a panic, falling over themselves in their hysteria. Screams and tortured cries fill the smoke-filled air.

A young boy trips in front of me and I help him up. "Find cover," I yell at him over the chaos. His eyes are wide and fearful and I'm not sure if he understands me when he runs away.

I need a sword or a weapon of some kind. I think I see Leila and her boys running along the tents, highlighted against the growing flames, but I can't be sure it's them. I head in that direction when one attacker starts charging at me.

The figure is shrouded in layers of ragged, stained clothing, like a monstrous form of a beggar on the street.

He waves a short spear in the air as he growls like an animal, bearing pointed teeth.

I step to the side and grab the spear when he thrusts it at me, and spin it out of his hands. I know instantly he isn't a trained soldier. I shove the spear into his chest and, as he drops limply to the ground, I throw the spear into another attacker's back. The motion almost trips me off my feet, but I manage to regain my balance, only irritating my ankle a little.

A familiar face comes to me, sweating and panting heavily. The long-haired young hunter, Freddick, grabs my arms.

"He's dead. He's dead," he says shakily, almost incoherent.

"Who's dead?" I ask.

Freddick shakes his head as tears stream down his face, which crumples into a pained grimace. "My father. They came out of nowhere. They're everywhere. They're..."

I grip his shoulders and urge him to meet my eyes to focus on him. I know he's in shock, and that he just lost someone he loves, but I need him to explain if I'm going to have a chance at saving others from the same fate. "Who are they?"

"B-bandits," he says. "Wildmen."

It hits me in an instant and a cold shiver ripples through me. These are the feral savages we heard of in the Oathlands. The uncivilized cannibals who roamed the Wildlands. The crazed men who are more animals than people.

I shake Freddick firmly to snap him out of his whimpering. "You're a hunter. They're animals. Find a weapon and take them down."

He looks lost and shaken, so I shake him again and lock eyes with him. My fierce glare thankfully sobers him. "Find a weapon. Take them down. Protect the people. You can do this."

He gives me a shaky nod. I let him run away, hoping he's heading for a stash of hunting weapons.

Some villagers have bows and are firing arrows at the bandits. And only some of them look like they know how to use them effectively.

My head snaps around at the sound of a woman's scream. A howling bandit is chasing down a young woman holding a babe in her arms. I run as fast as my legs can carry me and pick up a rock as I go, knowing I will not reach the Wildman in time. The rock soars from my hand and hits the bandit on his back. It's enough to distract him for a moment and give me time to reach him. The woman with the babe runs away into the chaotic night.

The bandit growls and roars at me, sounding like a feral animal. His knuckles bulge with a wrapping. Likely filled with rocks for more damage. This one has matted long hair and his face is covered with enough dirt to hide his true complexion.

Just before I meet the Wildman, a ball of fire cuts through the air nearby. It strikes the ground and catches onto another bandit, who begins to yell and convulse as the flames envelop him.

Yes, that's it, I think. *Use your gifts. Fight back.* I wonder if any of the bandits have magical abilities.

The Wildman before me throws a punch, but I easily avoid it and twist his arm to snap the bone. I slam my head into his and think I've almost knocked him out, but finish him off with a heavy punch to his gut. That drops him cold. No weapons that I can see on him. No time to search him.

I'm relieved to see some villagers are fighting back. Their hunters—the closest they have to soldiers—are fighting with long spears, knives, and axes. Both sides are carrying swords, but I don't know if they came from the Shanti People or the Wildmen.

Two children are standing and screaming, looking completely frozen with fear. I go to them and usher them towards the tents, telling them it's going to be okay. I turn a corner to see Aldus is among those on the attack now. He is rushing through a wide path between two rows of tents. A heavy-looking hammer is in his hand and he seems to know how to use it effectively.

A crying woman comes to me and the two children hug her. I yell at them to find cover and stay there. The sight of Aldus makes me think of Galene and Leila. A body is lying on the path with a spear sticking out of their chest, but I don't think it's them.

I head back out into the open area, away from the tents to where most of the bandits are. The hunters of the village are doing their best to fight back the Wildmen, but they are far from experienced soldiers. Neither are the bandits, but their wild savagery gives them an advantage over the peaceful villagers.

There she is. Galene. She's on the ground, pushing herself away from an approaching bandit with an axe held high. I charge at him and snatch the axe as he swings it down. With a quick twist, I plunge the axe into his chest and shove him to the ground.

Galene is shaken, her bright eyes wide and trembling. I pull her up to her feet and she falls into my arms, sobbing into my chest.

I take her face into my hands. "Are you okay? Are you hurt? Are you *hurt?*"

She shakes her head. It pains me to see her so distraught, her face smeared with dirt and tears.

"Are there any safe places in the village?" I ask. "Anywhere to hide?"

She looks too frightened to understand, but I'm relieved when she nods. "Ah, yes... The Nisshi's tent. They have a cellar."

"Round up as many people as you can. Get them in there. Stay hidden. Do you understand?"

Her shimmering eyes draw me in. I cup her cheek to reassure her everything is going to be okay.

"Go. Now," I say. "Stay hidden. Stay safe."

She straightens and her features grow serious. The fire and determination in her eyes take me by surprise. She nods sharply and pauses when she begins to move away.

We lock eyes, and in that moment, I feel a swell of emotion between us. Something powerful that takes my breath away. I give her a reassuring nod, and she turns and runs away. I don't have time to think about what had just happened between me and Galene. I need to save as many people as I can.

I make it a few steps before my legs buckle under me and I drop to the dusty earth. The growls of a bandit tell me someone is coming for me. I pick up a rock as I spin around and throw it into the man's head, knocking him down.

I try to get up, but another bandit tackles me back down. We tumble and wrestle, and I'm surprised at how strong and crazed the maniac man is. I'm used to fighting trained and controlled men with calculated intelligence. This is like trying to pin down a wild animal. But the instant my hands wrap around his head, it's all I need to snap his neck. He rolls onto his back and stops moving.

His coat falls away to show a knife tucked into his pants. I grab it and throw it at a Wildman chasing down two people. I catch the flash of a spear in time to roll away. It thuds into the earth where my head had just been. As the next bandit charges at me, letting loose a shrill yell, I snatch the spear and throw it at him. The bandit tries to catch it and manages to do so, but not before the spear tip plunges into his chest.

An arrow thuds into the dirt just below my armpit. As another bandit comes and reaches for me, I snatch the arrow from the dirt and thrust it into the crazed man's throat. He drops limply onto me, smothering me in his unwashed stench.

The earth shakes and trembles. I sit up and turn to see the ground rising across the field. A patch of earth lifts and causes two bandits to fall over. Villagers come with spears and axes and cut through the downed bandits. But they leave their backs exposed and don't see two more bandits coming from behind. I cry to warn them, but it's too late. Two of the villagers get knives in their backs while the others run away.

I finally push myself to my feet, managing to stand, and ignore the mud and dirt covering my clothes. That ground had to have shifted from a magic user. They hadn't mentioned someone with the ability to move the earth.

I head for a bandit who is grappling with a young man when a bright light fills the sky. A charged sphere of blue lightning flies into the bandit and explodes on his back. He's thrown through the air and lands with his body burning with blue and purple flames. I see with horror that the young man who had been grappling with the bandit had been caught by the lightning, and his arm is burned.

I search for the next person to help, and the next Wildman to attack, and it takes me a moment to realize the fighting is over. What's left of the bandits are disappearing into the night. Their howls and yells diminish as they flee.

We're left in the ruins of the burning village.

Chapter Eight

ROURK

The loss of Shanti people hangs in the air.

It is a long and arduous night of picking up the pieces of the village and helping the many injured. The dark, despondent mood of everyone can be felt in the air. I feel their pain and see it etched on their faces, and it fills me with anger. These are good people. They didn't deserve to be attacked like that.

What surprises me the most is how much Galene is doing, rushing about and helping everyone she can. I didn't know she had this caring, determined side about her. She is clearly in distress and looks like the ground has exploded in her face, but she seems to only care about helping others.

I see she has a commanding presence when she gives orders to others to fetch bandages and hot water, or where they can find what they're looking for. She's one of the few people who are keeping their composure while others are still in shock.

Galene meets my eyes at one point, and her face hardens. She scowls for a second before looking away and ignoring me. I guess whatever close moment we'd had tonight had been in my mind, or had meant nothing.

Leila is among those helping the injured, but she has to spend time calming her boys, who think the bandits are coming back at any moment.

I do what I can to help clear debris and begin the restoration process, but my legs can only take me so far and I need to rest at times, much to my annoyance.

By the time the sun has risen, I feel like several long days have passed and the weariness and fatigue have seeped into my bones.

Three people died last night. Three lives lost. It affects the village as deeply as if it had been many times more than that. Everyone here knows everyone. They all lost three people. And there are four more people who might not survive the rest of the day. One of the deaths was a young girl. Others spoke of her as a ball of sunshine. Someone who could never harm a hair on anyone's head. And she is gone. Dead because I couldn't help these people enough. Guilt settles on my shoulders. I have to be better for them, to repay them.

Despite the aches and stiffness in my legs, I'm determined to be as useful as I can in their time of need.

I see Aldus across the field, speaking with a tall, muscular man who looks vaguely familiar. They seem to be locked in a serious discussion, so I go over to them.

The powerfully built man is wearing a faded, weathered tunic that shows off his muscled arms. His rich skin tone is the closest to bright red that I've yet seen in the village. The sides of his head are shaved and a short mohawk runs along the top.

"Tarin, my boy. Good to see you still standing," Aldus asks when I reach them.

I nod to Aldus's right arm, which is in a cloth sling.

"Not to worry," he says. "I pulled my shoulder swinging that damn hammer. I'm not as young as I used to be." He grimaces before asking, "Have you met Bohan?"

"I have not," I say. The tall man shakes my extended hand. His grip is unsurprisingly very firm.

"Bohan is our Head Hunter. One of the best I've ever seen," Aldus says. "He is in charge of all our hunters."

"I remember you from last night," I say. "You're very handy with a spear. And an ax."

"I did what I could, just like we all did," Bohan says, his voice firm but low. Though he's trying to come across as humble, I can see he's posing himself as a heroic figure. Someone who needs no thanks, because they're so great. He towers over Aldus and is a few inches taller than me, but he carries himself like he's trying to take up as much space as he can.

"We were just saying," Aldus begins, "we cannot let these attacks continue to happen."

"And I was just saying," Bohan says wearily, "we need to move further north, to the coast."

"And I was telling you, we cannot simply move our lives a hundred miles away."

"Are these attacks common?" I ask, not caring about their argument.

Aldus shakes his head. "The last time was over two years ago. And before that, we had almost four years of peace. The bandits are not organized, or following any particular schedule, but they somehow know when to catch us at our most defenseless. They are whirlwinds of death and destruction. Thankfully, they didn't kidnap anyone this time."

"Aldus, I can't believe I'm hearing this," I say, fighting back the rising rage. "These animals have been attacking you for years and you've done nothing about it?"

He frowns at me, looking outraged. "We fight back! What else would you have us do? We do not invite them to slaughter us."

"I've been saying for years we need to strengthen our defenses," Bohan says.

Aldus wheels on him. "You are the one in charge of our hunters, Bohan. You speak of defenses as though it were someone else's duty."

"We are hunters," Bohan spits back, showing a flash of fiery anger. "We are not soldiers. We do what we can. Our job is to catch food to keep us alive, and that is what we do. Why don't *you* organize our defenses?"

Aldus doesn't back down, despite their height and size difference. "I will take this up with the elders and see that they know how you speak."

"I'll tell them myself," Bohan says.

"Hold on," I say, keeping my voice even. "Fighting each other will not solve anything. Let me get this clear. You know those bandits are out there and can attack at any moment, but you don't have people keeping watch on the surrounding lands?"

Aldus scoffs. "Maybe you have the capacity for that in your big cities, but we are not like that. We cannot have people sitting around all day in the fields and on hilltops, watching for bandits who may not be coming for years."

"You create shifts," I say. "Everyone takes a turn. You can make it part of your Tasks, for the younger generations to prove their competency. It's better than being caught unaware at any moment."

Aldus's cheeks have flushed red. "We are a village of farmers, craftsmen, and hunters. We have no soldiers to stand guard. We are defenseless."

"Not anymore," I say. That gets their attention. I let my words sink in for them. "Last night, I saw a glimpse of what your people are capable of. Some of you have been given special gifts. You can use them offensively when needed. But you need training."

"You would have us turn into something we are not?" Aldus says.

"That's not what I meant," I say, but I don't get the chance to explain.

"Why are you even here?" Bohan asks. "This is not your concern. We don't need you telling us what to do."

"Let's not go too far," Aldus says with some restraint. "I'm simply telling Tarin that what he's suggesting will change the fundamental mentality of our entire people. The world has changed, yes, but it does not mean our people have to change with it."

"You already have changed with it," I say.

Aldus continues as though I haven't spoken. "We will keep doing what we have been doing and pray for the support of the land to provide for us."

I want to say more to make them see things how I see them, but I know I can't interfere. They are stuck in their ways and it's going to take a hell of a lot more than me to change that.

"I've wasted too much time here," Bohan says. "I have work to do." He pauses and looks at me. "If that's alright with you?"

I give no response or reaction. Bohan sneers at me and walks away. I know that look. It said, 'If you challenge me again you will regret it'.

When I'm alone with Aldus, I ask, "Who threw the ball of blue fire last night?"

His brows crinkle in thought. "I did not see that. And don't know anyone with that power. Are you sure you saw correctly?"

I feign confusion and concede. Maybe I was mistaken. I get the impression he wouldn't tell me who had that power, even if he knew. And maybe he does. There's no use in asking who manipulated the earth either, as I don't think I'll get an answer for that. But I think he knows more than he's letting on. Whether it's about the magic last night or something else.

Aldus shakes his head in defeat and lets out a weary sigh. "There's Magdalena," he says, nodding across the way. "I have to meet with her to discuss what we are going to do about the festival tomorrow."

"Festival?"

"The Patron's Blessings Festival. It is a bi-annual festival to bless the world and keep us safe. Some are saying we would not have been attacked if we'd held the festival already. We're going to have to cancel it, however. We'll have to discuss that with the elders. A big party is the last thing anyone wants right now."

I chew the inside of my cheek and consider that. "Maybe it's exactly what you need. You can hold the festival in honor of those who died. And people will be comforted by the fact that you've blessed the land for support."

Aldus eyes me for a long moment, his blue eyes shifting in thought. He's assessing me. Perhaps wondering if he should listen to me or not.

"You're right," he eventually says. "I will bring that up with the elders."

"I don't suppose... I could meet them."

He smirks. "Do not push your luck, lad. Allow us our privacy and traditions."

I nod. "Of course."

He claps me on the shoulder and makes his way across the field to where Magdalena is waiting.

I take some time to feel the wind and the air, taking in the serenity of the moment after so much chaos. The birds are back in the trees, happily singing their song.

My ankle has begun to throb, so I go to find a place to sit for a while. Dark clouds are looming on the horizon. The air is alive with growing energy. A storm might be coming. Or it might shift away and miss us.

I feel like I've spent my entire adult life in this situation. Waiting for a storm to come or seeing if it will pass. Perhaps that old man Yovin had been right. Maybe I've been brought here for a reason.

Chapter Nine

ROURK

So quickly, everyone seems content to go on as if nothing at all had happened. As if three fresh graves were not just out of eyesight.

The Shanti People decide to continue with The Patron's Blessings Festival, and the next evening was a stark contrast to the dour day that preceded it. Though people still grieved their dead and nursed wounds, music was played, a feast was prepared, and the drink flowed.

I woke that day to find my legs were surprisingly more capable, despite the excessive use and strain on them recently. I figure I need to push the muscles to get them working again, and go through several periods of pain and rest on the road to recovery.

The large field between the tents and huts is alive with people mingling, filling bowls of food and cups of wine, and breaking into sporadic dancing. Those with the musical instruments are playing a jolly, whimsical melody that feels both fun and somber. I notice several small groups who are sitting to the side and clearly not engaged with the frivolities, the weight of the recent devastation and deaths keeping them separate from the rest.

I was told I should wear something green for the festival this evening, although of course I have no clothes other than my old uniform and what I've been given so far. Before the central bonfire is to be lit to mark the beginning of the festival, Leila approaches to hand me a forest-green tunic.

"This was my Geralt's," she tells me with a sad smile. "Might as well put it to some use."

"No, that's unnecessary," I say, taking a step back. "Thank you for the offer, but—"

"Nonsense," Leila says, and thrusts the clothes into my arms. "You must. Geralt would want to see it used for good rather than collecting dust, don't you think?"

"You don't even know me," I say slowly. "Are you sure you want me to wear his clothes?"

"I am sure," she says with ease, giving me a smile. "Besides, it would be rude to not wear green to the festival. It is meant to mimic the land. Do you know that? And your garb there reminds me more of rot. Not the growing, blooming earth around us." She pats my cheek lovingly. "Wear the clothes, boy," she says. "And do so with confidence. Geralt had good taste." She winks and pinches my face before strolling off.

People try to soak in the celebration, but I can see that it's not as easy for some people to ignore what happened as it is for others. Some look around with nerves, as if expecting Wildmen to appear any minute. The Elders insist they won't be back for a while, that no two attacks have ever happened so close together before, but it's easier to say something than it is to believe it.

I'm glad to see that they have listened to my advice and placed lookouts at regular intervals on the outskirts of the village. Each lookout has a horn they can blow the moment that any danger is spotted. I've never liked taking chances. In my experience, it's always best to be prepared.

I make my way around the festival in a slow stroll, taking in the merriment. These are not my people, but it is nice to be with them on this special occasion. While I've been learning so much about them in the short time I've been here, they are also fairly secretive about certain matters. Which I understand. I'm still a stranger to them and the Oathlands have not had a peaceful history with their people.

I come to one table laid with food and see Galene is there, filling her plate. She is in a flowing white corseted gown with emerald adornments, and leaf-like ornaments are in her dark hair which is smooth this evening.

She tenses when she sees me, but it is a subtle flinch that is almost imperceptible.

"Enjoying the festival?" I ask as I pick up a cup of wine from the table.

She focuses on placing vegetables on her plate. "The Patron's Blessings Festival is to bless the world and bring us good fortune. It is not for enjoyment."

"And yet, I can't help but detect a sense of merriment," I say, looking around. "Must be my imagination."

Galene turns to me and pauses, her face dropping. She storms up to me and jabs a spoon at me. "Where did you get that? That tunic does not belong to you."

"Leila gave it to me. She said she wanted me to wear it."

She looks at me with uncomprehending eyes. I can see her building up her next argument. She sighs and says, "You should not be wearing that. Geralt was a great man. A greater man than you'll ever be."

"Some people think I'm pretty great," I say with a playful grin.

Her scowl tells me she doesn't appreciate that.

"Speaking of clothing," I say. "That is a wonderful gown on you."

She glares at me and her eyes narrow mistrustfully. "I am relieved to know this garment, which I specifically wore for you, pleases you."

When she turns back to the table of food, I say, "I know you don't like me. But that doesn't mean we have to hate each other. Have I done something to offend you personally? If I have, then I apologize deeply."

A hint of hesitation passes on Galene's face. She shakes her head. "I do not think of you at all."

I consider pushing the matter further, but finally concede. "Very well." I take a step closer and she looks up at me with those bright blue eyes. "Despite it not being the purpose, I hope you enjoy your evening."

Our gaze remains locked for a long moment. Her chest heaves with her rapid breathing and her lips are parted. There is something infuriatingly interesting about this woman, and I really don't know what to make of it. I think I see something vulnerable buried deep within her stern eyes.

I take my chance to be the first to walk away and do so, not looking back. Firebugs dance in the night air. With the bonfire in the center of the field sending golden light into the star-filled sky, and the whimsical music in the air, there is a dream-like quality to the evening.

Either I have become severely weak lately, or the Shanti wine is fiercely potent stuff. This is my second cup this evening, but it feels like I've had an entire bottle of red.

I was told that the merriment of the villagers is the gift they give the land, to pass their festivities and good hearts into the earth and pray for goodwill to come back to them.

Aldus is near a round table speaking with a few elderly people I haven't seen before. A large canvas has been laid beneath the table and chairs, and there is a great bounty of food and drink on the table. This seems to be an important group of people.

When I see Leila rushing about nearby, breaking up a playful fight between her two boys, I go over to her. She has given the boys a stern warning to behave and sent them on their way by the time I reach her. She smooths out her floral dress and smiles at me.

"Those two boys are going to kill each other one day," she says with a heavy breath. "Or me."

"They are spirited," I agree, having to raise my voice as we're closer to the musicians. "I was the same with my brother." I catch myself before I mention Arthur. I still don't want them to know I'm the brother of Arthur Bearon, the new ruler of the Oathlands.

"I didn't know you had a brother," Leila says.

She has a pleasant air about her and a hint of a smile always on her lips. A stark contrast to the gruff stiffness of her sister. She is only a few years older than Galene, but there is a tired look to her smooth features, with faint dark circles under her eyes and distinct furrow lines.

I change the subject by looking over at Aldus. He kneels at the table, speaking with two of the five elderly people. They all have indistinct ages but look well into their nineties at least, fragile and shriveled with age.

"Those people with your father. They are the village elders?" I ask.

"They are," Leila says. "That's right, you haven't met them yet."

"To be honest. I wasn't even sure if they existed."

Leila giggles. It's a lovely melodic sound. "Of course they exist. I can see you want to speak to them, but I'll have to strongly discourage that. They are a highly private group, and we have our ways. They do not hold audiences with strangers."

She regards me while I study the old people at the table. "Trust me. You don't want to overstep."

I initially think that's a warning, but I realize her words come from a place of concern. "I do trust you," I say. I don't fully believe that, but I feel like I'm on my way to it. Leila and Aldus seem to be the most trustworthy people I've met in the village.

"Good," she says with a smile. "Because you should." Her face hardens when she sees something behind me. "Oh, those two are at it again," she says with a sigh, and rushes off toward her warring boys.

The boys' boisterous play takes me back to simpler times when Arthur and I would compete to see who was the strongest brother. For many years, as the oldest, I would hold that title, but after Arthur's growth spurt, he eventually had the largest physique.

In a way, that had pushed me to become my best self. I would train and work hard to prove I was not the weakest brother, and it wasn't until many years later that I would realize I was only competing against myself.

Leila looks back and gives me another smile as she goes away. I find myself smiling back. I can see becoming friends with her, given how easy she is to speak to and how pleasant her company is.

And yet...

Galene is near the bonfire, helping an older lady stand up. While she has a hard, prickly edge with me, I've seen how kind and caring she is. How good her heart is.

A somber smile comes to me. Galene's hatred of me reminds me of how I'd first met my wife all those years ago. Galene has a similar fire and stubbornness within her.

It has been over ten years since my Sia left this realm, and this is the first time I've seen a glimpse of her in someone else. I'm not sure how to feel about that, especially when the face I see her in is one I have no chance of a future with. Not any kind of future. She will be here, with the Shanti people, and I will be in the Oathlands. She will forget my name before the year is over, and I can only hope to have the same luck.

I stroll around for a while, greeting a few familiar faces and picking up my third cup of wine.

The festivities and crowd become too much for me and I feel like taking a moment to myself. I'd like to check on the watch guards to see if they are keeping to their posts and looking out correctly. I'm sure they are in need of a lot of advice and instruction, as no one here is a trained soldier.

I reach the path between a row of tents and see someone is ahead, walking up to me. The young girl has a cascading river of blonde curls that bounces about her as she giggles to herself about something. Her dress is low and cut in a flattering style that emphasizes her full breasts and shapely legs. I've seen her around, I think.

She perks up and stops when she sees me. "Oh. Hello there," she says, her voice breathy and light.

She slinks closer with a mischievous smirk and a gleam in her green-blue eyes. She knows how strikingly alluring she is.

"There you are," she says.

"And there you are," I simply say.

She giggles and curls a lock of hair behind her ear. She's come to a stop so close that I can smell the floral perfume in her hair, and is looking up at me with wide, captivating eyes. I can't help but stir at her proximity.

"I was hoping I'd run into you. We haven't met yet. My name is Wini."

"Tarin," I say.

She giggles again, making me think I've missed a joke. "I know who you are. You're leaving the festival so soon? It can be dangerous out here. You should really have a companion when you retire to bed." She bats her eyes at me, inching closer and closer.

"I've heard how dangerous beds can be," I say, "but I'm confident I need no companion. Thank you for your concern, Wini. Perhaps there is a young man out here in need of your protection."

"One poor soul to save at a time," she says, flashing her eyebrows.

"How old are you?" My guess is barely out of her teens.

She smiles demurely and leans into me, filling my senses with her floral scent. She takes my hand and presses it onto her considerable breast. "Old enough."

I feel myself drift closer to her parted lips, but I snap out of it and step back, retrieving my hand from hers.

She appears confused.

"You should go back to the festival," I encourage her.

Her scrunched face shows she is deeply offended. "What is wrong with you?"

I sigh. "My wife would not approve." It isn't technically a lie.

"She isn't here." Her alluring nature disappears. "*We* are here. Now. At this moment." She scoffs. "I thought you were a man."

"I am... old fashioned." And very uninterested. "And I am exhausted. Enjoy the festival, Wini." I give her a pleasant smile to tell her there are no hard feelings, but she scoffs again and strides away, shaking her head.

I do my best to put the young Wini from my mind, trying not to think of the wild night of fun I could have had with her, and make my way out to the nearest lookout spot beyond the trees. I have to admit it's been quite some time since someone has stirred me like that, and I have half a sense to go back and find her. But I know that wouldn't be right. I couldn't. My Sia wouldn't like what she sees when she looks down on me in the heavens. I couldn't do that to her memory. Not a torrid night of sex with a random voracious vixen. One whose name I've already begun to forget.

Once I'm happy with the mindset and skills of the person keeping watch beyond the village, I head back to find a place to rest. My ankle has started throbbing.

Later in the evening, one of the village elders, whom I learn is named Audric, makes a speech about their recent losses, and how they will come back stronger than before. They will honor their dead by thriving in their memory. That earns him a raucous round of applause. His speech ends with a blessing to their god. I'm surprised that they only have one god, rather than the many gods known to the Oathlands. I'm in no mood to get into a religious debate with them.

After the speech, the dancing and music begins and thrives through the night.

The table of village elders keeps my attention for most of the night. I can't help but think that these people are hiding something from me. What is the real reason I can't speak to the elders?

Another thought takes precedence in my mind. The thought of leaving. I will see how strong my legs are tomorrow and consider leaving, perhaps. I can't stay here. I have a life to go back to, and a daughter and brother to reunite with.

I just wonder what I'll be leaving behind here.

Chapter Ten

ROURK

I wake up with a pounding headache the next morning and see that I'm being watched. A scrawny dog is in the hut with me, panting lightly with its tongue out. I think I've seen this dog around the village but it's beyond me why it's so interested in watching me.

I get up, wincing at the throbbing in my head, and shoo the dog away. It stays in place and cocks its head curiously.

"Get out of here," I say hoarsely. "Go on." It doesn't look to be leaving anytime soon.

I push myself to my feet and wave my hand wildly at him. "Go!"

The dog gets spooked and finally darts out of the hut.

The Shanti People really know how to make strong wine. I take a while to find my clothes and get dressed. As I pull on my sleeveless shirt, I realize my legs haven't been bothering me. I don't think I can push myself too much, but it's a relief to not have any irritation or weakness in my movements.

The light is temporarily blinding when I leave the hut, with the sun a good way up the sky. Most of the village is already awake.

Several of the sister wives are at the main campfire in the center of the field, busy making what smells like a morning brew. The smoky aroma is drifting in the air and helping me wake up.

I stretch my lower back and greet the late morning sun, taking in the bird songs and low chatter of the mingling villagers. The short woman with the auburn hair, Magdalena, is standing between two of the tents, locked in a close conversation with two men. The oldest of them is Yovin, the old man who had told me I'd been brought to their village for a great purpose. The other is tall and robust, maybe a little older than me, with white streaks on the sides of his dark hair. I think his name is Colm. The three of them seem to be having a private, serious talk about something, tucked away in the shade between the tents. They notice me and disperse, their stern expressions softening into casual indifference and innocent smiles. I have to wonder what that had been about.

"You survived the festival," a familiar voice says.

I turn to see Leila walking through the field. She's wearing a faded brown apron, matching her long skirt that is swishing along the ground. A bowl of dark beans is in her hands. A friendly smile on her face greets me.

"I'm surprised, myself," I say. "You Shanti People certainly hold your liquor better than any Oathlander."

"Outsiders just don't have our constitution," she says with a smile and a wink. Her friendliness feels nice and is very welcome, especially compared to the scolding hatred I get from her sister. Her sister, who I have to fight to keep from looking around for now that I've thought of her.

I nod toward the bowl in her hands. "That's right. You're a sister wife?"

"Technically, yes," Leila says. "Although I don't partake in their activities as much as I should. Jonah and Milo take up too much of my time for that. I do what I can to be helpful, though." She pauses and gives me a mischievous grin, like I've missed a joke. "You were seen last night, you know."

I raise a brow. "I was seen?"

"Oh, yes, you were. With Wini Semassi. Out behind the tents."

I let out a weary sigh.

Leila chuckles. "How did it go?"

"Nothing went," I quickly respond, my mood souring. "Nothing happened. And she was very annoyed about that."

Leila nods. "That sounds like our Wini. Well, you did the right thing. She's certainly nothing but trouble." She regards me for a moment and seems to approve of what she sees. "I'm impressed, Tarin. Few men can refuse the charms and curves of Wini Semassi."

"I'm sure I'll regret it," I say, wondering how obvious my sarcasm is. "So... who saw us?"

She cocks an eyebrow. "Why? Are you worried my sister saw you?"

My face drops. "Huh? What do you mean?"

Leila chuckles lightly, enjoying herself. "Nothing. It was Abby Don'Dallen who had noticed the two of you sneaking around. She's not one for spreading gossip, I promise. Abby only told me as a friend, knowing about your association with our family, so your secret is safe. Don't worry, Galene doesn't know."

I frown in confusion. "I'm sure I don't care what your sister knows or doesn't know. I was only wondering if I would develop a reputation around here. I wouldn't want people to get the wrong impression of me. Your people have been very kind to me, and I wouldn't want to tarnish that."

She has that appraising look in her eyes again. "Want to help us?" She nods towards the sister wives.

I go with her to the campfire and help ladle the morning tea into several mugs. This is the tea they call farro-fan, which has a potent, aromatic kick to it and helps clear away the morning haze. Many people would either be making their own tea, simply not be interested in it, or not be old enough to consume it. But the sister wives cater to the thirty or so people who would be happy to take a mug from them.

Around us, people have begun repairing the broken huts and structures of the village. Several of the hunters and workers are cutting down trees in the distance. A large collection of trunks and branches has been collected and brought over by carts. A group of people are busy carving the wood into beams and poles with expert ease.

Eventually, I can't help but ask, "Why did you think I'd care if Galene saw? Or if she knew?"

Leila just smiles.

Cryptic. I take a tray with tea mugs and take it around the nearby huts and tents, allowing people to help themselves. The walk around the village is helping to clear my head, as is the heady aroma of the tea.

Around the back of the row of tents, I pass one and see Aldus is inside, speaking with a few people around a table. Wanting to know what they are talking about, I go in with the pretense of asking if they'd like some farro-fan tea.

I recognize Colm, the large man with the white hair at his temples, who had been speaking with Magdalena earlier. The Head Hunter, Bohan, is there with a sour look on his wide face. A stern-looking woman with a pinched expression, her hair up in a tight bun, is sitting beside Colm.

"I don't want to tell people we have run out of food," Aldus is saying. "Do you?"

The occupants of the table stop talking and turn to me when I enter the tent.

"Run out of food?" I ask innocently.

Colm sighs and says, "No. Far from it."

I stand there with the tray of steaming mugs.

"Tarin, lad," Aldus says. "We were just making plans to send hunters out. We are indeed going to be low on meat."

The muscled Bohan hisses at him. "Why are you telling this outsider our affairs?"

Aldus absently scratches at his beard. "Tarin is our guest, who saved many people in the attack. He can be trusted."

I'm not sure I believe that's why he's telling me these things, but I appreciate the gesture, anyway.

"We have plenty of meat," the woman beside Colm says, her accent thick and clipped. "But, yes, we can do with more."

Aldus gestures to a nearby stool. "Take a seat while you're here. I'll take some farro-fan from you. It smells intoxicating."

I place the tray down and take a mug for myself as I sit on the stool, keeping some distance between me and the table.

"Colm and his wife Deena look after our food supplies," Aldus says to me. "We've recently discovered that the bandits had taken several animal carcasses with them during their raid the other night. That has set us back a few weeks of food, and so we're having to arrange a hunt."

Colm shakes his head, showing a flash of frustration. "I've been telling you we need to send people out to find a farm with chickens." He turns to me and adds, "We've been at a loss since the Wildmen killed the last of our chickens a few years ago."

"I miss eggs," his wife mutters with a forlorn look.

"Joven Tektas said he thought he saw a boar a few days ago out in the northern plains," Colm tells them. "By the foothills of the Shadowstand Mountains."

"That area is known for several varieties of birds, also," Aldus says.

"I can take a few men and search the area," Bohan says.

They've forgotten I'm there, but I speak up to say, "May I go along? I've been meaning to stretch my legs more to test my strength, and I'd like to be helpful if I can. To thank you for your hospitality."

Bohan sneers fiercely at me, as if I've just insulted his mother. "We need no help from you, outsider."

"I think that's a good idea," Aldus says. He has a quiet commanding air about him, and doesn't need to raise his voice or force attention on himself. "I'm sure we could use the expertise of an Oathland's soldier."

Bohan scoffs. "Then you use his expertise here. We do not need him on a hunt."

"If I go on the hunt with you," I say coolly, not matching his hot tone, "I promise I will leave this village on my return. If I am capable of doing so."

Bohan scrutinizes me. He casts a look at Aldus and Colm before shaking his head and finally agreeing. He downs a mug of the farro-fan tea in one go, despite it being steaming hot. I don't show how impressed I am by that.

"I think Freddick should go, also," Colm says.

"He has not been on a hunt beyond our village borders yet," Aldus says.

I watch the two of them with some interest.

"The boy has been a wreck with his father slain in the raid," Colm says. "Going on his first proper hunt will help clear his mind. Give him something to focus on."

"Good point," Aldus says, and takes a sip of his tea.

"I want Zayne and Wills, too," Bohan says. He has the grumpy air of a child desperately trying to get their way.

Aldus nods in agreement. "Very well. I trust you can prepare to leave within the hour?"

"We can," Bohan says.

"Excellent," Aldus says. "I have but one more stipulation. I want my Galene to go with you."

Bohan opens his mouth to object, but Aldus raises a hand to cut him off.

"Her Task with Tarin is technically not complete," Aldus says. "I'd like her to go with you to continue watching over him. A hunt will help mature her. And, once you are back, that will be the end of her Task."

"She will not like that," I say.

Aldus grins at me. "She will not. But you leave her to me."

Chapter Eleven

GALENE

My fists are balled tight as I walk through the fields near the village. I tried pleading with my father not to make me go on the hunt, but he was adamant and had promised my Task would be complete on my return.

If going on the hunt means I can finally wash my hands of the Oathlander, then that is what I must do. Not like I have much of a choice anyway—if I said no, I wouldn't complete my Task. And after everything I've already done, everything I've already done for Tarin, that's not an option.

The sun is high in the air, drifting in and out of the heavy dark clouds, as we leave the fields and enter the barren grassland of the Brownlands.

I know why I'm here. It's because I am unwed and without a child. I'm seen by many as a disgrace and an unwanted pariah. What good is a woman who refuses to settle down and start a family?

It's not my fault I've never met a man I was interested in. And I certainly have liked none of the eligible men that others have tried to set me up with. Most boys are intimidated by me, and the older men want someone more agreeable and less opinionated.

We've spent half a day traveling so far, going slowly by foot. I've heard many stories about what hunting is like, but I never knew how boring it could be.

Bohan, leading the group, points ahead. "There. The foothills of the Shadowstand Mountains. That is where we will find the boar."

The other hunters, Zayne and Wills, are quietly surveying the surrounding land, their eyes constantly moving. I'm surprised that Freddick is with us, as he is a new hunter and has never been on a proper hunt beyond the village. He may be in his twentieth year, but he acts more like a naïve, innocent teenager. But now his expression is dour, and he hasn't spoken this entire trip. I can see how much he's mourning his father, and it breaks my heart.

Wisely, we have not given the Oathlander a weapon, so the hunters are the only ones carrying spears, knives, and bows and arrows. I keep my dagger sheathed on my belt, although I don't intend to use it.

I sense Tarin walking closer to me and ignore him until he finally speaks.

"I know you don't want my company," he says. "But you will be happy to know that I will be leaving the village once we return."

I turn to him sharply, and cannot help the exasperated sigh that escapes me. I shake my head. "My father told me my Task with you will be complete on my return. He didn't mention that you will also be leaving."

It was smart of my father not to mention that. I would have stayed behind if I had known that the outsider would leave regardless if I went on the hunt or not.

"I won't be happy until you have your back to the village," I tell him.

There's a strained, troubled look on him when he clears his throat. "I want to apologize."

"For your odor?" I say. "There is no apologizing for that."

"For my people," he says, which catches me off guard. "I... did not know of the murder of your mother ten years ago. Can you tell me more about it? I might remember something if I knew more about it."

"I care not what you know," I say. "Do not ask me about my mother again."

"Why are you always trying to get into our business?" Bohan asks, turning towards us as we walk. He adjusts the longbow on his back as he gives Tarin a challenging look.

"I mean no offense," Tarin shrugs. "I'm a curious creature. And I'd like to help where I can, as I have your people to thank for being alive."

Bohan sniffs violently. "You can thank us by shutting up and staying out of our way."

I think that should be the end of it, but Tarin surprises me by continuing to speak.

"I might know a few things about hunting and fighting that I could teach you."

A booming laugh explodes from Bohan. Zayne and Wills join in with low chuckles.

"There is nothing an outsider can teach me," Bohan says. "Enough with this nonsense."

I'm glad Tarin has the sense to leave it at that. He must have sensed what I did. If he'd continued to push Bohan, the Head Hunter would likely have attacked him.

We walk for some time with the sun beaming down on us. I watch the shifting shape of a group of birds passing through the sky. The pack over my shoulder is beginning to feel heavy and annoying.

Zayne addresses Tarin. "What part of the Oathlands are you from?"

It takes Tarin a few seconds to answer, which tells me he is thinking of a lie.

"The city center," Tarin says. "Are you familiar with the Oathlands?"

"I visited when I was younger," Zayne says. "I was not born a Shanti. I grew up in The Kingdom."

Tarin raises his brows, and my expression matches his. I never knew Zayne was from the Kingdom. He stands at over six feet with a powerful build, deep-set dark eyes, and a thick square jaw. His complexion is lighter and creamier than an average Shanti, but I've never considered that to mean he was an outsider. From the non-reactions of the other hunters, I take it that Zayne's heritage has not been a secret from them.

"A Kingdom folk among the Shanti?" Tarin says. "How did that happen?"

"I... did not enjoy my upbringing," Zayne says. "I decided to leave in my late teens. I traveled the land for a time. I met many decent Oathlanders. Your people are very welcoming, and you like to feed people."

Tarin chuckles. "We do."

"Eventually I found the Shanti People, and I was accepted among them," Zayne says. "I have been one of them for almost thirty years now." His voice drops into melancholy.

I want to ask why Zayne is being so open with him. Why are we entertaining this Oathlander?

Something draws Bohan's attention. He straightens and takes a few steps toward the rolling hills in the south. The land steadily grows greener with an abundance of life, and it's through a thin woods that I see what Bohan has noticed.

Far to the south, a hundred or so soldiers are marching in close formation. They are hard to see, but their gleaming white armor catches the sun and makes them stand out against the rolling fields.

We stop to watch the distant figures through the trees.

"Are those... Kingdom Soldiers?" Freddick asks, a hint of fear in his low voice.

"What are they doing?" Wills asks.

"It doesn't concern us," Bohan says with some annoyance.

"They are training," Tarin says. "Soldiers will often march across the surrounding lands to remain familiar with the land and keep their fitness up. Also, it acts as a reminder to anyone who may be looking that the military is present and organized."

"He is correct," Zayne says.

"I didn't think the Kingdom ventured this far out, so close to the Wilderness."

"They are far enough away not to bother us, so we do not need to bother them," Bohan says, and nods for us to keep walking.

"Our Oathlands Military would also march," Tarin says, half in thought. "But we do so less for the show of it, unlike the Kingdom."

Bohan seethes through his teeth. "You think you Oathlanders are so much better than everyone else. Better than us Shanti."

"That's not true," Tarin says. "I just think we have our customs, and you have yours."

Bohan points a frustrated finger at him. His other hand is on his longbow, I note. "You are not here to speak, outsider. That is enough from you."

Tarin's gaze and his tone remain cool. "I was simply saying there is nothing wrong with training and discipline. You wouldn't understand that, though. Because you know so much already."

Bohan's eyes flash with murder. He unslings the bow and quiver of arrows and strides toward Tarin. "I said that's enough! I will show you who the stronger fighter is."

I tense and back away, not wanting to be near the ensuing fight.

Bohan shoves Tarin in the chest, but Tarin moves like a flash of lightning and suddenly Bohan's hand is twisted and he has dropped to a knee. Tarin stands there calmly with Bohan's bent wrist in his hand. I can see Bohan wants to break free, but the hold looks to be too strong.

"That's enough!" I yell.

Tarin remains there for a second longer before releasing his hold. Bohan pants heavily and rubs his sore wrist as he stands and backs away, his blazing eyes locked on Tarin. I've never seen someone so easily overpower a big man like Bohan before. I have a feeling that Tarin could have easily broken his wrist if he'd wanted to.

Freddick blows out a breath. "That was a really cool move. Can you teach me that?"

"Perhaps another time," Tarin says with a slight grin.

We continue toward the foothills of the mountain.

Along the way, we check the rabbit traps hunters had set up across the area. Every now and then, the hunters take us off course to check a metal box hidden in the underbrush.

Zayne and Wills explain to Tarin that the small cages contain kimisol flowers within. The violet petals emit an aroma that helps people sleep and dulls their senses, and is also used to help injured people recover faster. We place the kimisol petals in the cages to entice small critters like rabbits and foxes, and when they enter, the cage door drops and traps them inside. They peacefully fall asleep until we come and take them. We pick out a few rabbits from the cages as we go, and place them in a sack.

"The smell is familiar," Tarin says to me. "Do you put some in tea?"

"In the tea I made for you," I nod. "The one you refused on account of it being poisoned."

"The one you threw across the tent," he pushes back. But then his voice softens. "My fault for not trusting you."

That almost sounds like an apology. I turn away from him and no longer pay him attention. But I do eventually find myself gazing over at him. I note how toned his arms are, which speaks of years of training. And how plump and pouty his lips are. I have to admit how impressed I am at the keen intelligence in his eyes as he studies the surrounding land. I'm beginning to see there is more to this Oathlander than I realized.

After some time, I see Tarin has fallen behind with Freddick. I listen to their talk without looking back.

"How are you holding up?" Tarin asks.

Freddick doesn't give a response.

"I know this isn't an easy time for you." Tarin's voice is filled with surprising warmth and compassion. "Losing a father is never easy. I want you to know that it's okay to mourn. To feel bad. It's okay to do whatever you want. There's no right or wrong way to grieve."

Freddick sniffs. "I don't know what to do without him. He did everything for me. I wouldn't be here if it weren't for him."

"When my father passed," Tarin says, his strained voice showing great depths, "I lost myself in the bottle. I lost sight of myself completely for a while. My brother tried to get me back, but in the end, only I could help myself. I realized I should make my father proud and work to become the best man I could be. For him."

"When does it get easier?" Freddick asks, sounding like he's close to tears.

"That's different for everyone," Tarin says. "In some ways, the pain is always with you. But you learn to live with it." He claps Freddick on the shoulder. "You will get through this. I can see there is a great warrior inside you."

I glance back to see Freddick giving him a confused look.

Tarin points at Freddick. "It's in your eyes. I've seen it before. That warrior inside. Trust me."

That seems to cheer Freddick up and he walks with his shoulders higher. I watch Tarin for a moment, wondering what kind of a man he really is. That was a nice thing he'd done for Freddick. I hate how it shows some goodness in his heart. Unless he has an ulterior motive for acting so nice.

He is a man full of surprises.

We eventually reach the rocky foothills of the Shadowstand Mountains, the peaks of which loom over us and block out the sun. We won't have to climb high up the mountain as the wild boars are known to stay low within the winding paths of the foothills. They feed off the rich weeds and shrubs growing between the rocks.

Bohan and the others hear something that I don't, and he directs us up a pathway. We enter a passage filled with trees and come out to an open glade surrounded by jagged rock.

Something enormous crashes through the tree line above the jagged rock and comes hurtling down toward us. A massive boar lands and roars at us. But this is no ordinary boar, this one is three times bigger than any I've ever seen, and it appears to be highly enraged. My muscles soften like jelly at the sight of the powerful beast.

The boar roars and charges at us.

Chapter Twelve

GALENE

The hunters scatter and ready their weapons as the boar charges at us. I run as fast as my legs can carry me to get out of its way, heading for a collection of trees and shrubs in the open glade.

For an enormous beast, it is surprisingly fast and lively. Long tusks protrude from its thick-lipped snout. Beneath its short gray fur, powerful muscles give the animal a robust, intimidating look. This can't be an ordinary boar. The way it's shaking its head and huffing makes me think it is unhinged, looking to tear us all apart.

The hunters' arrows deflect off the boar's thick hide. Freddick has a spear in hand, but he becomes frozen with fear when the bull charges at him. Tarin is there in a flash and tackles Freddick to the side just before the boar reaches them. It ends up crashing into a rock wall and becoming dazed for a few seconds, which only serves to anger it further.

Bohan spins a rope overhead and throws it at the boar. The wide noose catches on the boar's head and holds tight. Bohan stands firm and yanks the rope to steady the boar, which gives the others a chance to fire more arrows. But the arrows continue to deflect off its thick skin and fall to the ground. The boar jerks its head and Bohan is forced to release the rope before he's pulled off his feet. I see Bohan's pain as he gasps at the rope burn on his hands.

I stay by the trees and shrubs, even if I know they will serve me no safety if the boar comes for me. I leave the dagger in its sheath, knowing it will be useless in my hands.

Tarin has a spear in his hands now, possibly taken from Freddick, and he manages to jump on the boar and stick the spear into its back. The spear stays in place as the boar roars in anger, but it doesn't slow it down. Tarin drops to the ground and rolls away from a thrusting tusk. My throat catches. Tarin looks injured. Had the boar struck him? No, he must have hurt his ankle. He can't get up.

The other hunters try to distract the boar from the other side, but they can't get close enough to effectively use their spears. The boar notices Tarin is on the ground still and that gets its attention. It takes a few careful steps toward Tarin before breaking into a heaving run.

I rush out from the trees and head for Tarin, not knowing what I'm going to do. I can't just leave him to die there though. Spit flies from the boar as it nears Tarin, who is struggling to stand.

It's too late. We're out of time. I reach Tarin a split-second before the boar flattens us. I scream and instinctively hold a hand over myself.

A blinding golden light comes to life over me, taking the form of a solid square. The boar crashes into the square of light and gets knocked back several feet, as though it has struck a solid rock wall.

I blink back my focus as the light disappears. It came from my arm, I think. A solid barrier of golden light. Tarin looks just as surprised as I feel.

Freddick's cries fill the glade. He has grabbed hold of the rope around the boar's neck and is being dragged through the rocky dirt.

"Stay back," Tarin says to me, now on his feet. "And thank you," he adds as he makes his way to the boar. He can hardly walk, but he looks determined to help. He must be a madman.

I'm looking back at the boar as I rush toward the trees, and suddenly I find myself falling. I roll and drop into a low ditch I hadn't seen before. My vision spins for a sickening moment before I settle with a thud on the muddy ground, my legs up on the rim of the ditch.

I look up and can just about see the boar barreling out of the glade with Freddick still being dragged with it. The boar crashes through the trees and disappears from view. Everyone takes chase, not looking back. Not noticing I am not with them. I call out but they don't hear me. They have left me.

The crashing sounds of the boar fade, and the glade becomes very quiet. I call out again, but there is no one to hear me. My head drops back in the mud. I'm a complete mess and stained with mud and dirt all over.

Movement catches my eye. I look up to see I am not alone. Tarin stands over me, blocking out the sun. I become very aware that my legs are up and my skirt has dropped and become stuck in the mud, revealing more of my thighs than I'd like.

"Need a hand?" he asks.

I drop my head back with a sigh. "No. I am perfectly fine here, thank you."

"Okay then." He steps away.

"Hey!" I yell. "Come here. Where are you going?"

He can't seem to help the smirk on his face as he takes my outstretched hand and helps me to my feet.

"You didn't chase after the boar?" I say.

"An Oathlands soldier would never leave their squad," he says.

His firm sense of duty is almost impressive.

I pick up the sack of supplies I'd dropped. "We should go after them." I can no longer hear the boar or the hunters, but they can't have gone far. They must be somewhere within the rocky foothills.

"Go, but I can't run," he says. "I think I twisted my ankle during my heroic acrobatics."

"You mean you tripped," I say. I watch him carefully, wondering if he's telling the truth about his ankle.

I shove him. He staggers back a few steps and his left leg buckles under him. I quickly reach him before he falls to the ground.

"What in the hells..." he says in surprise.

"Sorry, just checking," I say, and look at the tree line we'd entered from. "I can't hear them."

"I think they're a good distance away," Tarin says. "They were so intent on catching the boar and helping Freddick, that I don't think they're going to be back anytime soon."

"You don't know that," I say defiantly.

"Come on, let's see if we can follow their trail."

I walk with him. My adrenaline is still high from the boar attack. My dress is caked in mud and my hair feels like a matted mess. "Is that something you can do? Follow their trail?"

"It depends on the trail."

I can't believe I'm stuck here with him, of all people. But I have no choice but to work with him if we're going to get out of here in one piece. And I know it means something that he was the only one to stay behind. Perhaps he isn't such an evil man after all. Perhaps.

He eyes me as we pass through the trees. "So... would you like to tell me about that golden light you summoned?"

I hold my chin high. "No."

And that's that.

Chapter Thirteen

GALENE

I follow Tarin through the rocky pathways for some time. I'm not sure where he's taking me exactly, even if he says he's checking on prints in the dirt and broken branches. At times, I insist on going in one direction, and we bicker for a while before one of us gives in.

The only weapon we have is the dagger on my belt, but I prefer to keep that to myself. If I'm going to be alone with this man, I prefer to be the one with the weapon. Even though he could likely kill me with his bare hands before I pull the dagger from its sheath.

The sun has already dipped toward the horizon and has long since hidden behind the higher points of the mountain. All around us are rock walls and rough pathways that incline or decline. I feel like we're trapped in a maze. The only sounds are the clumps of dirt shifting under our steps and the low howl of wind.

"I can't believe they vanished like that," I say, shaking my head. "Be honest. Are you really following their trail, or...?"

"Or what? You think I'm purposely keeping us here?"

I shrug.

He grins at me, which makes me grow hot with anger.

"What?" I demand.

"You pout when you have no response," he says with a smirk. "It's cute."

Cute? Did he just use that word? I eye him mistrustfully, feeling flustered. "You didn't answer my question."

"Because I thought it was a foolish one," he says, his smirk growing wider. "Am I following their trail or keeping us here on purpose?" he asks.

I nod.

"I will answer that if you first answer my question."

I know what's coming.

"What was that golden light?" Tarin asks.

I shake my head in defeat. We step through a narrow gap between the rocks and come out onto the other side to find more open pathways and high walls. I don't like that we're going higher instead of lower.

"Can't you let it go?"

"Can't you put a little trust in me?" he retorts.

"No," I snap.

"Then no," Tarin murmurs.

I sigh, then say, "I was one of the few who discovered their magical abilities when the world changed," I admit. "I've hardly tested what I can do, but... When I concentrate, I can summon light from my hands. Sometimes it happens without me thinking about it."

"Your father has the same gift?"

I nod. "Similar. Maybe it's the same. I don't know. I never asked for it, anyway."

"What you did back there," Tarin says, watching me carefully. "That was more than just light."

"I know. The light... hardened. It became solid."

"Very solid," he says. "It didn't even jar you, did it?"

I shake my head and shift some muddy hair from my face. I'm beginning to notice how bad I smell.

"You can probably do a lot more than that if you explore your powers," Tarin says.

"No thanks. Not interested," I say, but hate how stubborn I sound. "My father keeps telling me I should master my powers. I just want to stay the person I was before."

"You still are that same person," he says, and watches for my response. Why does his gaze feel so heavy and powerful?

"You don't know me," I say, then turn sharply away. "Oh."

I spot a pool of water on the rock. My guess is it's collected rainwater, but it'll do me just fine. I drop the bag of supplies and bend down to wash some of the mud from my arms and hair. My skirt is ruined and my blouse has fared little better, but it feels good to clear some of the mud away. Tarin looks around us while I clean myself.

I feel somewhat better with my arms and legs cleared of the mud, and some of the larger chunks removed from my clothes. My blouse is soaking now though, and I notice Tarin's eyes roaming my body, though he tries to hide it. I dismiss him and finish cleaning myself as best I can.

"I might know you better than you think," he finally responds.

I feel myself flushing with annoyance and turn to face him. "Oh, really? Go on, then. Tell me who I am, if you know so much."

His face tenses with something earnest, like he's stripped away his arrogant mask and showing his true self. His true self that startles me.

"I know you have a big heart," he says, "and care too much for others. You are one of the most selfless people I've ever met. But you hide your kindness and care behind a tough, stubborn exterior because you're afraid of getting your sensitive heart hurt."

That leaves me speechless for a second before I compose myself. "Generic," I simply say, and fold my arms over my chest. I can feel the cold air seeping into my wet skin, but I fight back the urge to shiver.

"I can see what kind of child you were," Tarin says. "I can see it clearly. Full of life, and very cheeky. Too smart for your own good. I bet you were a girl who played with dolls and made sure each one was happy. Because you have to make sure that everyone is happy."

A chill washes over me. My mouth has fallen open. How could he have known that? My voice is low when I admit, "My favorite dolls were called Mave and Socks. Socks was the scared one, and Mave would always cheer her up."

"It was you cheering Socks up, not Mave. You used them both to process your own emotions of fear and confidence."

I cannot fathom how he could possibly know this about me. It feels like he's seeing right into me and I don't like it.

"Above all," he says, "you just want to be accepted for who you are. You want comfort and safety, and someone who accepts you for everything you are."

I raise an eyebrow. "Generic again." But he is right. Everything he said was right.

Is he reading me? Does he also have that ability? I focus on him and try to connect to that feeling of a spark within me.

"What?" he asks when he notices how much I'm staring at him. "You want to have a go at me? Tell me about my childhood?"

A thrumming vibration reverberates through my mind as I feel a connection passing between us. I expect to hear a voice, like an inner thought, or feel an emotion, but there is none of that. He is surprisingly hard to tap into.

Then something reaches out to me. There. An inner thought. I think. It's a flash of a feeling, but it hits me with great clarity. I straighten.

"Your name is not Tarin," I say in surprise.

His face hardens, like a shield crashing down to protect him. His eyes are wide and it's the first time I've seen him so shaken.

The word 'How' passes silently on his lips.

My danger senses kick in. He isn't who he said he is? Who is this man?

In the distance, thunder rumbles in the sky and softly echoes around us.

I realize I shouldn't push the matter because it might force him to take action. He might get violent or end up running away and leaving me here. I have to stay calm for now. I can't show how afraid I am.

"Anyway, it doesn't matter what name you go by. What matters is that we get off this mountain. Any suggestions?"

He regains his composure and replies, "It seems that the others went a good distance away before noticing we weren't with them. If they have killed the boar, they may have chosen to return to the village with it."

"They wouldn't leave us!" I'm horrified at the thought.

"Well, they won't care about coming back for me," he says. "If they are out there now, looking for you, we would have heard them by now."

A shiver shakes my shoulders. I hug myself, realizing how cold it is getting.

Tarin…or whatever his name is…studies the sky, and doesn't seem to like what he's seeing. I don't like the growing dark clouds, and how cold it's getting. Maybe I'm feeling the cold because I'm dripping wet.

"It will be night soon," he says.

"Oh no," I say. "Don't say it."

"We will have to find a place to stay for the night, and continue at first light."

My shoulders sag. "You said it."

"It isn't ideal," he says, "but we have no other choice at this point. We don't want to be out here in full darkness."

"I'm not spending the night here alone with you," I say stubbornly.

"We won't be alone," he says. "We will have the coyotes and vultures and snakes and a number of other creatures." He grins at me.

I narrow my eyes at him, weighing my options. He's right that we can't be out here once it's dark. We could try to leave the mountains before full night comes, but then we'd be out in the wilds with no cover, completely exposed to the elements.

I sigh and meet his gaze. "If we stay here tonight, I want something out of you first," I say. "What is your real name?"

He regards me for a moment, his mouth a straight line. I see this isn't easy for him.

"My name is Rourk," he says.

I feel like the name is familiar, but I can't be certain. "That wasn't so hard, was it?"

"No," he says. "But please, keep this between us. It doesn't matter who I am. Just know that I don't mean you or your people any harm. None at all."

"If it doesn't matter, then why hide it?" I ask.

"I've been told many times by your people to allow you your privacy. That goes both ways."

"Fine," I grit out, but am not fully happy.

A cool breeze blows through the mountain path, causing me to shiver and hug myself. My teeth begin clattering. With the sun behind the mountain, the weather has shifted fairly quickly.

"Alright," I finally say. "We can find shelter here for the night."

"Fantastic," he says with a smirk. "I have some good scary stories."

I roll my eyes and follow him through a descending slope in the rocks. It's fairly steep and my boots don't seem to hold well on the gravelly slope, so Tarin takes my hand and helps me down.

Rourk. Not Tarin. I have to get used to that. Why would he hide his name? Was he afraid we would know who he was? I can't think of any Oathlander I know by name, other than its ruler, Arthur Bearon. Even his Fae Queen's name is beyond me.

"You must have a strong magical lineage," Rourk says as we search for a suitable resting place.

I continue hugging myself against the cold. "My father used to tell Leila and I how we were descended from a famous heroine. Someone from the old world. It was just a story, though. Or we thought it was, anyway. And when magic returned to the world, we found his stories to be true."

"Leila has the same abilities as you?"

"My gifts came in the form of summoning light from my hands," I say. "Same as my father. Leila, on the other hand, has shadows. And she can sometimes sense what a person is thinking or feeling."

He turns to me. "Like you."

I'm not sure if he truly knows that or is just testing me. I shake my head. "Not like me."

"But that's how you knew my name wasn't Tarin?"

"I see how you respond to your own name," I lie. "As though you're not used to hearing it."

I don't meet his gaze as he watches me.

Not comfortable with the silence, I continue, "Leila has hardly used her ability, anyway. It mostly comes without her trying. She doesn't like the idea of invading people's privacy like that."

I don't tell him that Leila and I are unusual. It seems that everyone who received magic unlocked one major magical gift, while Leila and I both received two. The ability to summon light, or in her case, darkness, and to sense people's thoughts.

I had been the first to show my light power to the public while Leila had managed to hide the fact that she could do the same with darkness from everyone but me. And when the villagers wondered why Leila had not attained light-summoning magic like our father and me, she had eventually admitted her ability to sense things in people's minds, but hid the shadows she carried in her veins. I'm glad I was wise enough not to reveal my own mind-sensing abilities. I still don't know how it works. I just get glimpses of feelings from others sometimes.

The light has faded rapidly around us, and the wind is picking up. Angry dark clouds are building overhead. We are less than a day away from the village, but this feels like we're trapped in another world.

"Here we go," Rourk says.

He points to a small crevasse in the rock, like a tiny cave, hidden by shrubs and gnarled weeds. The gap is long and narrow, small enough to barely fit one of us.

"You want us both to get in there?" I ask, raising an eyebrow.

"It'll help us stay warm, at least," he says, but looks just as doubtful as I am.

My heart begins to race.

Chapter Fourteen

ROURK

I have to be careful how I lay next to Galene, as I don't want to risk overstepping or making things any more awkward than they already are. Although our options are limited in the small gap in the rock wall, and it feels like we are laying in a coffin-shaped hole with a rocky ceiling close to our heads.

It's awkward to press our shoulders against each other, so I lift my arm to curl it around Galene to allow her head to rest on my shoulder.

"Hey," she says when I move my arm over her.

I give her an innocent look and continue moving, but very slowly. It's hard to deny that my arm being around her has made the space more comfortable for both of us. Regardless of how inappropriate it feels.

We watch the light slowly fade on the mountain and feel the howling wind picking up. The far-off rumble of thunder echoes in the air.

"I have a question," I say gently. "But you will not like it."

Galene sighs. "No, we will not rub our bodies together for warmth."

That catches me off guard. "What?"

She looks up at me. "What?"

I give her a bizarre, confused smile. I'm not sure why her mind wandered there.

"No, I..." I take a second to reconfigure my thoughts. "I would like to ask you about your mother. And the Oathlander who killed her..."

She takes a long moment to acknowledge my words. Her voice becomes low and strained. "She was out with my uncle, her brother. They were picking berries in The Greens, before the Wetstones that divide the Wildlands from the Oathlands. She was due to give birth in another two seasons and wanted to go on a foraging trip before she would have to stay home and wait for the baby to come. The Oathlanders... they were dressed in weathered cloaks, like Wildmen. But they were clearly not Wildmen. They attacked and cut my mother down, like an animal."

"How do you know these details?" I ask, hoping the question doesn't offend her.

"My uncle had his arm cut off. He was left for dead with my mother. But he managed to return to our village. He... died three days later from an infection."

"And what did your uncle say about these Oathlanders?"

She keeps her head tilted low so I can't see her face. "That they wore the uniforms of the Oathlands military beneath their cloaks. He described the man who had slain my mother. The man had a scar on his neck, so was easily identifiable."

I stop breathing for a moment. "A scar?"

Galene draws a line down her neck with her finger. My heart is pounding hard in my chest. I hope she doesn't notice.

"My father led a group to infiltrate the Oathlands," she goes on. "They managed to find out the name of the man. But they were told the man had been struck with an illness and was not accepting visitors."

Despite the cold, I've started to sweat. This all sounds far too familiar. But she can't be speaking about what I think she is. This can't be happening.

"You... learned the man's name?" I ask, my voice sounding hollow. I clear my throat.

"Yes. The man who murdered my mother and unborn brother is named Delton Alacante."

My breath catches in my throat. It feels like I've been dropped from a great distance.

"Are you certain?" I ask, barely able to speak now.

She meets my eyes. "Do you know him?"

Yes. I know my father's name.

"They said he had been someone close to Queen Moira," Galene says.

I have to force my voice to remain calm, despite the screaming devastation in my mind. "I know that Delton Alacante did pass from an illness," I confirm.

"You knew him?" she asks, sounding mistrustful.

"Not really," I lie. "But, yes, he was known to me."

I struggle to process what I'm hearing. My father had murdered Galene's mother? He had slain a pregnant woman in the Wildlands? That can't be true.

Moira Bearon had taken my father's name when they wed. After she was murdered by Kingdom assassins, Arthur and I disbanded our royal lineage, and the Oathlands had become a military-led nation. We have gone by our mother's name of Bearon ever since. My father had become a broken man after his wife died, and he was content to let us break the royal line. I knew his mind had been failing him in his final years, particularly in the lead-up to his illness taking hold of his body.

Could he have slain a Shanti woman in his final year of life? Why would he have done such a thing? I want to tell Galene she must be mistaken, but I can't reveal what I know.

The sound of heavy rain interrupts my train of thought. Our view of the mountain becomes filled with thick raindrops thudding on the ground. The sparse shrubs around the crevasse sway in the wind. My boots get spattered with wayward raindrops, but at least we know we are safe and covered in here.

Galene shivers against me.

"Here," I say, and put my hand on her arm to keep her warm.

She flinches away from me and knocks her elbow into the rock. She winces and seethes at me.

"Now, don't get the wrong idea," I say, and gently place my hand back on her arm. I shift my body so we're pressed more together. Her body is covered in goosebumps. There is a distinct muddy smell around us, but I don't bring that up.

"You're the one who shouldn't get the wrong idea," she says. "You understand?"

"Yes," I respond. I would only admit it to myself, but it does feel good to have her in my arms.

The rain picks up and a flash of lightning highlights the rocks outside. It's become a full storm out there. For a while, the only sound is the crashing rain.

Galene stirs beside me. "How did you know those things about me? About when I was younger."

"Maybe I'm magic, too," I say. "Or, well... I've always been able to read people well."

"Can you... Leila says she gets a feeling within her, like a vibration, when she hears someone's thoughts or senses their feelings."

I smile. "It's no magic trick." Then I consider that. "I think."

She yawns and sleepily nuzzles into me. I can see she is more comfortable around me, but I can't stop thinking about my father being the one who killed her mother. I can't tell her, because we're only just starting not to hate each other and I don't want to ruin that.

"You should sleep," I say, noting how tired my voice sounds.

"I can't sleep while you're awake," she says.

"What are you afraid of?"

"I'm not afraid," she says, and yawns again.

Something howls in the night, sounding very close. Galene flinches and knocks her head on the low ceiling.

She has leaned into me in her fear, and my hand is gripping her side. I become aware of how closely pressed together we are, and how close our faces now are. Her sweet breath and the floral hair scent mix with the mud caked in her hair. Her cheeks are smeared with dried dirt.

I know I should move away from her. We're better off leaving our hesitant friendship just the way it is. If not for the past, for what my father did to her mother, then for the future. I'm going to be leaving soon, and she's going to be staying. There's no use starting something that will undoubtedly end.

But no matter how sure I am that I should pull away from her, I'm even more sure that I can't. Galene's always been the one who backs away, and for good reason.

I just don't have it in me.

"It's okay," I say. "We're safe here. The night has many sounds. You're... safe."

I become lost in her captivating blue eyes for a long moment and feel myself swell with arousal. Her full lips look so inviting. The power in this moment between us is like nothing I've ever known, and I know she feels it too.

We've stripped away our armor and have nothing left but each other. We're so close. I drift toward her. But there is something pained in her eyes. Something that causes her to hesitate.

I swallow and lick my lips and drift away from her. The moment passes like a breath in the wind.

We finally break eye contact, and she rests her head on my chest. I think it's so she doesn't have to look at me anymore, but there is a nice comfort in the way she's wrapped herself around me now. This is nice. This feels good. I'm surprised at how comfortable we are now, pressed into each other like lovers.

We say nothing more, but we don't need to.

It's clear that something has shifted between us.

Chapter Fifteen

GALENE

A foggy haze fills my mind as I drift out of sleep and I find myself entangled with Rourk. My thigh is pressed between his legs and his arm is wrapped around me, his face almost touching mine. I'm still mostly asleep, but I'm aware of him gently moving against me. He is also stirring awake, I think. He hasn't opened his eyes yet.

Rourk groans softly and pushes my head closer to him. I feel my core dampen as he groans and sleepily moves a hand over my body, lifting my blouse and running his hands along my skin. His touch is nothing more than a gentle caress, but I feel it *everywhere*. I *want* it everywhere. I writhe against him and quietly moan with pleasure when one of his hands drifts between my legs and brushes softly over the fabric that shields me from being bare to his touch. I feel like this is a dream, or we're somewhere caught between sleep and a dream. A place only for us.

Our lips touch, and a wave of heat washes over me, igniting a passionate and tender kiss. I breathe him in and taste his salty, sweaty goodness. He holds my face in his hand and kisses me firmly. I can feel his control slipping and know that I'm not far behind him. My hand shifts down to feel his cock swelling against me. Knowing what I do to him is almost intoxicating. I rub him hard over his pants and gasp when he presses even harder against me. "Fuck," Rourk groans. "Galene."

My name on his lips brings me back to my senses. My eyes snap open and I jolt upward. I yelp when I crack my head against the low ceiling.

Rourk's eyes fully open, too, and I watch him fully settle into his body. Like... like he was still asleep before. His hand flies off my breast as if burned.

What the hell were we doing? "Shit," I mutter. I quickly shuffle out of the crevasse and crawl into the morning light. There is a gray tint around the mountain, telling me it is a little after sunrise.

Rourk crawls out after me, but I don't turn to look at him. I just run my hands frantically through my hair as I pace the rock.

"Morning," Rourk says, and I turn sharply to face him to see him squinting against the low light. The mountain is very quiet in the early morning.

"I didn't..." I begin, flustered. "I wasn't... We weren't..." *We weren't about to fuck each other's hands.* What would that be like? The taste of him is still in my mouth.

But Rourk gives me a confused look. "I don't remember anything happening. Do you? I just woke up. Why? Did I miss something?"

Several emotions pass through me before I control myself. He doesn't... remember anything? I don't understand the disappointment that settles into me at the revelation. I give him a stiff smile. "No. Nothing happened. I—I just woke up, too." My eyes flash downward, to the stiffness clearly showing in Rourk's pants, but I quickly look away, chewing on the inside of my cheek as the sight reignites the fire inside my belly.

I'm such a fucking idiot.

"Can we return now?" I ask, deciding the best route to take right now is to change the subject entirely and pretend that nothing—not a single thing—happened.

"We can," Rourk says. He picks up the pack of supplies and pulls out two water skins, handing me one. He finds a chunk of bread and offers me some, but I shake my head. I can't even imagine eating right now. Rourk chews on the bread as we make our way down the mountain.

Rourk tries to make some small talk to avoid the awkward silence that has settled between us, asking how I slept and how I feel today, but I can only give brief responses back. Every time our gazes clash, I remember the feel of his skin against mine. His hands were just a layer of fabric away from where I wanted him the most.

Until he said my name, and I remembered who I am. Who *he* is. Where he comes from.

Once we're finally out of the foothills of the mountain, we make our way through the rocky landscape and into the surrounding hills and valleys. The atmosphere feels heavy with energy, like something has changed. A part of me wonders if I've been feeling this change for some time, but have only been noticing it more as each day passes. It's a hard thing to pinpoint.

My thoughts shift to what had happened between me and Rourk. I don't understand why I can't bring myself to regret it quite as much as I should. He's an *Oathlander*. I shouldn't even want to be alone with him, much less let him kiss me—and much, much more.

Rourk stops us when he sees a rabbit darting through the tall grass. It takes him three tries to finally convince me to hand over my knife. And it only takes a quick flick of his wrist to throw the blade into the rabbit. It dies before it can even process what just happened.

"So they can't tell us we've returned empty-handed," Rourk explains, picking up the limp rabbit.

The sun clears the mountain and bathes us in its warm glow. The air feels heavy and charged with energy from the lingering remains of the storm. Our boots squelch in the soft wet earth. The awkwardness has cleared with the rising sun and the time spent walking behind us. Besides, I have Rourk to myself right now. I might as well use it to my advantage and try to get to know him a little better.

"Are you really just a soldier?" I ask as we walk.

"I've been in the military for over twenty years."

I nod, unable to help the small smile that curls at my lips. "I forget that you're an old man."

"Hey," Rourk says, his features sharp with the sting of my words.

But I just laugh. I think it's the first time I've ever laughed in front of him. "Well, I may be twenty and five, but I've always felt older than I am."

"You have an old soul," he agrees. "Only twelve years between us."

"I suppose you're not that old," I say. Then, still smiling, I cup a hand to the side of my mouth and yell, "I said, I suppose you're not that old."

Rourk blinks at me with wide eyes before a bark of laughter escapes him. I can't help but laugh again, too. I don't think I've seen Rourk so... at ease before, and I have to admit that it sets something free in me as well. A chain reaction. Something that connects us.

Rourk wags a finger at me. "I see how you are."

After some lingering chuckles, I sober up. "That trick you did with Bohan. Where you bent his wrist. Can you... show me how you did it?"

"I feel like the Shanti people are going to have a lot of broken wrists if I do that."

I smile, and Rourk smiles back. I can't help but stare at him, and he stares right back. I'm not so sure I would agree with Kris when she called Rourk handsome. No, he's... beautiful.

"I promise only to use it in life or death situations," I eventually say, and press my hand over my heart in a swear. But then I add, "Or when someone truly deserves it."

Rourk gives in, leading me off the trail and to somewhere just a little more protected. Private. We reach the shade of a cluster of trees and face each other. Birds chirp and rustle above us.

Rourk goes through the motions of slowly throwing a punch to show me how to grab his wrist, where to place my fingers, and where and when to exert force. It only takes me a few tries to get the hang of it. Within minutes, I have him down on one knee with his wrist twisted back.

"I can get used to this," I say with a wicked grin.

I gently apply more pressure to his wrist before releasing him with a sweet smile.

"But can you do it at speed?" Rourk asks, and we try a few more times with him throwing fast but soft punches at me.

I adapt to the change of pace quickly. "Like a natural warrior," he praises. I hate how good his words make me feel.

"What else do you have to teach me?" I ask, bouncing lightly with adrenaline.

Rourk stares at me for a long moment, then shakes his head and grins. "Okay, Galene," he says. "Let's see what else you can do."

He shows me how to throw a punch, and then a combination of punches, but then I ask about self defense. So he teaches me what to do if someone grabs me.

He comes at me from the side, moving slowly as he explains what he's doing and what I should do, and reaches for me. He shows me how to raise a hand to intercept his arm and how to twist his arm with both of my hands, forcing his arm to bend. I admit that I take a little too much pleasure in twisting his arm, in watching him fold from my actions.

"Now, if someone grabs you from behind," he says, "you can twist your body to give yourself room to jab an elbow in their ribs."

With his arms around my neck, he shows me where to place my feet and how to position myself. I restrain myself from hurting him when I elbow his side to get the feel for what I'm supposed to do.

He shows me again, and this time I don't resist. I let him wrap his arms around me and he presses himself against my back. And then we just... remain there, with his face close to mine, breathing against my ear. His arm is resting gently on the top of my breasts and each breath presses them firmly against him. As I turn my head to meet his eyes, I see his expression turn hooded, and I know that if I stay here even just a few seconds more, his lips will be on mine. I want that.

But I can't let it happen.

"I think that's enough," I say, becoming shy and quiet as I ease away from Rourk.

I don't give him the chance to say anything before turning back towards the path we were taking and striding away, refusing to look behind me but knowing with every bone in my body that Rourk is there, just a step behind.

We crest a tall hill and finally see the edge of the woods that leads to the Shanti Village far in the distance. We still have a way to go, but we're making good progress.

When we come across another rabbit in the underbrush of a small woods, I insist on catching this one.

Or trying, anyway, because when I toss the knife, I miss. The rabbit scurries away.

"We'll make a soldier of you yet," Rourk says encouragingly.

"If only the rabbit had tried to punch me," I reply, fighting off the smile that threatens to cross my face. "I'd know how to twist its wrist at least."

We go through the sack of supplies and find some dried meat and hard bread. Along with the water skins, there is a coiled rope, and a rough spun blanket. Neither of us mention how we could have used the blanket last night if we'd known it was in there. I wonder if either of us regrets not having it.

We eat as we walk for a time before my stomach starts to twist. I can't help the groan that escapes my lips.

"What's wrong?" he asks. The concern in his voice is palpable.

"I get this when I walk and eat," I explain. "I'll be fine."

"We can rest for a bit," Rourk says. "We've been making good time. Unless... you want to get back as soon as possible?"

I know I should tell him we should push on. I know I shouldn't want to be alone with him a second longer than I have to. But what I *know* and what I *feel* are two entirely different things. I say, "I'm in no rush to get back."

Rourk grins rakishly at me, and I regret, for just that moment, pulling away from him this morning. What would it have felt like to let him have his way with me? He says, "Neither am I."

There's a group of high rocks ahead which will give us shade and something to lean against while we rest and eat. We sit beside each other and enjoy the quiet stillness of the air. We're quiet for a long while until Rourk speaks up, as if the silence is wholly unacceptable to him.

"Tell me, Galene," he says while chewing the tough meat, which I think is some kind of venison. "What do you want most out of life?"

I give him a confused, thoughtful look, silent for a moment. "What do *you* want most out of life?" I finally ask.

Rourk looks up at the bulging clouds in the sky. "To not be forgotten. To not die alone."

I watch him for a while as his words settle within me, soaking into every bone in my body. *To not be forgotten.* I want to promise him I will always remember him. But I say instead, "Do you have anyone back home? To go back to?" *Someone else to remember you? Someone to be there when you die?*

"My daughter," he says. "She'll be worried about me."

I nod, though I'm truly panicking on the inside. He has a daughter. Which means he has a lover—and he and I—this morning... I swallow thickly. "I'm sure your wife will worry about you as well."

"She would always worry about me," Rourk says. "She had the biggest heart I've ever known. She worried about everyone."

The past tense is a sharp knife. A burning question I cannot ignore. But he doesn't make me ask, either. He continues, "She was taken by an illness. The red cough. It's a disorder some people have. There was nothing we could do for her."

"I'm so sorry to hear that," I say, my voice full of emotion. How horrible is it I feel relief just as much as I feel sadness for him?

"That was ten years ago, though," he says. "We find ways to move on after loss. Even if the person is always with us."

"Around the same time my mother was taken from me," I say dully. I'm trying to sympathize, to show him that some small part of me understands even a little of what he went through, but...

Thoughts of my mother race through my head.

I can no longer meet Rourk's eyes.

"Galene," Rourk says. "I want you to know that I'm deeply sorry for what happened to your mother. I know it won't bring her back, or ease your pain, but I will look into the matter when I return home. I will find out why she was killed."

I shake my head. "There's no need. It happened and cannot be undone." I swallow thickly and force myself to meet his gaze. "For what it's worth, I can see you're not who I thought you were. You helped us during the Wildmen attack, and you helped repair the village in the following days. You looked out for Freddick, who was grieving his father. And you stayed back for me when the others left. I can see you are a good man, Rourk. But that does not mean I can truly trust you. Or like you."

He stares for a long moment, then nods. "Fair enough," he says. "I'll take what I can get."

I give him a small smile. Some of the tension has seeped away, leaving a warm familiarity.

"You didn't answer my question," he says finally. "What do you want most out of life?"

I chew the inside of my cheek while I go back to considering the question. But the answer is more obvious now than it was before. "To have a peaceful life, filled with love and acceptance. And safety."

Rourk slowly nods. "I like that. I hope you find it someday."

We finish the last of the food and decide it's time to head back. A golden ribbon of light in the sky catches my attention. It's like an eel, I think, but it's drifting casually and intentionally through the air. Its scales are golden and a faint golden aura is emitting from it.

"What is that?" Rourk asks, pointing.

I study it for a moment, absorbing the details before I give him an answer. "A sky eel, of a kind I have never seen before."

"You've seen a sky eel before? I didn't think there were any around here?"

"Once. Far to the north, near the coast. When I was younger. When the world felt safer. This, however... must be a fiorin."

"You mean a magical creature?" he asks.

I nod.

Some time passes with us walking in comfortable silence. But as we draw nearer to the village, I tell Rourk about the surrounding lands and the names of places, and share a story or two about each place we pass.

The village finally becomes clear in the distance when we exit a small forest and head down an inclining path. We'll be there within the hour.

"Are you looking forward to your Task finally being complete?" he asks me.

I shrug. The answer is more complicated now than it was yesterday. Yes, and no. It's not so simple. "It's a lot of pressure. It will be a relief. You will leave once we return?"

"Aye. I made a promise to your father."

I don't know why I'm so disappointed by his answer. His knuckles brush against mine, and I know it's not an accident. I can see it in his gaze. It feels like an apology—an apology, and something else. Something I'm unwilling to even try to identify. My mouth tightens as I look away, falling silent. The idea of him leaving hits me hard. I know he has to go. I know that a friendship with me would never be enough to hold him here, especially with a daughter in the Oathlands.

But I also know that I will think of Rourk for years to come and ask myself—*what if*?

Chapter Sixteen

ROURK

We reach the village to see people stopping to look at us, happiness and relief coloring their faces. It feels like we are lost heroes returned from the war.

Leaving the treeline, we head across the primary field to the tents and huts. Many are busy at work with the reconstruction of a few huts and cabins. The villagers have carved blocky shapes into the ends of the wooden beams to allow them to connect the beams together, like pieces of a puzzle. I'm impressed at how they can chisel the wood into the joints needed, and how they can firmly join the wood together with no need for screws or any bindings. They've made significant progress in a matter of days.

Aldus hurries over to us, his red and black robe-like coat swishing about him. The ground looks soft and muddy in places, telling me the heavy rain made its way to the village.

"Thank god," Aldus says with a relieved sigh. He takes Galene in his arms and studies her for any injuries before finally relaxing. He hugs Galene and shakes my hand firmly. "I was furious with Bohan when he told us how he'd left you both behind."

"Did they return with the boar?" I ask.

"They did. Thankfully. We will feast well for some time with the size of that thing." Aldus turns to Galene. "I'm so relieved to see you well, my dear."

"Thanks to Tarin," she says. "Where is Bohan? I have a few words for him."

Aldus frowns deeply. "The hunters were very sorry to return without you. Their priorities were with the entire village."

Galene's face remains impassively resolute. "I understand," she says, though her tone speaks of anger and frustration.

Freddick runs up to us with an excited bounce and a bright grin. He pulls us each into a tight embrace.

"I knew you two would be okay," Freddick says. "I'm so sorry we left you. I wanted to look for you, but Bohan was adamant about taking the boar back."

"It's alright," I say. "No harm was done."

"It wasn't easy dragging that thing back," Freddick says. "That spear that you stuck in it, Tarin, slowed it down and eventually weakened it enough to allow us to finish it off. We couldn't have done it without you."

"I'm happy everything worked out," I say.

Freddick perks up, his eyes widening. "You both must be exhausted and hungry. I'll get you some water and something to eat. Hold on."

He gives us an encouraging nod and rushes off.

"He's a good lad," Aldus says, and turns to us. "We sent some people out to find you both. You didn't see them?"

"No, we didn't see anyone on our way back."

Aldus frowns. "We were about to send a second team out to search for you both. But some disturbing matters have distracted us."

The severity of his tone and expression gives me pause. "What disturbing matters?" I ask.

"It's better if I show you," Aldus says.

He leads us across the field to where the grass thins and the ground becomes rockier and muddier.

Galene and I share a concerned look. The familiarity and comfort between us is clear now. At least, it feels that way to me. I no longer feel her hatred toward me, I believe.

Aldus shows us several large fissures that have spread through the ground. Like the earth has been cracked and split open. They are narrow fissures, but troubling nonetheless.

"We had a tremor last night," Aldus tells us. "The ground was torn apart in places. One of our huts collapsed." He shakes his head severely. "We are still repairing the damages from the Wildmen attack, and now this has happened. The world is not in our favor."

Galene has her arms wrapped around herself. A gesture I've come to learn means she is disturbed and uncomfortable. "I should go see Leila and the boys. They will want to know I am back and unharmed. And, dear gods, I've never been in more need of a bath."

Aldus nods. "Stay safe, my dear. It's good to have you back."

Galene flashes me a quick look before leaving. I wish I could read what that look meant. I don't even know if it was a friendly look or a 'stay away from me' glare.

"I see you both are getting along better," Aldus says, watching me closely.

"We haven't killed each other yet," I say.

The sounds of grunts and footfalls reach us on the wind. In the distance, up on a hill, I see the outlines of several hunters. They are practicing with spears, going through attack combinations. I've seen them do this once before, during my time in the village. It irks me how sloppy their forms are and how they are not being taught correct techniques.

"So, I have returned," I tell Aldus. "That means I can fulfill my promise to you and will be on my way back home. And Galene's Task is also complete. Correct?"

Aldus slowly nods, his expression tense and sorrowful. "Correct on both. It will be a shame to see you leave, outsider. You are a good man. Are you certain you can manage the journey back?"

It should take me over a week to reach the Oathlands on foot, if I don't push myself too much. "Yes, my legs are stronger now and I am confident I can make the trip."

"You will be missed, Tarin," Aldus says. "But I understand you need to return to your home. I will prepare provisions for your journey. You will be well resourced."

"Thanks. I have one request before I go," I say. "I hope you don't mind me saying that I've noticed how poorly trained your hunters are. They are in dire need of better training and discipline."

Aldus's thick eyebrows rise. "They are not soldiers, Tarin. Our hunters have proven more than capable for generations. We wouldn't be alive and fed as well without them."

I detect the defensiveness in his tone, so I tread lightly. "They can be better. They need to be better. The Shanti People pride themselves in working together and helping each other for the greater good, but reality is that they compete against each other and each wants to be the best to prove their worth. Helping each other is not their highest priority. They know little about working as a team, from what I've seen. Some are undisciplined and a danger to themselves and others."

So much for treading lightly. Aldus is frowning deeply at me, as if weighing my words. But he doesn't look happy.

I let out a weary sigh and add, "What happens when the Wildmen next attack? You take your losses and move on, as usual? Mourn your dead? Wait for the next time? Would you not prefer your hunters, or any of your people, to have some skill to better defend themselves?"

Aldus slowly nods, as if he's decided. "Yovin is right. You were brought to this village for a purpose. I believe we've found that purpose. Very well. You may try to train our hunters before you leave. Hopefully, you can impart some wisdom to them. I will spread the word. Anyone else who would like some formal combat training may attend your session."

"It would be my honor," I say. But I know it won't be easy. Some of their hunters have proven to be brutally stubborn and resilient. I will need to rise to the challenge.

I see Freddick rushing up to us from across the field with a jug of water in his hand.

A crow is up in a tree, and I realize it is watching us closely. Once I notice it, the crow abruptly looks away, as if pretending it hadn't been staring at us. Strange reaction from a bird.

"For now, rest and regain your strength with some food and drink," Aldus tells me. "I will let Bohan know of the training."

"He won't be happy about it," I say.

"You leave him with me. I will get the approval of the elders, and then no one will be able to disagree with the decision."

He nods a farewell and heads toward the tents across the field. There was something in Aldus's eyes, and his tone, that gives me pause. I can't help but feel like I'm missing something. Something right in front of me, hiding in plain sight. I can guess that this village holds many secrets, but it is not my business to know them all.

I eye the cracks in the ground and feel troubled by them. That feeling is coming back. That sense of heaviness in the atmosphere. The feeling of the world changing.

It's like we're waiting for a match to be struck and set the world on fire.

Chapter Seventeen

ROURK

It's late afternoon when I begin my training session, up on the hill where they usually train. The twenty hunters in the tribe have shown up, promise, along with six villagers who also want to learn from me.

I give a speech about what we'll be aiming to achieve during the training: Form. Awareness. Resilience. Discipline. It's a speech I've given countless times before to new recruits, and it takes me back to simpler times in the Oathlands.

These hunters and villagers do not know I am the General Commander of the Oathlands Military. They think I am a simple soldier. But that's still enough to get the attention of half of them. The other half clearly do not want to be there or listen to a word I have to say.

We go through footwork first. The first lesson to learn is balance. The second is awareness. To be aware of your surroundings and know where the enemy is, and where your allies are. I take them through a few basic attack and defense combinations with a spear to begin with. Some show surprising promise while others seem to not have entered this life equipped for combat. But I work with what I have.

Bohan is the most vocal against me. Which isn't surprising. He seems intent on undermining or questioning me at every turn. He has a few hunters on his side while others seem to be genuinely determined to do well.

As we move on to sparring in pairs, I find myself looking out over the village, hoping to see Galene down there. I wonder what she's doing, and who she's with. And, I have to admit, only to myself, I wonder if she's thinking about me.

I notice two women watching us from afar. Magdalena and Abby, the young blonde woman whom I've hardly spoken with. I note how I've never seen the two of them together before and have to wonder why they're so interested in the training session. But I note now that many others are also watching my tutelage.

I take my would-be soldiers through their sparring sessions and move on to unarmed offensive and defensive techniques.

At this point, Bohan throws his spear into the ground with a powerful huff. "This is pointless. This man knows nothing of actual combat." He paces as he waves a meaty hand at me. "We do not spar with a wolf, like knights in a palace courtyard, and we do not use our bare hands to catch a fish or snatch a bird from its perch. We are not Oathland soldiers and we do not wish to be."

Freddick steps up. "We can learn a lot from Tarin. I mean... no one else told me about balance and awareness."

"He's right," Zayne says. "We should learn what we can from Tarin as the man speaks from experience."

Wills shakes his head, his wavy hair flapping around his ears. "Have you gone mad? Bohan knows more than this outsider. We do not need to learn the steps of a dance to hunt." He shoots me a murderous glare. "This is no man. We shouldn't listen to anything he says."

"Have I done something to offend you, Wills?" I ask, feeling like I'm missing something. The young man hadn't shown this much hostility toward me before, and now he appears on the edge of rage.

Freddick leans closer to me and mutters, "He is Wini Semassi's brother."

My stomach drops. I understand now. Rumors have spread about me being seen with that young vixen, Wini, during the festival. And I can sense there is nothing I can say to defend myself, as others seem to have made up their minds about my character. Arguing with them will get me nowhere.

I step away from the main group and clasp my arms behind my back as I address them. "New plan. Bohan and Wills, I will engage with you both in combat. No weapons. If either of you can land a blow on me, I will cease the training and leave the village immediately."

I'm met with concerned and confused faces as a heavy hush falls over them. Some share uncertain looks. "What?" I challenge. "Does it not sound fair to you?"

They ignore the question. Bohan's dark eyes have a wild gleam in them. "And if we lose?"

When, I almost correct. *When you lose.* "Then you will listen to what I have to say and do as I instruct with no push back. Do we have a deal?"

"We accept," Wills says eagerly.

He has a strong build for a man in his mid-twenties, but he is eager and undisciplined. Although he has speed in his favor, he will be a sloppy fighter, going for the heavy hits without thought to defense or counters. And his rage against me will blind him to my actions.

"You don't have to do this," Freddick says under his breath with urgency and fear in his eyes.

I give him a small, reassuring nod.

"We accept," Bohan says, wanting to be the speaker for them both and show his dominance.

I instruct the others to form a circle around us, giving us a makeshift arena. That will help keep our skirmish hidden from the rest of the village.

Bohan stretches his neck and arms as he steps up. He is taller than me, with a more powerful build, and he has the experience behind him. He is the Head Hunter for a reason. But he will underestimate me, and I have a few surprises for him.

Bohan flexes his hands and cracks his fingers. "I, Bohan Boronoro, will show you the might of the Shanti People."

I cock my head. "Your name is Bohan Boronoro?"

He pauses. "Yes. Why?"

I let out a chuckle. "No reason. I just think that's funny."

Bohan flushes with rage and charges at me. His anger will make him careless. But also formidable. I'll have to be careful to use his anger in my favor.

Bohan goes for heavy punches, which I easily evade, while Wills rushes up with a jumping knee thrust. I move swiftly between them, gauging their prowess and thought patterns. They are brash and are openly indicating their moves to me, as expected. I side-step to avoid their attacks, block a punch and use the momentum to throw them off balance, and at times have to twist or dive away from them.

Wills comes at me with a thrusting kick, but I raise my leg to intercept, plant my foot against his, and push him back. He rolls through the dirt and knocks into the surrounding watchers.

Heavy grunts and footfalls tell me Bohan is charging from behind. He goes to grab me, but I spin around and bring my arms up under his arms to clasp my hands behind his neck. That traps his arms and renders them useless while my hands remain firmly locked behind his neck.

But he is a fiercely resilient opponent, and he tries to shake me off. I'm still not as strong as I used to be, but I manage to hold the arm lock. Bohan throws his head back as I quickly shift my head away. He would have knocked me unconscious with that blow.

I finally release him and shove him away. Wills has picked himself up and is coming at me from the side. I catch Wills' punch and twist his arm, careful to not put enough pressure to break the bone, and flip him over my shoulder to slam him on the ground.

Bohan charges at me like a mad bull. I leap up and flip over him, twisting in the air, and bring my foot down to kick him as he passes. That elicits some impressed gasps from the spectators.

Wills fires off a series of punches and kicks, but he is growing tired and I evade them easily, not even needing to raise my arms. I start to sense the growing approval from those around us, as I show them what they could be capable of doing.

When Bohan charges at me again, I duck low to hook my arm under his leg and roll us both to the ground, bringing him into a firm lock with his arms and leg trapped. I allow him to stay helpless for a second, making sure others see what I've done, and release him when I sense Wills coming for another attack.

Wills comes low from the side. His arm flashes out and a cloud of dirt and grit hits my eyes. The shock of the impact stuns me and I feel myself drop hard to my knees. My vision is gone, and so is my confidence. It feels like my eyes are bleeding.

I throw myself to the ground to evade a punch from Wills, which I just sense coming. Then I have to roll to avoid angry foot stomps from Wills. I push myself to my feet, clearing the dirt and dust from my eyes, and manage to see distinct shapes through my blurry, stinging eyes.

A boot lands on my back and knocks me several feet through the air. My breath leaves me as I hit the ground hard and roll in a heap. I cough into the dirt, kicking up more dirt into my face and mouth.

"It's over," I hear Bohan say, his voice strained and exhausted.

I take a moment to clear my eyes, my vision gradually returning.

"That's not fair," Freddick says.

"There are no rules in battle," Bohan says.

"We won. We landed a blow. That was the deal," Wills says, panting heavily.

"They are right," I say. "They won, fairly, even if they played unfairly."

Zayne's deep voice carries over the crowd. "Tarin showed us he is a capable, experienced fighter. Far beyond the skills of any of us. Even myself. Even the great Bohan."

"That doesn't matter," Wills says. "A deal is a deal."

"But that flip," someone says.

"Or that lock he had Bohan in," another says. "I want to learn that."

Others chime in, making it clear they want to keep learning.

"Enough," Bohan barks, forcing a silence. He glares at me, his chest still heaving from the adrenaline that must be coursing through him. His tone softens slightly when he says, "I don't know anyone who could take on two opponents like that. You made us look like fools. Even if we won, I... I would still like to learn from you, outsider."

"This is bullshit," Wills says, seething. "You're going to listen to *him*?"

"We all will," Bohan says sternly, staring Wills down. He turns to me. "Yes. Tarin lost. He will leave as promised. However, before he goes... I would like to know how that arm lock move works."

I smile at him and nod, relieved at the understanding and respect showing in Bohan's eyes. "I'll be happy to show you."

"Very well," Bohan says with a small nod of his own. There is no more aggression emanating from him. "Let us continue the training," he yells to everyone, once again needing to be the leader of the group.

I continue the training and we go for hours, until almost dusk. This will be my last night with the Shanti People. I make arrangements to leave in the morning.

A steady rain picks up that night and a howling, fierce wind keeps the village inside. I want to find Galene, to spend more time with her, to see into those eyes and hear her voice, but I know I shouldn't. I will be leaving and that will be the end of it.

The previous night spent with Galene plays through my mind. Despite my words to her denying remembering it, I can still feel her against me, and taste her lips. My hands remember the feeling of her.

Snap out of it, Rourk, I finally tell myself. I'm getting ahead of myself and building a fantasy in my head.

My time with the Shanti People is over. I will give my goodbyes to the villagers in the morning and be on my way.

A face flashes through my mind. Striking blue eyes and a wicked smile.

It was always meant to end.

But the idea of that ending sours my stomach now. Of turning away from this village, these people...

Galene.

Chapter Eighteen

GALENE

Leila and I hang laundry on the line and pretend we haven't noticed that everything around us is changing.

Or maybe it has *been* changing since the very day Rourk was brought into the medic tent. Since the moment it was declared that his livelihood was my Task.

Maybe I've just been avoiding that truth since the very heartbeat when I first set eyes on him.

I'm busy tossing a blanket up and pinning it down, wrestling against the damp fabric as it billows in the wind—so busy that I don't notice someone has joined us until they clear their throat.

I jolt away from the noise—or, in other words, right into the billowing blanket. The person laughs, a deep, throaty sort of chuckle. Then an arm wraps around my waist and pulls me backward while untangling me from the fabric.

I recognize the feel of his skin against mine. Or perhaps not the feel of it, but more the way my body reacts to having him so close to me.

Rourk.

"Let go of me," I mutter when I'm free, but the words come out so weakly that even I don't believe them. Can he tell that I say it out of habit rather than disgust now? That I'm just trying to protect myself?

Still, he does. His arm falls away, and he takes a step backward. "Sorry."

I cut a look at Leila, who tries to pretend she's not watching us as she hangs one of our father's shirts up. "It's fine," I mutter, straightening my shirt out. "What do you need?"

"It's more of a want, actually."

I raise an eyebrow. "Okay," I drawl. "What do you *want*?"

"To go on a walk," Rourk says simply.

Now I'm confused. "Then go."

His mouth quirks up into a devastatingly handsome smile. "I meant with you."

I blink. "Oh."

He nods. "Yeah. I'm leaving soon, you know, and... I think we should talk. Before I go."

"Oh." The syllable falls from my lips dumbly. I quickly look at Leila again. She's given up pretending to hang the clothes and now just watches us blatantly. "I can't. I have chores."

"Just go," she calls out. "I'll cover for you." She winks at me.

"I don't think—"

" —Please," Rourk cuts in. When my eyes meet his again, those dark irises are pleading. Earnest. "Come on," he says, his voice teasing but not quite hiding the serious note behind it. "Didn't you hear me say I'm leaving? I'm giving you the chance to say whatever the fuck you want to me without having to see me later." A not-quite-believable grin sprouts on his lips. "This is your only chance to finally get out all those insults you've thought of since the day we met. Formally, anyway."

But none of those insults feel true anymore.

Still, I nod. "Okay," I say. "Let's go."

Rourk tentatively offers me his arm.

I hesitate. Look into his eyes and can't quite read the question within them.

Then I wrap my arm around his, let him pull me a little closer and lead me away.

Away is ten minutes away from the village, tucked into the treeline. Rourk walks us toward a fallen tree before releasing my arm and sitting.

I gingerly take a seat beside him. "What did you want to talk about?"

"Don't want to get your insults out first, Galene?" he asks, his voice light.

I stare at him for a long moment. "No," I say finally. "Not anymore."

He nods and falls silent again, but I can't sit inside that quiet any longer. "Rourk, you brought me all the way out here. Just... say whatever it is you want to say."

Gently—hesitantly, like he's waiting for me to pull away—he rests a hand on my knee. The touch is electrifying. He says, "I wanted you to know that I will always remember you."

His words sear through me. There's something about the stark honesty, the vulnerability, that melts my heart even as I freeze. It's not even the words themselves, I don't think. It's the intention behind them. All the layers of meaning I could peel back if I wanted to. "What?"

"I will remember you," he reiterates. "Forever. Fondly. I will tell stories about you to anyone who will listen. I will detail your eyes and your sharp wit and your determination to never be less and to always be more than the others around you."

"Rourk," I say. My voice is soft. "You don't have to say that."

"I mean it," he says roughly. "And I only ask one thing in return for this—this lifetime of *longing* I am to be subjected to from the very moment I walk away from you."

My throat feels dry, but my eyes don't. I have to fight back the tears that build. I realize now, in this moment, as Rourk gives me his version of a goodbye, that I don't want him to leave. And that I will remember him, too. Forever. Fondly.

So I whisper. "Okay." I let myself soak in the feeling of his thumb brushing against my knee. "What do you ask?"

His dark eyes stare deep into mine as he says, "That you remember me, too. I don't care if it's in fondness or fury. I don't care if it's only in passing, as you're tending to wounds similar to the ones I had, or if it's only when someone mentions my name. Either of them." His voice is earnest now. "Just remember me, Galene, *please*."

My hands shake as I fight back my tears. I can't help myself as I reach for Rourk and press each palm to one of his cheeks, cupping his face in my hands. "I will remember you every day," I swear to him. "And I will miss you every night."

Rourk doesn't try to kiss me, though I think that, in this moment, I would let him.

Instead, he pulls me tight to his body and wraps me in a hug.

It somehow means more to me than a kiss ever could.

Chapter Nineteen

ROURK

I spend my final night in the hut I've called home for the past week and a half, listening to the rustling trees and heavy rain. I was told that rain, especially storms, are rare in these parts of the Wildlands. I lay there, far from sleep, wondering what this unfamiliar sensation is that's been coming over me. This anxiety and uneasiness.

The low sounds of a heated argument stir me awake early the next morning. A few voices are disturbing the quiet air, and they don't sound happy. I crawl off of my bedding and inch toward where I can see outside through the gaps in the hut flaps. The light is low, with the sun barely over the horizon, and the main field looks empty.

I try another angle and see some people across the field. The old man, Yovin, is there sitting on a log far to the side. He is speaking with Colm and Magdalena.

"This is ridiculous," Colm is saying, his voice low but angered.

"And yet it is real," Magdalena says. Her voice is normally bright and casual, but now she sounds almost unrecognizable, her tone dark. Far more commanding and controlled.

"We must see the facts," Yovin says wisely.

Colm huffs. "I will not discuss this out in the open."

"I agree," Magdalena says. "We should find the others."

I assume she means the elders, but it sounds like she's talking about someone else.

They head across the field. I keep low and still as I peek out at them.

"I will prepare the thoro-seer," Yovin says.

"We'll wake up Aldus and Abby," Magdalena says.

I sit there for a while after they've left, wondering what a thoro-seer is, and what it has to do with Aldus and Abby.

I throw on a sleeveless shirt and head out, keeping my actions quiet. A pre-dawn blue-gray haze is over the world, making me feel like I'm walking through a dream. The birds in the trees have only just begun their morning songs.

The field is muddy in places from the rain last night, so I stay on stone pathways to reach the rows of tents. For a while, I hear nothing but the sounds of the quiet morning birds as I creep along the tents. When I round the back of one, I catch sight of Aldus and Magdalena heading into a small tent on the outskirts of the village.

I make my way to the tent and listen by the side of it. I think this is one of their supply tents, used for hunting tools and general storage, as it's smaller than the others and I don't think I've ever seen it frequented.

Aldus's grumpy voice sounds very disturbed about something.

"For the record, I still don't believe this is happening," Magdalena says challengingly.

"Let's just trust in the thoro-seer," Aldus says. "That's what it's for."

"We should send people immediately," Yovin says. "We need to know what is really happening out there."

There's a rustle in the leaves nearby. I duck to the side of the tent as two figures come into view. It's Colm and Abby. They enter the tent with the others.

Something isn't right here. This seems like a strange group for a secret meeting. I've seen them all in smaller groups before, but never together at the same time. It sounds like something very important is going on, and I wonder why they aren't involving the elders.

"Colm told me what's happening," Abby says from within the tent. Like Magdalena, her voice is also different now. Slower and more severe, without her girlish lightness. "Are we sure this is real?"

"That's what we want to find out," Aldus says.

"We should make an announcement," Magdalena says.

"And get everyone worried?" Colm asks skeptically.

"It's too soon for an announcement," Aldus says. "We shouldn't bother the elders for such a thing. Not yet."

"I'll get Bohan," Colm says, "and begin forming a hunting team for the western plains."

They agree on this and say they will stay close to the thoro-seer to see what else they can discover.

I'm not sure what I'm hearing, but it doesn't sound good. And why aren't they involving the elders?

I step back into the dim shadows between the tents as Colm leaves and makes his way to the other side of the village. The sky is lightening around us and the morning gloom is gradually dispersing like mist burning away.

I consider following Colm to hear what he tells Bohan, but a flash of golden light gets my attention. I look around, wondering where it came from. It was like a faint lightning flash.

I wait a moment until another flash lights the air. This one is coming from down in the valley beyond the village. I make my way there and look down the hill to see a cluster of trees below, beyond a field of tall grass. Someone is there within the trees.

Another light flashes. The golden vibrancy of the light tells me who this person is. My heart begins beating faster.

I head down the hill and cross the tall grass to get a better look at the figure. A golden light begins to grow, casting a warm glow in the field and sending long shadows out from the trees.

When I reach the edge of the trees, I see Galene is there with a glowing light emanating from the bottom of her boots. She is several inches from the ground, standing on the solid light. Her arms are fully shrouded in a golden glow of light. Her long dress gently billows in the wind. My eyebrows rise at the sight of her in the air.

She sees me, and the light instantly vanishes. She drops and scowls at me, though there is a look of shock and embarrassment on her tense face.

"That is very impressive."

Galene pants softly and catches her breath. "What are you doing here?"

"Morning stroll. How about you?"

She looks around, reminding me of someone trapped and looking for a way out. But she softens a little when she regards me. "I... thought I should learn more about my... ability."

"Good for you." I step out from the trees and approach her.

"It is not just channeling light." She looks at her hands. "If I concentrate enough, I can harden the light. Make it solid. And... it doesn't just come from my hands."

I make a show of looking her up and down. "Where else does it come out from?"

Galene rolls her eyes, unimpressed with my humor. "Take a look at this."

She raises a foot as if she's showing me her boot. A look of deep concentration crinkles her brow.

A square of golden light appears beneath her foot. Seeing it materialize makes my breath catch in my throat. Galene pushes against the light and rises, as though she is going up a step. Her arms glow, as if the light is emanating from her skin. The light gradually lowers with her weight before it vanishes in a puff. She falters and steadies herself.

"Well, I'm still working on it," she shrugs.

I'm guessing my presence is making her distracted or nervous, and likely affecting her ability to wield her magic. Something about her arms being fully encased in light nudges at my memory, but I can't place it.

"I stand by my assessment. Very impressive. What made you decide to practice your magic? I thought you were against it."

"I never said I was against it. But, I was thinking about the boar attack, and how my magic saved us. If... If I knew more about what I can do, maybe I can help other people. And I can finally stop my father from telling me I should practice more."

I nod in agreement and step closer. "You have a good heart, Galene."

Her breathing has increased, I see, like she's nervous. But I also feel how strong our desire is for each other. How the air burns between us.

"You are a good person," I say, my voice low. "And you are strong of heart. I don't think I've ever met anyone like you before."

She holds my gaze, her lips quivering. I can feel my heart being pulled toward her. My lips part as I inch closer, breathing in her warm, intoxicating scent.

Galene's face shutters and she steps back before we touch. Her eyes burn with anger.

"I don't know what you've been thinking, or feeling," she growls, "but I want no part of it. You are an Oathlander, Rourk. All Oathlanders sicken me. I could never befriend someone like you."

The coldness in her voice strikes my heart and freezes me.

"I thought you were leaving. Why are you still here?" she continues.

My chest tightens, making it hard to breathe. It feels like the world has just tilted and I'm having to reorient myself.

"Yes, I am leaving today," I say hoarsely.

I search her eyes for the truth and see nothing but turmoil and pain in their depths. I know I have to accept her words and her wishes.

"Not all Oathlanders are the same," I tell her.

"I have seen no evidence against that," she says, her voice shaky. She faces me challengingly, as though she wants me to argue with her.

"You're alive, aren't you?" I ask.

"I could say the same thing."

"Your integrity isn't the one being questioned," I point out.

"You've done nothing to prove you aren't like the other Oathlanders."

"Bullshit."

She just glares.

I think she's lying to me and herself. This charged energy between us cannot only be felt by me.

I take a step closer and raise my hand to place it on her side and bring her closer, to convince her of what we are feeling. Galene flinches and slaps me hard on the face.

"That is enough," she says through her teeth. Her trembling eyes are filled with emotion. "Leave, and never look back."

With that, she storms away furiously.

I ache to make things better, but it's too far gone for that. I shouldn't have pushed things. I know I have to accept the truth, not the fantasy I've been making up in my head. I've been a fool. It's time to return to my life.

There is nothing for me with the Shanti People.

The village has awakened by the time I reach the central field, with many people mingling and going about their chores for the day.

Aldus is pulling a cart with a mountain of wooden blocks, taking it to one of the huts being rebuilt. He pauses when he sees me and waves me over.

"I have the sister wives preparing a care pack for you," he says. "You will have provisions for your journey home. And the map I promised you."

"You have my thanks, Aldus," I say. "For a great many reasons. I'm happy to help with the pack."

He smiles and shakes his head. "They have it handled."

"Is Leila around?" I ask. "It would be good to say goodbye."

"She has already left with the boys. They have gone to tend to our crops in the northeast."

I ask him to send my regards to Leila and her boys once they return, as I follow him to one of the huts being rebuilt.

Several people there are trimming thick wooden beams into shape. The woodworkers are cutting gaps in the wood to allow other parts to fit into place. I'm still amazed at how they can construct their huts by fitting wooden beams firmly into each other, with no other bindings required.

Aldus leaves to attend to some business, so I help those setting up the new beams into place while I wait for my travel pack to be ready.

A small girl watches me curiously and cautiously. I recognize her as the one who has mostly been watching me fearfully from behind her mother's legs. Now she is smiling at me, which makes me smile back. She must have become accustomed to my presence. It makes me think how much I'm going to miss this village.

I notice a familiar face watching me from across the field. Wini, the young girl who had tried to seduce me during the festival. She stops to stare at me when our eyes connect. A passing look of what I guess to be regret, longing, or perhaps disgust, crosses her soft features. She strikes a strong figure with her blouse hugging her full chest and wide hips curving beneath her dress. Wini settles on a sneer and swiftly turns away. I guess that explains what she thinks of me.

A sister wife comes over to me, with a bowl in her hand instead of a heavy travel pack.

"Leila requested you keep your strength up," she says, handing me the steaming bowl of stew. Large chunks of boar meat are mixed with the rice and vegetables. It smells delicious and hearty.

I take it from her gratefully.

"I thought Leila was away this morning," I say.

The woman blushes. "Well... I'm not supposed to say, but Galene was the one who requested the meal for you. She told me to say it came from Leila."

That brings a smile to my face. Though it makes me more confused than ever.

I sit and eat for a while, taking in the atmosphere, knowing these are my final moments in the village. A few familiar faces nod hello's to me as they pass, while others are firmly trying to avoid eye contact with me.

Aldus comes over to me by the time I've finished the bowl of warming stew. He hands me a medium-sized backpack with water skins hanging from the sides.

"The map is rolled up inside," Aldus says as he comes to me. "It will show you the best routes to take and where you can camp each night. I put it together myself." A pickaxe and a knife are hanging from the back of the pack.

I thank Aldus for all his help. "Is everything okay in the village?" I ask, watching his reaction. "I thought I heard something about the elders making an announcement?"

His face hardens enough to make him appear like a different person. He eyes me firmly, his mouth a tight line.

"Not sure where you heard such a thing. I can assure you everything is well here. You can leave knowing we are in a good state. And we feast on boar meat thanks to you."

Aldus notices me looking around. "I'm sure Galene will miss you, as well." His countenance softens with a smile.

I raise my eyebrows. Does he know Galene and I have been getting closer lately? "She will be relieved once I'm gone, more than anything."

"Women are the greatest mystery of the world," Aldus says. I have to agree with that. "Galene is not here, anyway. She just left to spend time with Leila and the boys in the fields. She said something about wanting to clear her head. You wouldn't know what that meant, would you?"

I shake my head. "The greatest mysteries, indeed."

We shake hands firmly. Aldus wishes me well and I thank him once again for getting me back on my feet.

With no desire to drag out the goodbyes or find anyone else, I make my way out of the village without ceremony. I notice some people watching me go, but mostly, I can simply disappear from among them.

When I pass the last of the tents, I hear heavy footfalls coming from behind me. The young hunter, Freddick, is rushing up to me, his long hair flapping about him.

"You're not leaving, are you?" he says, catching his breath.

"That's the plan."

His face is struck with horror. "Y-you can't. We need you here. Now, more than ever."

"What do you mean?"

Freddick hesitates, as if wondering if he should say something. But the moment passes quickly.

"There is talk of a great disturbance out there. Like a darkness devastating the land and tearing up crops. People are saying it's some great evil. Like... like the magic in the world is breaking."

"What are you talking about?" He sounds like a madman.

"I don't know. There are just whisperings. We're waiting for the elders to tell us what is happening. But I've heard its something to do with everyone's magic. Like it isn't working properly. Or... I don't know. But it isn't good. We're getting a group of hunters to take a look at the western fields. We think we're going to find something big there. Something dangerous. We could really use your help, Tarin."

The false name he uses tells me what I already know—I don't belong here. I never have. I place a hand on his shoulder. "I'm sure everything is going to be fine. This sounds like superstitious and unwarranted rumors." I swallow. "Besides, I'm just some military soldier from Oathlands. There's not a lot I can offer you guys."

"You know that's not true," Freddick argues. "I've seen what you've done here. How you helped us with the Wildlands attack. We need you."

I swallow thickly. "I can't stay. This isn't my home."

He looks physically hurt.

Galene's furious glare flashes in my mind. I sigh and add, "Look, Freddick. I have a home to go back to. I have my family waiting for me. They think me dead. If I go back with you, I'll never go back home. There's always going to be something keeping me here with you all. I have to go. I wish you a good life. You will be a formidable hunter one day. Feel free to visit the Oathlands whenever you like. You will always be a welcome guest among us."

Freddick shakes his head and steps back. "I cannot believe this."

I frown, seeing how much I'm disappointing him. He lost his father a few days ago and I can see my departure is hitting him hard. Much harder than I thought it would. He's shaking his head and his eyes have reddened.

I want to tell him something encouraging, but he moves away from me.

"Just go," he yells, shaking with fury. He turns and runs back into the village.

I stop myself from going after him. There is nothing for me back there. I need to look ahead and move forward.

I begin my long journey home.

And I pretend that I don't regret every step.

Chapter Twenty

ROURK

I walk for over an hour without looking back. I have to keep my focus on the future. On getting back to my daughter, my brother, my soldiers. My people.

I've already begun to imagine my reunion with May and Arthur. If all goes well, I will be with them again in a week. And yet, I can't deny something is pulling me backward. There's energy in the air that feels like it's almost calling to me, but I can't fully detect what it is. It might not even be there. It's as though the more I focus on it, the less I feel it, and when I try to empty my mind or think of other things, that energy is there lurking in the back of my mind. It's lingering in the air, all around.

Freddick's pained face sticks in my mind. I hate I had to leave him like that.

I've been wondering if the growing danger that Freddick mentioned is related to whatever Aldus and the others had been discussing. I've never heard of a thoro-seer before and guess it's a device of some kind. A secret of the Shanti People.

It was odd that they hadn't wanted to involve the elders. Maybe they were going behind the elder's backs. Could they be looking to overthrow the elders? No, that doesn't feel right.

Whatever the case is, I'm sure I shouldn't care. The Shanti People will keep their secrets and I will go on my way.

As I cross through a field of yellow grass, my thoughts shift to Galene. She has been a constant presence in my mind, lingering in the back at all times. I can't deny how alive I'd felt in her presence these last few days.

I tell myself this has just been a moment in time. Something I'll have to move on from. *You are an Oathlander, Rourk.* "*All Oathlanders sicken me. I could never befriend someone like you.*" Her words echo through my mind and churn my stomach. Images of her are replaced with that seething hatred she'd shown in our last meeting this morning.

My boots squelch in the soft mud. I take a look at Aldus's map to be sure I'm going the right way. The recent rain might have shifted the land a little, meaning I would have to adjust my bearing slightly. The last thing I want is to divert my course without realizing it and add more time to my journey.

From the look of the map, it seems that I'm going to have to cross this muddy area. I take a few more steps before I stop again.

A print in the mud gives me pause. It takes me a few seconds to realize what I'm looking at, and my pulse rises. A large indentation is in the mud, in the shape of an animal footprint. Except it is larger than any animal I've ever seen.

There is a distinct shape of a wide round paw and four individual toe prints. Sharp lines from the toes tell me the paw has long claws.

A second paw print is nearby. I inspect the prints and find a partial third print. These indentations are fresh, and they are pointing north. I check the map and realize the prints are leading toward the fields to the north, where I was told Leila and the boys would be. Where Galene was heading.

This could be a coincidence, and the large animal may have changed course between here and the crops. But I can't take that chance. Not with Galene, the only woman who has ever reminded me of my wife. The only woman who—

I cut the thought off.

My heart races now at the thought of Galene, Leila, and her sons being in danger.

I don't know if I can make it in time to help them, but I have to try. I can't just keep going home now. I can't ignore this.

The Oathlands are going to have to wait.

I break into a run, heading north to intercept the giant animal. I just hope I'll make it before anyone gets hurt.

Chapter Twenty-One

GALENE

"Are you sure you don't want to talk?" Leila asks me.

I give her a tired look. "I'm fine. Really. Why is it so odd that I wanted to come and spend time with my sister and nephews?"

She narrows her eyes. "Alright. You keep your secrets. We won't talk about how you probably didn't want to say goodbye to Tarin. He likely would be gone by now, so you can head back if you like."

"I couldn't care less about Tarin," I say, a little too heatedly.

I can see from her knowing look that she knows this is about Tarin. About Rourk.

I had just wanted to go for a long walk to clear my head, and spend some time beyond the village. Rourk will have left by now so I can begin putting him behind me. A familiar warmth washes over me when I think of our close moment in the mountains. How passionate we had been. It had felt more like a dream than anything real, so I have decided to keep it that way. It was just a strange moment that had happened, exactly like a dream.

I will not have an Oathlander complicating my life. No matter how good his heart is, and how strong and selfless he is. How heroic. How physically appealing.

I don't want any of it.

The boys, Jonah and Milo, are picking berries from the field, placing them in baskets. They have made a game out of it to see who can pick the most berries. The wind has picked up and a cool breeze is struggling to fight against the warmth of the sun. The dark clouds on the horizon make me frown, reminding me of the storm over the mountain.

The world seems to be changing a lot these days. I'm not sure what to think about it.

"Have you thought of what you will do now that your big Task is done?" Leila asks as she digs the soil with a pick.

"I'm not even sure if this is my big Task," I say. "I wouldn't be surprised if father finds another way to test me. To push me. At least your big Task was straightforward." I sigh and shake my head. "My fault for being such a disgrace to the family."

"Hey, I'm also unwed," Leila tells me. "People think oddly of me as well. And my Task was *not* straightforward."

"You're widowed. You have two children. That's different. You're a sister wife. That holds respect."

"We put too much emphasis on doing what's best for the village," Leila says. "And not enough on what's best for ourselves."

"Careful. You'll have the elders burning you on a pyre."

Leila scoffs. "Let them try."

I smile at her, feeling a little better about myself. The more time I spend away from Rourk, knowing he is getting farther and farther away from us, the more I'm able to relax.

So why am I looking around, as if I'm expecting to see him at any moment? What would I do if I turned around and saw him here? I shudder at the thought.

"Hey, boys," Leila calls out. "No pushing. Come on."

That settles them somewhat, but I can see that competitive look in their eyes and their smirks.

Leila looks up at me. "Well, if you're going to be here, you might as well be helpful."

Something shifts in the air. I look around to find the source of what suddenly started bothering me, but there's nothing I can see. Maybe it was just my mind playing tricks on me.

The ground trembles.

Leila and I share a fearful look. My first thought is that another earthquake is imminent. The boys have stopped squabbling and are looking around them, more curious than concerned.

The ground rumbles and shakes again, sending a shiver through me. I hear muffled, heavy breathing a second before something enormous breaks through the trees in the distance.

A giant animal raises its head and roars into the sky. The deafening, reverberating roar shakes my bones and the force of it ripples my clothes. This is like nothing I've ever seen before. It has the size of an oversized elephant and the brown fur and paws of a great bear, with huge curled horns on its head and a snarling bull-like snout.

Leila screams for the boys and rushes to them. My bones rattle with jarring fear as the giant beast growls at us and breaks into a run on all-fours. The ground shakes enough for me to struggle to keep standing. Leila reaches the boys and drags them back as I run to them, but there's no avoiding the beast. It bounds at us and rises for an attack, raising a massive furred paw.

The beast jolts and pauses as a knife plunges into its side. I turn to see a figure sprinting across the fields to us. My heart swells at the sight of Rourk running with a pickaxe in hand, muscles tense, his long hair flared in his wake.

"Find cover," Rourk yells without looking at us.

The behemoth rears back and faces Rourk, its snarling face full of fiery rage. That gives us enough time to take the boys to a low rock wall surrounded by tall shrubs and a tree stump.

Rourk rolls away from a swiping reach from the beast and he comes up, swinging the pickaxe and slicing its arm. The beast roars back and prepares for another attack.

I cannot believe Rourk is really here. It feels like a vivid dream. How had he found us? Had he known of this behemoth? I reach for the knife on my belt and realize I have not brought it. I've left it back home. There was no thought of possible danger when I'd left earlier. I'd just wanted to get away from the village. Leila's pick is over by the crops. Maybe I could run out and grab it before the beast notices me.

"How did he find us?" Leila asks me, echoing my thoughts.

"What is that thing?" little Milo asks, his voice quivering with fear as he hugs his mother's dress.

Rourk leaps away from a paw swipe and sticks the pickaxe into the side of the hulking beast. As he lands and maneuvers away, a swinging arm slams into him and sends him flying several feet through the air. My chest tightens instantly with fear. Rourk rolls through the field and crashes into a tree.

The behemoth charges at him. I flinch, half considering running out to help Rourk, but what can I do? I don't think I can summon my magic with my heart beating so fast. Rourk gets to his feet and dives to the side in time for the beast to miss and get its horn stuck in the tree. It shakes its head and wrestles to free its horn, and ends up ripping the bark into several pieces as it releases itself.

Rourk is now without a weapon. I take my chance and rush over to the pick in the ground. Leila calls me back, but I ignore her. My heart threatens to burst from my chest as I throw myself to the ground and grab the pick.

"Rourk!" I yell, and throw the pick as hard as I can to reach him.

Rourk has to sprint toward it while it spins in the air, and the beast turns and chases after him with surprising speed. It rises onto its back legs, raising both paws to slam them down on him. Rourk leaps and snatches the pick out of the air. He twists and manages to plunge the pick into the beast's paw, getting knocked back by it at the same time. Rourk falls to the ground and rolls several times, heading toward me. Fear jolts through me at the sight of him on the ground, but I'm relieved to see him get to his feet. The man is made of strong stuff.

I ignore Leila and the boys calling me back and rush to Rourk. The summoning of my light takes hold in my mind. I have to help us both. Rourk looks dazed and unsteady, but there is a fierce determination in his eyes when I reach him.

We have no time for words as the beast barrels toward us. In an instant, it is rising up and blocking the sun, about to trample us. I raise my hand to summon a shield, but nothing happens. A split-second of absolute terror dawns on me when I realize I cannot help us. The beast's paws slam down on us. I'm shoved by Rourk and feel the rush of air as I fall to the side. The massive paws crack into the earth. I roll and throw myself to my feet, my head spinning, and see Rourk managed to get clear of the attack.

He has pulled out the knife from the beast's side and he stabs it again into its arm. Dark blood pours from several places, but the beast doesn't seem to be slowing down or concerned by its injuries.

"Get back," Rourk calls out, waving me away.

He dives and rolls and pulls the pickaxe from the beast, causing it to roar in pain. The behemoth rises on its back legs and watches us both with its beady black eyes which are surprisingly alert and show intelligence. It focuses on Rourk, who is running backward and waving the pickaxe to get its attention.

I'm left there as the beast bounds towards Rourk. He can't do this on his own. One direct hit is all it would take to end Rourk's life.

"Hey!" I scream.

It isn't enough to distract the beast. A shiver of fury washes over me and I throw my arm out in frustration. A spark of golden light shoots out and spins through the air like a thrown stick. It thuds into the mud by the beast's paw and gets its attention. It turns to me and growls, baring its teeth.

"Oh gods," I mutter, stepping back.

Rourk calls out, but the behemoth is no longer interested in him. It breaks into a bounding sprint, shaking the ground and sending tremors of fear through me. Spit flies from its snarling mouth, its beady eyes wide and crazed.

As I start running back, I search for the light within me. That charged energy that comes from the spark deep within. But I'm too shaken with fear to think or feel anything clearly.

The huge beast leaps toward me and covers my view. Rourk is running for me, but he's too far away. I scream as the beast crashes down on me, flattening me into the ground. Everything goes black. And then a blinding golden light fills my vision. A pillar of solid light breaks through the beast and bursts out from its back, shooting into the sky. The light instantly vanishes, leaving a gaping hole in the beast.

Crippling pain keeps me in place as my strained mind tries to focus. Blood and guts are covering me and sticking my clothes to me. The hot stench of blood and meat stings my nostrils.

I blink back my focus and see I am beneath the beast, pressed deep into the mud. I see dazzling daylight through the hole in the beast.

Someone comes to me and I yell out, my sense of danger spiking. It's too hard to think clearly. But relief swells within me when I see Rourk is there. He takes my arm and pulls me out as he shoves the beast aside.

I still can't believe he's really here. My heart swells with joy.

He pulls me up and I wrap my arms around him. Our lips slam into each other and we kiss hungrily, holding each other close. I pull his face to me, breathing him in and tasting his hot sweat and sweet lips. His powerful arms hold me close. I'm lost in the moment and I don't care. I just want him. I need him. Every part of him. I've never needed anyone more. I need his hands on me. Need his body pressed against mine. There's no amount of closeness to satiate my desire.

I become aware of the sound of our kisses as my senses come back to me. I pause suddenly and break free from his mouth. I turn, slowly, and see Leila and the boys staring at us with slack-jawed mouths and raised eyebrows.

I startle and shove Rourk away. "No," I say. My mind races with thoughts, but I can't verbalize any of them.

But he nods, understanding as he always is. And yet something lingers in his eyes, in the way he clenches his fists and the way he averts his eyes from mine.

I wonder, at that moment, just what it is that I think I'm doing.

Chapter Twenty-Two

ROURK

The walk back to the village is tense and filled with unspoken comments. Galene has been avoiding my gaze mostly, and whenever our eyes meet, she quickly turns away as if burned. And yet, there is no more sense of anger or hatred from her. Her small smiles and soft eyes are telling me that. The air is different around us and the only tension is the embarrassment we're feeling from our passionate kissing earlier. I still have some smears of blood and guts on me from being pressed against Galene. We've managed to clear the worst of it off her with a pail of water in the field, but it's hard to ignore the lingering stench of death on her.

Little Milo has stopped whimpering and looks more composed now as we go through the fields. Jonah has a disturbed expression, his brows constantly furrowed, which makes him look older than his ten years.

"So," Leila says. "We were just almost killed by the biggest monster I've ever seen. And yet that somehow is not the most surprising thing to happen." She regards us. "When did this happen with you two?"

Galene has developed a shaky, awkward air about her, which I find adorable. "When did what happen?"

"The kissing." Leila raises an eyebrow.

Galene focuses ahead, as if she hasn't heard her sister. "It's new," I mutter.

Leila wraps her arms around herself, reminding me of Galene. "She called you Rourk. I'm guessing that's your real name."

I nod. "But please, do not tell anyone."

"Why? Why is your name a secret?"

I turn to Leila. "For the same reason I have not been able to speak to your elders."

Leila nods with understanding. They've asked me to let them keep their privacy, and I'm hoping they will do the same for me.

"Did you recognize that beast?" Galene asks after a time.

Leila cocks her head.

"I did," Jonah says, looking up. "That was Aramet. From Grandpa's books. Is that right?"

Galene nods, and says to me, "Aramet is an ancient magical being from our legends. It was known for causing destruction wherever it went."

Leila gasps. "Those are children's stories. Folktales."

"That wasn't Aramet, though," Galene says. "It was a behemoth like him, but not the same, I don't think. Aramet was meant to be able to trample towns. This one was much smaller. I think it was a similar behemoth to the famous destructor."

"How would this creature from legends be here now?" I ask, but I feel like I already know the answer.

Leila and Galene both believe it had returned to the world with the resurrection of magic.

"Speaking of magic," Leila says. "How in all creation did you summon that light to kill the beast?"

Galene shrugs. "I've been practicing lately. And I think the more I try, and the more I summon, the easier it gets." She gives a small grin. "Plus, a bit of panic seems to help summon it."

Milo perks up. "Can you do that, too, mommy?"

"No," Leila says quickly. "No. I didn't inherit light magic. Instead, I got darkness."

The world has been changing lately, and that disturbs me greatly. It must be that energy I've been feeling in the atmosphere. Ever since... the journey to the mountain foothills? Or before?

When we eventually reach the village, we see there is a disturbed murmur among the crowd gathered in the central field. Something seems to trouble the villagers.

A large stone pedestal has been placed in the field. A bowl shape is carved into the top of the plinth, which is filled with silvery water. A group of elderly people are standing closest to the plinth. The village elders. It's a rare sight for me to see them among the other villagers like this.

Aldus comes to us as we make our way through the crowd. He hugs his daughters and grandsons, and claps me on the shoulder, full of relief. "What happened?" he asks when he sees the bloody remains on Galene's dress.

"It's of no concern now," I tell him, as it's clear something very important is happening here.

"What is going on?" Leila asks, pulling the boys to stay close to her.

"We are in danger, my loves." Aldus turns to his daughters. "Our worst fears are coming true."

He takes us over to the plinth of water. Magdalena is standing nearby, while Colm and Yovin are on the other side of the crowd. It takes me a while to find Abby among them. I wonder if they're purposely keeping themselves separated now.

Aldus's eyes are wide and he has a trembling look about him. He's almost unhinged. I've never seen him this shaken. But I suppose the idea of losing your family will do that to a man. That beast was headed in their direction. If I hadn't got there as quickly as I did...

"We were just talking about the disturbances in the air," he says. "You have felt it?"

Leila and Galene look confused and uncertain, but I nod. "I've felt it, yes. What does it mean?"

Aldus places a hand on the plinth. "The thoro-seer has spoken. It has shown us the danger we are in."

"What does it say?" Galene asks.

At my questioning look, Aldus explains to me what the thoro-seer is. I think he does this to delay the news he has to tell us.

"The thoro-seer is a relic from the old world that is known to be able to sense ripples in the atmosphere, and even through time itself. It can show images of the future, or the past, when accessed by someone who knows how to command its power and read its images."

"There is no easy way to say this," Aldus continues gravely.

"Magic has betrayed us," one of the elders says. "We have proven this is so."

Leila's lips tremble. "What does that mean?"

Galene is silently stunned and horrified.

"You know the stories," Aldus says. "The ancient king, Thanek Deidamos. The dark king who once ruled this world."

"From the stories, yes," Leila says. "I know Thanek once lived, but that was so long ago. What does that have to do with-"

"The thoro-seer has shown us," another elder says, his face dark and heavy. "Thanek has risen again. His forces are back in this world."

Galene and Leila look to the five elders, as if pleading with them for help.

One woman in their group, whom I believe is Magdalena's mother, says, "Magic has been a blessing and curse to us. And it has allowed ancient forces to rise from their deep slumbers."

Like that behemoth, I think, a chill washing over me.

"You've had access to this thoro-seer this whole time?" I ask.

"We've had it," Aldus answers, "but it has only been usable since magic returned. It has shown us very little until now. One thing it showed us... was a man in an Oathlands Military uniform. That was a few days before your arrival."

A stunned hush falls on the crowd.

"You never mentioned this," I say. But I shouldn't be surprised about that.

"We did not know what it meant," Aldus says. "Or if it foreshadowed something good or bad for our village. We had to wait to see what kind of man you were."

"The thoro-seer never lies," a hunched elder says, his voice strikingly gravelly. "Thanek Deidamos has returned to the world, and he will mean to take it once again."

Galene shudders. "Thanek was slain, wasn't he? You said so yourself, father. That's what the stories say. Dashna Strongblood defeated him and banished him from this realm."

"That's right," Leila says, trying to sound hopeful. "Irina Dashna, the heroine whom we are descended from. That's what you tell us, right?"

Aldus nods, his expression severe. "Correct, my loves. We are descended from the heroine Irina Dashna, whom the stories call Dashan Strongblood. That has no relevance to our situation, however. And, yes, she defeated Thanek. But it appears the dark king has merely been slumbering all this time. And the resurgence of magic has somehow allowed him to grow in power and return to our world."

"And you saw this?" I ask. "In the water?"

"We did," Aldus says. "Only a few of us are capable of interpreting the images, but it was confirmed. Thanek and his forces roam this land. And they are intent on destroying everything. They will not stop until Thanek rules over the rubble that remains, so that he may rebuild this world for himself. He has done so before."

I'm still struggling to take in all this information. The grave looks on everyone tell me they fully believe this, and the danger is very real. I take my cue from Galene, who seems shaken and horrified. That tells me I need to do something about this, for the sake of us all.

"Do we know where this dark king is heading?" I ask.

Aldus nods and pulls out a folded slip of paper. "We received a message earlier. A messenger came from The Kingdom."

My brows shoot up. "The Kingdom? Here?" I didn't even think the Kingdom knew of the Shanti People's presence.

Aldus unfolds the note and holds it up. "It is a plea for help. The Kingdom seeks our aid. I believe they have sent messengers across the land, like the one who came to us. Their Kingdom is in great danger. Thanek's army has been seen coming to them."

"A Kingdom messenger came all the way here, to deliver a note?" I ask. "How do we confirm the note is true?"

"The thoro-seer proves the truth," an elder says with some annoyance.

"Can I take a look?" I ask, although I know the answer before I finish speaking.

The same annoyed elder glares mistrustfully at me. "It is not for outsiders. Shanti only."

I try to keep my voice even. "This is no time for customs if we are in such danger-"

"Shanti only," the elder hisses.

Aldus raises a calming hand to me. "You will probably not see anything."

"I've seen it work before," Galene says. "It's real. You can trust it."

I have to take her word for it. The elders have been staring at me hard with wary frowns.

"We must help the Kingdom folk." Leila voices what must be on many of our minds.

"We want to," Magdalena says. "But we can offer no support to them. We will go there to die."

"We have to help," Aldus says sternly. "We believe the Shanti People have the most concentration of magic out of anyone else in this land. We have the means to help, and to actually be useful in the fight."

"We will go to die," someone calls out.

"The Kingdom will fall," an elder replies, surprisingly calm. "And the rest of the world will follow."

It would make sense for an invading army to go after the center of the continent first. Take out the biggest challenge, and the rest will be easier. Maybe Thanek can sense the power and influence of the Kingdom and is drawn to it.

Aldus is right. The magic users among us are likely the best defense The Kingdom has. The Oathlands will have their own magic users, but they are too far away to be helpful in time. And The Kingdom, for all its gold, power, and influence, has never been known for its magical heritage. They will not have the forces to defend themselves from this ancient army.

"How long do we have?" I ask.

"Thanek's forces are swift and unyielding, but they ride no animals," Aldus says. "The messenger came on horseback and said the invading army should reach the Kingdom by nightfall today."

"It would take us a day to reach the Kingdom," I say. "We have no animals to ride, either."

"To the south, there are farmlands," Leila says. "In the Sundown Ways. They have many horses there. We can ride them the rest of the way to the Kingdom. That will cut our journey by half. We could arrive at the Kingdom by tonight. In the middle of the night."

"What army does he have?" I ask.

Aldus's brows crease. "Horrors of the old world."

That unsettles my stomach. "You need to contact the Oathlands," I say. "They are the nearest military. And they have the largest force to aid the Kingdom. Koprus and Syraxia are too far away."

Aldus frowns at me. "The Oathlands, coming to the Kingdom's aid? Preposterous. You are both sworn enemies."

"This is different." I shake my head. "If this is all really happening, then it means our entire world is in danger. We can't let innocent people die and then wait for the invaders to come to the rest of us. If the Kingdom falls, we will all be slaughtered."

"The Oathlands is too far," Magdalena says. "We will waste much time going there, and then the time needed for the Oathlanders to reach The Kingdom. Thanek's forces will have taken The Kingdom before our message can even reach the Oathlands."

"We have to try, though," I say. "Please. Send a message to the Oathlands. Even if it takes a week. Even if The Kingdom has already fallen. They have to know. Tell them what is happening. And my... people will ride out." I almost said, *my brother*.

Aldus is watching me closely with narrow eyes.

"We need to go now," I say.

"You are right," Aldus agrees. "We Shanti People are the only ones in this land who can sense the returning power of Thanek and the other forces among others. We are the most in tune with ancient magic. The Oathlands will not have detected Thanek's return. And the only reason the Kingdom knows of the attack is that they have seen the approaching army on the horizon. That's why they have positioned themselves so high above everyone else, so they can see approaching armies from miles away."

"The Oathlands have their magic back also," I say. "Perhaps they have sensed Thanek's return."

Aldus shakes his head. "The magic in this world is newer. It is diluted and filtered. I speak of ancient magic. The kind that runs through our Shanti blood."

I frown in thought, coming to a dark realization. I must do what I hate. I have to defend the Kingdom and save everyone there.

All I wanted was to return home, and now fate has brought me back to this village. If we don't help the Kingdom, death and destruction will spread across the world.

Galene shares a concerned, deeply troubled look with me. I can see the fear in her eyes. I want to reach out and comfort her but have to hold myself back.

One part bothers me. A Kingdom messenger coming all the way out here and knowing where to find the Shanti People. But that is the least of my concern, and far from the most outlandish thing I've heard today.

We make a plan to send as many people as we can to the Kingdom. We must do what we can.

Chapter Twenty-Three

ROURK

The villagers spread out and prepare to go to war for the first time in their history.

It takes us some time to decide who will go and who will stay. All the hunters are tasked to make the journey to the Kingdom, except for the three who will remain to keep guard of the village, and two who will become messengers. Several able-bodied men and women step up and request to go with us. They have no training or combat experience, but they can wield a weapon and are fit enough to not become a burden. I'm aware that everyone may well be going to their deaths, including me, but we are all willing to take that chance.

The Shanti People may be secretive and keep to themselves in this world, but they have a code to help others. They cannot let the Kingdom get attacked without aid.

They've kept out of the affairs of the Oathlands and Kingdom for centuries, but this time it's different. The fate of the entire world is at stake.

At my insistence, a message is sent out across the village. Everyone with a magical ability should step forward and join the party heading to the Kingdom. No one is forced to do anything they don't want to do, but I know we need any advantage we can get. The villagers are asked to attune to their abilities in the time they have, to be certain they know how to wield them without being a danger to themselves or others. We don't have long before we leave, so every minute counts.

Two hunters are tasked to go as swiftly as they can to the Oathlands to deliver a plea for help. Freddick was initially tasked as one messenger, given his lack of experience fighting, but he firmly insists on going to the Kingdom. He wants to help fight the invading force. I see that killer look in his eyes. That world-weary, battle-hardened look that's mixed with spiking fear and adrenaline. There's no way of stopping him from going to the Kingdom.

It's unlikely the Oathlands will reach the Kingdom in time to help in the battle, but we have to take that chance and let them know what is happening.

Travel packs are prepared, along with food and water for the journey. Others are quick to fashion more arrows out of wood and sharpened rocks for blades. The entire village becomes a hive of preparation.

I meet Aldus's eyes and we step aside to speak to each other.

"We have forty-five people to go to the Kingdom," he says. "That's all we can spare. And more than I thought we'd get. I'm not too happy about some of the younger ones, or older ones, with us, but they're insisting they want to help."

"If they don't slow us down or get in our way, they will all be helpful," I say, looking around. "It will have to do. All we can do is all we can do."

Flashes of magic cut through the dwindling afternoon light. A blast of fire strikes a far-off tree. A sphere of lightning launches into the air. I've discovered more people showing abilities they've never revealed to me before. The one who can fly, a young girl named Delis, is spiraling and looping in the air. The hunters have been teaching her how to throw knives down with accuracy.

"Before we go," I say to Aldus, "I'd like to know something."

He regards me with a hard look.

"The elders," I say. "They are not really the elders of the village, are they?"

His face is impassive. "What do you mean? What is this?"

"I've seen how the elders work here. And how you work. You, Magdalena, Colm, Yovin, and Abby. Abby was a hard one to figure out, as she really didn't seem like someone who holds any influence or power. But I noticed it was just a mask. A mask that you all wear. You five are the genuine leaders of this tribe. The elders are just the faces of the village."

Aldus eyes me for a long moment, visibly troubled and thoughtful.

"I do not understand why you are doing this, now," Aldus responds with enough subtle heat that tells me to back off.

"I just want to know the truth," I say. "We need to trust each other. Yes, it doesn't change our fates. I guess... I just wanted you to know that I know."

"You speak of Shanti people's business like it is your own."

He's right. And I have nothing to say about that.

He sighs and shakes his head, taking a moment before turning to me. "Elders have always led our people. But for almost a century now, others have become the true leaders of our tribe while the elders remain as the figureheads. It is the secret way of our people, and none need to know about it. This is our way."

"I do not mean to interfere with your ways," I say. "I simply want us to trust each other. You have to trust the man at your side in battle."

"You have my trust," Aldus says. "There should be no doubt of that. I suggest you spend our last moments here helping prepare for the battle, rather than search for secrets."

He searches my face with a questioning *what will you do next?* look. It makes me wonder what he is capable of.

I nod. "You are right. Forgive me for my prying. I'm glad we are both in agreement. Trust is what matters."

Aldus eyes me for a moment longer before walking away.

I look around at the busy village, alive with people preparing to go into battle for the first time. These are not soldiers or warriors. They are peaceful people trying to do what's right. To not have innocent bloodshed.

Outside of the Kingdom, we may be the only people in the entire world who know of this imminent threat.

Galene catches my eye. She is heading toward the rows of huts across the field. She's watching me as she goes, her eyes alive with communication. A small smirk is on her face. I know that look. She wants me to follow her. She wants to talk about something. That smirk of hers, and the shine of her eyes, stir something deep within me.

I go to follow her when she disappears behind the tents, but hushed, heated words make me turn to the side. I straighten at the sight of Wini Semassi approaching me with her brother Wills hissing at her.

"Leave me," Wini is saying to him. "I will do what I like."

"You will listen to me," Wills snaps under his breath. "Mother said you must."

"Go take it up with Mother," she hisses back.

Her countenance shifts when she reaches me, the tension of her sibling squabbling, shifting to a soft smile and relaxed shoulders.

"Hello again," she says, almost diplomatically.

I nod, not knowing what to say or what is happening. Wills is trying to murder me with his eyes.

Wini is effortlessly well put together in a low-cut blouse and hip-hugging skirt, both weathered and worn and possibly fashionable a long time ago. She brushes a golden lock behind her ear as she smiles, though not in a seductive way.

"I wanted to tell you something," she says. "I... want to go with you. With you all. To the Kingdom."

Wills steps up. "I told her she can't just-"

Wini snaps at him and stomps her foot. He retreats, shaking his head. She looks around five or six years younger than him, probably not even in her twenties yet, but she has the air of the boss in the family.

I take a second to register her statement. I hadn't been expecting that. "It is going to be very dangerous."

"I know. I can handle it." She bites her lip before continuing. "And... I can... Well, I have a magical ability."

Wills runs his hands through his hair as he paces.

"I was not told you had a magic gift," I say.

"That's because no one knows," Wini says. "I have told no one but my mother and brother. I... didn't want anyone to know."

"Why is that?"

"It's... well I didn't..." She settles with, "I am, now."

I wait for her to say more.

She catches the question on my face and says, "I can connect with animals."

That makes me raise my brows. "Can you elaborate on that?"

"It doesn't matter," Wills cuts in. "It isn't helpful to anyone. Tell her she needs to stay here."

Wini shoots him a violent look. I hold a hand up to calm them both.

"I can... see through their eyes, sometimes," Wini says. "It's like I'm in their bodies. I can hear what they hear and feel what they feel. Sometimes I... Sometimes it's like I can control them. For a short while. I've been practicing, and I've been getting better."

I regard her with skepticism, but things are starting to connect. That wolf who had been watching me sleeping in my tent the other morning. The crow in the tree who'd caught staring at me. And a few other occasions where I've felt like I was being watched. They were her. Wini. Watching me through the eyes of animals. It's a little disconcerting how easy it is for me to accept such a thing. The world really is a new place.

"Okay," I say. "But we are still heading into a lot of danger. It's no place for a young girl like you."

"You don't know me," she says with her chin high, glaring. "I'm not a little girl. And I... I want to help. Please. I know I can help."

Wills looks like he's going to interject, but he catches himself and sighs, going back to pacing with agitation.

I look into Wini's deep blue-green eyes, searching for the truth of the strength that lies within. Her determination is certainly admirable. "Very well," I say. "If your mother allows it."

"She does," Wini replies quickly with a big smile and a bounce. "Thank you. I promise, I will be helpful. I think. I won't let anyone down."

Wini steps forward and looks like she's going to hug me, but stops herself. She smiles awkwardly with a nod and rushes away with excitement. "Thank you," she calls back.

Her brother glares at me for a moment with pure contempt and disappointment. As he turns to walk away, I say, "Wills."

He stops and goes back to glaring.

"I will do everything I can to protect her. To protect all of you. I hope you know that."

His face softens for a moment before he sneers and walks away. For a second, I thought I'd gotten through to him. But he has a rigid stubbornness that I've come to know as a common Shanti quality.

So, Wini can connect with animals. An interesting ability. I wonder who else in the village has been keeping their magic a secret, either from me or the rest of the tribe.

I turn and walk in the direction Galene had been going.

It takes me a while to realize she has gone past the rows of tents and ventured down the hill to the secluded glade below. A flash of her golden light tells me she's down there.

I make my way down to find her hidden behind a dense collection of trees. The area is quieter, with the low din of the village behind us, beyond the top of the hill.

Galene is holding onto a square of light with one hand, her feet dangling a good six feet off the ground. The sight of her in the air gives me a strange sense of unease.

"There you are," she says. "I... I think I'm stuck."

I cock my head curiously and can't help but grin. "Stuck? In the air?"

She sighs but doesn't hide her smirk. "I managed to step up this high, using hard light steps, and I thought I would try holding onto the light with my hands, and... then I lost the light steps and now I'm here. It's a long way down."

I position myself below her. Her long layered dress wavers softly in the breeze. "I'm here." I hold my arms out. "I'll catch you."

Galene focuses for a second, and the light in her hand vanishes. She falls into my arms.

I wince and hiss when her weight hits me. "Shit. My ankle."

Her face widens with horror. "Oh, no, are you okay? I..."

"How much do you weigh?" I ask, grimacing in pain and hobbling. Then I drop the act and grin at her while lowering her down to the ground.

Realization slowly dawns on her and the horror goes from confusion to shock, and settles on gleeful surprise.

"Hey!" She slaps me on the shoulder.

I laugh. "I couldn't help myself."

Her pouting mock-frown comes across as adorably cute. "Anyway, I still have a lot to prove, it seems," she says. "I guess that's why father is insisting that I go with you all to the Kingdom."

"What makes you think he is looking for you to prove yourself?"

Galene lets out a weary breath. "I thought my Task with you would be my big final one. But now it seems that saving the Kingdom and fighting an ancient army that's only meant to exist in storybooks is my final task. But I wonder if my father will just find something else after. If we both make it back."

"Hey," I say. "Of course you'll make it back."

"He just wants to keep pushing me. As a punishment for being unwed and childless at my age. Do you know what Leila's big Task was?"

I shake my head.

"Leila's great Task was to collect golden apples from a region where ferocious bears and wolves roam, high up on the Westfall Mountain. She hadn't technically been Tasked, as it was too dangerous to go alone, but she chose it herself as she wanted to prove her worth. She spent two weeks out in the wilderness on her own and collected twenty-four spirit apples. Those are the big golden ones, three times as big as an average apple. She almost got frostbite in her fingers and toes, but came back victorious. We planted the seeds of the apples we ate and grew our own golden apples from there on, and had a large festival to eat the apple pies made from them. She was a hero to everyone, and from that day, she was Proven. I think my father keeps waiting for me to do something crazy like that."

"Everyone is different," I say. "You don't need to prove anything to anyone."

Galene sighs and shakes her head.

My hands slip around her waist to comfort her. I do it so easily without thinking, like it's the simplest action in the world. If she's surprised by my hold, she doesn't show it. She melts into my arms, stroking my upper arm and shoulder.

"Careful," she says demurely. "Don't get too close. I hate you, remember?"

"I do have problems remembering things," I grin. We lock eyes and hold our gaze. The feeling of a deep, overwhelming connection hits me firmly in the chest.

I nod to where she'd just been hanging from. "That was an impressive feat. You've been practicing."

She shrugs. "It seems to get easier the more I try."

She has a conflicted, distant look that makes me ask, "What is it?"

"I just want to know what I'm capable of. To help others. To know that I can protect others. And myself."

I tighten my hold, pulling her closer. I can smell her light sweat mixing with her usual floral and earthy scent.

Our hips press together and I stir and grow against her. A gleam in her eye tells me she's noticed.

"You are the most courageous woman I know," I tell her, my voice low and soft. I want to tell her not to come with us to the Kingdom, but her father has already insisted she go. Leila will stay behind with the boys, but Galene, who has become most in tune with her magical powers, will be among those going to the Kingdom. "I just hope I can protect you. While you're protecting others."

Her glistening lips part. "And who will protect you?"

She slowly inches closer and I lean in. The world melts away around us as our lips meet. I lose all sense of myself as I take her in my arms and kiss her hard. Our heavy breaths bounce off each other as our pulses quicken.

My tongue teases at the seam of her mouth and she presses her body tighter against mine before slowly opening her mouth and letting my tongue slide against hers. She moans when I run a hand down her back and arch her hips against mine, pressing her against my hardness.

I pull my mouth away from hers to kiss her cheek and neck, moving down her neck to her collarbone. I lick and nip at her skin before sucking, her hands gripping my hair as she gasps. She tastes sweet and smells intoxicating.

Galene slides one hand from my hair and down my body, sneaking it between us. She gropes at my pants and rubs my cock through them, which grows even harder beneath her hand.

I'm pushing her back and she presses against a tree as we kiss. My hands don't know where to settle. I run them from her waist down to her ass, squeezing and kneading before sliding up and under her dress, running them over her breasts, pleasure rolling through me when I meet bare nipples. She has nothing on beneath the dress. My fingers tease at her peaks before pinching, just enough to get a squeak out of her and for her to press against me even harder. Her hand is pressed between her hips and mine, and I have to wonder if she's teasing herself at the same time as she is me.

I can't believe this is happening, but I'm too lost in the ecstatic moment to think clearly. To wonder if maybe it shouldn't be happening at all.

Fuck, I wouldn't give this up for anything.

Especially as she helps me pull down my pants, her delicate fingers popping the button and pushing them down. Her eyes rest on my cock and her breaths become heavier. Shakily, she rests a hand on my bare cock and pumps it once, her gaze turning upward to stare at me from beneath lowered lashes. Those blue eyes tell me everything I need to know. She really wants to do this. That burning neediness is clear in both of us. That strong magnetism that spurs us on. There is no amount of closeness that will satiate us, but we will have to make do with this.

She pulls up her dress and barely allows me a single glance at her hardened nipples before she turns around to press her front against the tree, revealing the full curves of her smooth, bare ass. "I want it like this," she says to me. She spreads her legs slightly.

I groan at the sight of her, black hair falling down her back, smooth skin and that ass that I've thought about countless times before. I suck in a breath and run my hands down her body. I wrap one around her front and brush my fingers across her navel before sliding lower and finding her wet folds. I slide my fingers through them, hearing her gasp and feeling her squirm, her ass backing up against my cock when I find her clit and flick it with my fingers.

I settle my mouth against her neck and groan. "Fuck," I whisper. "I cannot wait to be inside of you."

"Then get inside me," she gets out, breath hitching.

"Fuck," I say again, but I hold myself back. I brush her hair to the side and suction my mouth to her neck as I swirl my fingers at her clit, slowly building pressure with both my mouth and my fingers until she's writhing, unable to keep still. Her legs grow shaky, and I slowly adjust my hold on her until I can sink a finger into her entrance. She lets out a low moan and clenches around that finger.

"Gods," I groan, unable to stop myself from sliding my throbbing cock against her ass, just to give myself something to hold me over. "You're so tight, Galene. I need to stretch you out a little if I don't want to hurt you."

"Yeah," she gets out. "I saw you."

I chuckle darkly and pump that finger inside her as I scrape the heel of my hand against her clit. When Galene starts to move her hips against my hand, I let her take over. I'll let her have that now so that she's all mine when I'm inside of her.

Her hips move quickly as she grinds my hand against her, her wetness soaking my skin. I give her clit another flick and listen to her cry out before I sink another finger into her. She rides them with wild abandon before I nudge against that spot inside her, and then she's coming undone.

I don't wait for her orgasm to die down before I enter her from behind and she moans. I press a hand to her mouth as I pump, softly at first, before the writhing of our bodies increases and I thrust into her, harder and harder. She gasps against my palm. I breathe in the scent of her hair and kiss all along her neck, listening to the small sounds she makes and relishing in the feel of my cock pressed deep inside of her.

I rejoice in the warmth of her and the feel of her skin against mine. I don't think I've ever been this hard before, or this excited. The thrill surges through me as I thrust into her, pressing her more and more against the tree.

I want to see her face. To taste her. To be more with her. I pull out and quickly spin her around, listening to her gasp of surprise, and lift up her legs around my waist as I position myself to enter her once more, sinking into the hilt in one smooth motion. She moans low and her eyes flutter closed I grip her thigh and pump into her, my other hand reaching out to feel the soft swelling of her breasts, those nipples she'd barely given me a glance of earlier. Galene wraps her arms around me and kisses me firmly, our sweaty faces pressing into each other.

"Harder," she mutters beneath her heavy breaths. "I want you."

"I want you too," I groan, holding her cheek and kissing her over and over. My hand lowers to her throat and I see a thrilled flash in her eye as my thumb presses against her skin. That sends her to another level of ecstasy, causing her to cry out with a shaky groan. Her eyes roll back as she gasps into the sky.

Our moans mingle together in a symphony of pleasure and desire as we reach the heights of ecstasy together. My legs weaken as I shudder and convulse, my thrill reaching its climax.

After a pause, I lower her down and we rest against each other as we calm, catching our breath. Our shoulders and chests heave against each other. I soften inside her before inching away and pulling my trousers up.

Galene steps away and shifts her dress down and adjusts her blouse. I play my fingers through her thick hair as I watch her, overwhelmed with satisfaction and contentment. We share playful grins and chuckles. The chuckles become hearty laughter as we hold each other and kiss a few more times. Neither of us wants to stop touching the other.

I want to stay in this moment forever.

"That was... something," she says, her voice hoarse.

I clear my throat. "It was not nothing."

There's so much I want to say to her, but nothing feels like the right time.

We kiss until we realize we have to stop, and the impending journey and danger we're about to face finally forces us back to the village.

We can't hide forever. No matter how badly I might want to.

Chapter Twenty-Four

ROURK

Forty-six of us make our way south toward the Kingdom late in the afternoon. We keep a fast pace, but it will be a long walk to the southern farmstead where we can procure horses for the rest of the journey. I keep myself near Galene, but not close enough to draw attention to us both. A thrumming energy courses through me still when I think of what we had just done against the tree. Her firm hold of me and her powerful eyes as our bodies became one. I hadn't realized how much I'd yearned for her, and how thrilling the ecstasy would be.

And to think, just a week ago, she had hated me with every fiber of her being. But that had been before I'd known the measure of her, and before we'd become accustomed to each other. Before we'd acknowledge the mutual goodness of our hearts, and the strength of our resolve. Now, I can't stop thinking about her touch and the taste of her lips. I even have her soft, strong voice playing in my mind.

Swaths of deep reds and oranges fill the sky, telling me that something terrible will happen tonight. The red sky at night summons the blight.

I look around at the familiar faces around me, proud of how many we have with us. Almost every able-bodied adult from the tribe. Those who do not have young ones or elderly to care for. It does bother me how few hunters we left to keep the village secure, but we focus our efforts on helping the Kingdom. It's a strange thought to think I have an army with me again. A strange army of peaceful farmers and hunters with no soldiers and minimal combat experience.

I sense Bohan stepping closer beside me. He gives me a small nod.

"Some people think I'm hardheaded," he begins, "and an oaf."

"I can't imagine why they think that," I reply with a touch of humor.

"Well, it is true," Bohan shrugs. "But I also know when to admit I was wrong. I was wrong about you, outsider. You're a good man. And you have the experience we need with us. I just hope you know what you're doing."

"So do I." I give him a respectful nod. He returns the nod. "I had the wrong impression of you, also," I say. "I know you want to help your people and do what's best for them."

"I will fight beside you. We will do what's right. Even if that means we are helping the Kingdom."

"I don't like the idea of helping them any more than you," I say ruefully. But we both know why we're doing this. If the Kingdom falls, the rest of the world will follow.

This is more about stopping Thanek's re-forged army than saving the Kingdom. And none of us can let innocents die doing nothing to help.

It's been over two years since I was last at the Kingdom, and even then I hadn't entered the city gates. We had stolen grain from a storehouse and left with no one knowing. That feels like a lifetime ago.

The one among us who can fly, the girl named Delis, takes to the blood-red sky and swoops around. She had chosen to walk with us rather than fly ahead, but I get a sense of restlessness from her and the need to be in the air. If I could fly, maybe I would prefer being up there to being down here, too.

I notice the strained grimace on Freddick nearby. He looks to be on the verge of tears, or the end of quiet sobs. He notices me watching him and doesn't hide his emotions.

"We're not all coming back, are we?" He asks, his voice quivering.

"Battle is brutal," I say. "There will be blood. And death. On both sides. That cannot be helped. But I promise I will do everything I can to protect you all. We must protect each other."

Freddick's bottom lip trembles. He gives me a shaky nod. "I want to be strong. Father would have wanted me to fight. He always fought for those weaker, or less able to help themselves. I know I'm doing the right thing. I just..." He looks up at me with shimmering eyes. "I just don't want to die."

"Dying in battle is an honor," Bohan says stiffly.

I place a hand on Freddick's shoulder. "If we are all doomed to die, we will spend our last moments doing something good. That's more than many people do in their entire lives."

"That's better than what I said," Bohan shakes his head. "Ignore my last comment."

Freddick nods and smiles at us. He looks to be in better spirits.

We continue through the hills and valleys and reach the southern farmsteads before the last of the light fades from the sky. Dozens of horses are grazing on the land.

We have no time to ask for permission or search out the family of farmers, so we will have to seek forgiveness later. If we manage to save the world and return.

I give brief instructions to all on how to mount and ride a horse, as few Shanti People have riding experience. It takes a frustrating amount of time to get everyone mounted. There aren't enough horses for us all, so several of them carry two people.

Delis now flies freely as the rest of us ride the horses. I note how the act of flying doesn't seem to fatigue her. We make slower progress than I'd like, as the villagers need time to acclimatize to the horses, and many of them lack the confidence to push harder. It isn't ideal to ride without a saddle, but we only need to cover the distance to the Kingdom. And now is not the time for comfort.

We stop on one occasion when someone falls off their horse. I begin to wonder if I need to race ahead and leave the villagers behind, although I want to keep us all together.

I shout out instructions and advice for horse riding as we go. Then we somehow start making swift progress. The horses speed up and the villagers no longer seem so out of control. Soon, we are all racing onward at a surprisingly fast pace, the horses swift and strong.

I have no explanation for this, and the villagers look just as bewildered as I am, but we are making good time, so I don't question it.

Then I see a strained, tortured look on Wini's face. The young girl is low on her horse, her brows creased and mouth twisted into a pained grimace.

"Stop this," her brother Wills calls to her. "Wini. That's enough."

"No," she says through her teeth. "I can do this."

I realize what she's doing. She is connecting to the minds of the horses.

"They need to know how important our task is." Wini's eyes are squeezed shut. "They want to help us."

The horses pick up their pace even more and race faster than any I've ever known. Faster than the greatest horses of the Oathlands. I wonder if Wini is also imbuing them with extra strength.

"How are you doing this?" Wills asks her uncertainly.

Wini shakes her head and gasps. "I don't know."

After a time of swift galloping, Wini almost slides off her horse. She looks weakened and drained. Her determination is evident and admirable. Her brother tells her to back off before she hurts herself, but she remains resolute.

Somehow, the horses are not tiring. It makes me guess Wini is somehow absorbing their fatigue. Her magical gift seems to be a multi-faceted mystery.

I'm surprised at how strong Wini is, and I realize I had underestimated her character. She is far more than the voracious vixen who had tried to seduce me. It speaks of the strength of the Shanti People in general. These are good people capable of good things, who have kept to themselves for too long. Now is their time to show the world what they're capable of. I just hope I don't get them all killed.

We soon crest a hill and see the Kingdom far along the horizon. The sky-piercing white towers are highlighted against the flames surging through the city. The battle is well underway. The biggest city in our world looks like a glowing ember in the darkness.

Something is flying over the city, a dark shape against the firelight. It isn't until I focus on it more that I realize it is a dragon of some kind. Other smaller creatures cover the sky over the city.

This is going to be a battle unlike anything that's been seen in this world. We pick up our pace and race to reach the Kingdom before it's too late.

Chapter Twenty-Five

GALENE

My first battle. I feel numb to the idea. My heart threatens to burst from my chest as we reach the outer gates of the Kingdom. The sheer scale of it is like nothing I could have imagined. The illustrations in the books I've seen do not do this place justice. It could be a very beautiful, magnificent place under other circumstances, when there aren't fires raging through the buildings and monsters tearing through the streets.

Wini stays behind as she is on the verge of unconsciousness. Wills stays with her by the outer gate, although as we rush by, I hear Wini telling her brother to join the battle and forget about her. I don't hear the rest of their talk as the booming sounds of chaos bombard me. I tighten my hold of the spear in my hand as we run through the inner courtyard to the nearest streets. Impossibly tall buildings loom over us in the distance, some of their tops disappearing into the dark clouds.

A screeching dragon roams the sky overhead, joined by smaller dragon-like creatures who are throwing themselves into buildings to destroy as much as they can. One of the smaller dragons has picked up someone in the distance and drops them. The destructive madness around us drowns out their screams.

Through the remains of a broken building, a ten-foot troll barrels through the smoke and debris to swing a gnarled club at white-armored Kingdom Guards. Short, stout creatures are among the invading army. Their pointed ears and mottled green skin make me think of goblins from the old stories.

Rourk calls for us to charge forward. His fierce, confident voice gives me some strength, but doesn't remove the crippling fear coursing through me. This is already too much for me and my legs are weaker than I'd like. But I have to stay strong.

The vast city has a pyramidal shape, meaning we have several levels to climb if we're going to reach the center. We come to a wide abandoned street with short buildings on either side, the paved stones cracked and scorched. Ahead, Kingdom Guards battle with an enormous troll. Frightened civilians rush through the street, ducking into alleys or hiding behind carts and barrels. Some are banging on doors to be let in.

Several cackling goblins burst out from an alley and charge at us, waving metallic clubs and oversized hammers.

When we get close enough to engage with the goblins, I see their forms are decayed and rotten. These are not living creatures. Some have eyeballs half-hanging out of their sockets while others have gaping holes in their bodies. They all have white-glazed eyes.

"They are undead," someone yells shrilly.

"The undead army of Thanek," someone else yells.

None of us had been expecting this, but we engage in the battle with vigor. We fling arrows into the charging goblins and attack with axes, knives, and spears.

Bohan is surprisingly brutal and effective in combat, cutting down several of the undead army with his broadaxe. Small creatures drop from the roofs above, falling onto those around me. These have the petite three-foot frames, pointed noses, and sharp teeth of vicious elves. They wrap their claws around necks and sink their teeth into flesh. I rush up and stab an elf in the back with my spear, causing it to fall to the ground, writhing and shrieking. Another stab ends its thrashing. Then the thought comes to me. Will these undead stay dead?

An axe swings down and cuts the downed elf in two. I startle and look up to see Zayne is there with the ax.

"The more pieces, the better," he barks, and rushes off.

The enormous dragon swoops down to us with a blast of hot wind. Delis is in the air, flying toward the dragon. My heart jolts at the sight of her charging at the dragon head-on. The dragon snaps its long mouth at her, but Delis cuts to the side at the last second and spirals away. The dragon veers and takes chase, no longer interested in us. I lose sight of them both when they clear the rooftops. I hope that crazy brave girl will be okay. She's given us time to fight without the dragon bothering us.

I look for Rourk but don't see him anywhere. That sends violent shivers through me. When we reach the Kingdom Guards, their white armor gleaming in the glowing firelight, we help them fight back the giant troll and surrounding goblins. It's then that I see Rourk, who has picked up a sword and is diving under the feet of the troll, slicing its shins as he goes. My heart swells at the sight of him. I want to stay close to him, but I don't want to be dependent on him.

If there's any sense of surprise or confusion from the Kingdom Guards at the sight of us, it doesn't show. There's no time to explain who we are or where we've come from. I look back to see some villagers at the back of our group battling more of those cackling elves. The roar of another troll echoes through the street, though I cannot see where it is. That sends more dark fear through me. The sounds of death and destruction are all around, and no place is safe.

The sight of my father barreling through the undead army with his axe gives me a tremor of hope. He is proving to be a surprisingly formidable warrior. I need to be more like him.

Someone falls down near me. It's Geron, a fisherman, who has lost his spear and is on the ground, crying out as a goblin leaps on him. I swing the spear and knock the goblin away, but see that Geron has been slashed in the chest. Others help him up.

A body is on the ground. My heart leaps into my throat. It's Tan, Yovin's son. His stomach has been cut open, and he lays there with frozen fear on his pale face. We are all rushing around him, ignoring his dead body. I think I'm going to vomit.

Ahead, the huge troll is swinging its club at some of our group. I've never seen a creature so big and angry before. It's enough to make me want to freeze with fear, but I don't let it. I look inward and summon my light and throw it at the troll. A cube of golden light cuts through the air and smacks into the troll. It knocks it off balance, but it isn't enough to damage it. The troll soon regains its balance and is angry, thrashing and growling, with spit flying from its mouth. My arms glow with a vibrant light as I run, ready to throw the light for offense or defense at any moment.

Huddled dark figures in an alley are whimpering and cowering. They look to be a large family, hiding from the devastation. As we fight back skeletal soldiers, we help the family into a nearby house, where an elderly couple hurriedly welcome them in. Everything is moving in a blur, but it feels good to help people. To do some good.

Someone's pained yells catch my attention. Freddick has become overwhelmed and fallen to the ground. His opponent is a new enemy. This one is a hulking man-beast with fur covering its forearms and shins, and a pig-like snout on its dark-skinned face. A long black mane runs down its head, wavering as it stomps toward Freddick. It raises a hooked sickle-like blade. I try to rush to him, but several people are in my way.

Zayne rolls beside Freddick and comes up to slice his axe across the furred beast's leg. The beast drops to its knees but looks more angered than pained. Freddick gets up and joins Zayne in planting his axe into the beast before it can attack them, helped by two more villagers coming from behind.

We keep moving forward and reach marble steps that lead us up to the street above. A blast of fire shoots through the street, telling me that Yelena is still with us and using her fire magic. The ball of fire misses a goblin and hits a building, blowing out its windows and doors. I know there's going to be a lot of collateral damage, and that none of us have yet to master our powers, but I just hope we don't end up hurting each other or innocent people.

A shrieking creature with fluttering butterfly wings heads for us from the street above. It has sharp blades for arms and legs and is like something out of a nightmare. The ground shakes a moment before a chunk of the ground bursts upward and strikes the fairy creature, knocking it out of the air. I look around to see who has manipulated the earth, but don't see who has that power. Whoever they are, they have yet to reveal themselves.

We ascend to the street above and see a hulking troll that has to be over fifteen feet tall. It's tearing through the buildings with its meaty fists, and pauses when it sees our large group approaching. The sight of it holds me back and sends fresh fear through me. I can't believe we are all here in the middle of this war. And it pains me greatly that it feels like there are fewer of us. I don't want to think about who we've lost already, and who has fallen back with grave injuries. We're moving too fast to look back or pause.

Rourk leads at the front. He pushes off a wall and leaps into the air to avoid a swinging fist of the troll, and flips to the ground with a spin to slice it across the torso. He moves with impressive athleticism and prowess, making me realize how unskilled the rest of us are.

The giant troll swings its club and knocks down several villagers, throwing some through the air like dolls. A dark shiver crashes through me. This foe could easily kill us all.

I rush forward and summon a square of light in the air, which I use as a step to climb into the air. I push off a second light square and then a third, climbing higher as I reach the raging troll. There's no time to think of my actions. I just need to do what I can to save others. I push off the highest square of light and fall onto the troll, wrapping my arms around its neck. It bucks and twists violently, trying to shake me off, but I manage to hold on. My head swims with nausea and fatigue. I summon a thick slab of hard light into my hands and, in a flash, the light cuts through the troll's neck. I drop to the ground and roll away as the troll crumples in a bloody heap, its head almost torn from its shoulders.

I can hardly believe what I've just done, but I'm thrilled with myself. I get up and pump a triumphant fist into the air. Freddick comes by with wide, impressed eyes. Rourk is ahead, watching me. He gives me a sharp nod and there's a hidden smile that's meant only for me.

Rourk raises his sword and leads us farther down the street, toward where Kingdom Guards are battling skeletal soldiers in battered, torn armor. They are like warriors fresh out of the grave, re-animated with some kind of dark, ancient magic.

A charged ball of lightning strikes one of the skeletal soldiers and causes it to explode in a shower of sparks and bones. That fills me with hope. We are all using our abilities, combined with the tactics and skills learned from Rourk. Maybe some of us have a chance of surviving this.

A light in the sky causes me to stop. My face drops and horror grips me. A streak of fire is falling toward us, as if thrown by an unknown force. We cry out and dive away as it crashes into the ground near us. My vision blurs as I'm thrown through the air. I hit the ground hard, my breath leaving me as I roll into a wall. A piercing whine rings through my ears while I push myself to my knees. I cough through the smoke in the air, my eyes stinging. It feels like I've just been struck by a boar. My bones are jarred and rattled, seeping the strength from me.

Bohan is groaning loudly. His shoulder is reddened and burned, his face and torso blackened with soot. Others are helping him up.

"Keep going," Rourk calls out to us. "Head for the center."

I look up to see him ducking into a side alley, away from us. Where is he going? Why is he leaving us?

I follow him into the alley.

Chapter Twenty-Six
ROURK

My mind races with thoughts of what I think I've just seen. A familiar face. Someone from the Oathlands, here in The Kingdom. I saw a young girl on the other side of the alley, being ushered by two adults. Could it really have been little Tabetha? She had gone missing a few weeks ago and her father, Captain Tryphon, had been worried about her. Could she have somehow found her way to The Kingdom?

I burst out of the alley and check the next street to see no one is there. Broken rubble is strewn about, but there are no civilians or enemies here. The building next to me has a staircase winding its way up to the roof, so I head up for a better view of the surrounding streets. Maybe I can see where Tabetha has gone.

The rooftop feels particularly high up as the ground lowers on one side to the inclining levels of the city below. I check every side but don't see Tabetha anywhere. Perhaps it had been my imagination, but I was sure I had seen her.

Then I catch a glimpse of the young girl and the two adults crossing a street. It's a quick glimpse but I see

Tabetha clearly. It really is her. Same curly brown hair and button nose. Same dark eyes that match her father's. I lose sight of them when they turn around the corner of the building.

I want to go to her, but a flash of magic takes all my attention.

A figure is on the roof of a far-off building, its dark form is shrouded in pulses of black magic. Several Kingdom Guards are battling the armored figure, who must be at least seven feet tall. The armor is thick and robust, full of sharp edges and spikes, and gives the figure a powerfully imposing, monstrous frame. It's hard to see everything through the darkness, but nearby flames and flashes of magic highlight him clearly. I know instantly that this person must be Thanek, the Dark King of Old.

He was once a man, but now he is beyond the realm of my understanding. I wonder if he has been re-animated by some ancient magic, or if he has gained mastery of the magic he wields. Bursts of black light explode over the rooftop, knocking back the guards and throwing them through the air like dolls. Thanek's arms are glowing with the same inky black light. Strangely, it reminds me of the golden light that covers Galene's arms when she wields her magic.

As I consider my route to reach Thanek, the roof jolts suddenly as something large lands on it. One of the hulking man-like beasts is across from me, its forearms and shins covered in thick black fur. This one is over nine feet tall, with a long, heavy vest that wavers about it like a cape. It raises a double-edged spear as it approaches me, its pig snout snarling. Half of its face is scarred and rotten, and the long vest is heavily worn and falling apart. The faint blue light emanating from its eyes tells me of the sorcery controlling it.

I ready the longsword and prepare to face this beast. A splash of golden light hits the furred beast's back and causes it to stumble.

My brows rise at the sight of Galene on the roof, behind the enemy. She must have followed me to the roof.

"Get away," I yell to her.

"No," she yells back. "I'm with you."

That floods my heart with joy and terror in equal measures. If anything happens to Galene... If she gets hurt... I can't think about that. I need to focus.

I meet the giant beast and my sword clashes with its spear in a succession of attacks. Each block jars my bones and shifts me back several inches. The hulking beast is a surprisingly formidable foe, like nothing I've faced before. Both skilled and ferocious, with the keen intelligence of a seasoned soldier.

Flashes of golden light crash into the beast, knocking it back and sideways. They cause minor damage, but they give me a chance to strike blows that find their mark. I slice through the beast several times, but it doesn't slow down.

I need to keep my distance to stay safe, but I also have to get close enough to use my sword. When a cube of light cracks into the beast's head, stunning it for a second, I rush in and unload a combination of attacks. It isn't until I sense the spear swinging to my back that I know I've left myself exposed to an attack. But as the spear comes, a square of light appears and blocks it, inches from me.

I dive away from the next swinging spear attack, thankful to have Galene there with me. The spear crashes down onto the roof as I leap away.

The beast growls at Galene and stomps toward her, raising its spear. She steps back, looking at him with wide-eyed fear.

"Hey!" I yell at the beast, trying to get its attention.

It raises the spear and brings it crashing down into Galene, who dives away in time to avoid being skewed. I reach the beast and plunge the sword into its lower back. It rears back, howling into the dark sky. I manage to withdraw the sword and avoid a fierce backhand as it spins around.

I clear the space between us and then rush forward again. Galene's arms are shrouded in golden light. She gives me a quick nod.

I jump into the air and a square of light appears at my feet. I push off the light to leap higher, avoiding a spear strike as I push off another step of light and soar over the beast. It looks up as I fall toward it and plunge the sword into its head.

The beast stumbles and falters, dropping the spear. I push off it and land on the roof as it drops, causing the edge of the roof to crack and crumble. The roof collapses on one side and the beast falls with it, becoming lost in the crumbling debris.

I breathe a sigh of relief and share an elated smile with Galene. She comes over to me, but staggers when the crumbling roof continues to spread. Galene screams as she too falls out of sight amid the rising dust and smoke. A guttural cry of fear bursts from me. I sprint to the edge of the broken roof to see her summoning a bed of light to catch herself halfway down, easing her fall. She falls the rest of the way when the light gradually vanishes. She must be at least 6 floors down now, on the street below.

"Galene!" I call, a frisson of fear sending shivers through me. Please be unharmed. She's so far away that I don't know how quickly I can reach her.

"I'm okay," she calls back, though her voice is strained. Dust settles around her. "Just some scrapes."

"Stay there," I yell down. "I'll come and get you."

"No. You keep going. I'll find my way to the others."

I don't want to waste time arguing, so I nod. "Stay safe."

"You too," she says. Even from this distance, I can feel the intensity of her blue eyes reaching into my soul.

A group of Shanti are battling skeletal soldiers in the next street, so I know Galene won't be on her own for long. From this view, I can see the breadth of the devastation across the city, and the smoke from the raging fires billowing into the night sky. Screams of terror and pain fill the air.

I wonder if we've come too late. If The Kingdom is already lost. But we need to keep fighting while we can. As long as we draw breath.

I notice Aldus has separated from the others. He is entering a dark alley, one level up from the rest of the fighters. I frown, feeling like he's up to something. Something not good.

I make my way to the alley.

Chapter Twenty-Seven

ROURK

When I reach the mouth of the alley, I pause and quietly peek inside. Aldus is there, speaking with a tall man in gleaming white armor. The insignias on the armor tell me this man is a Grand General of The Kingdom Guard.

"I got them here," Aldus is saying, his heavy voice sounding angry. "I've done my part. Now you need to do yours."

"It is not that simple," the Grand General says. He has the lofty air of arrogance of many Kingdom Folk I've known. "You cannot simply tell The Dark King what to do. If you'd care to try, be my guest."

"We are in this together, Lok," Aldus says. "We have worked for too long to stumble at the final hurdle. If you cannot bring Thanek to my daughter, then I will bring her to him."

I tense up at those words. They are plotting something concerning Galene? Rage rushes through me as I enter the alley, no longer concerned with hiding.

Aldus's eyes widen at the sight of me. The Grand General places himself in front of Aldus. He glares at me from beneath his plumed helmet. I wonder that he seems vaguely familiar, but I don't think I've seen him before. The alley is wide enough to fit two men shoulder to shoulder, with little room to maneuver.

"I will dispatch him." The Grand General steps forward, withdrawing his ornamented broadsword, but the alley is too narrow for him to fully release the blade from its scabbard. The Grand General's eyes widen when he realizes how confined our environment is.

I dart forward, grabbing the hand on his sword hilt, and readying my sword for a slash. But he lashes out with an elbow to my brow, drawing blood with a flash of pain. I drop my sword with a clatter to better use both hands. We wrestle for a second before I manage to grab his arms as he attempts to withdraw his blade from a different position. I twist them and bring his blade across the gap under his helmet, slicing through his neck.

He had been expecting a show of swordplay, no doubt, but hadn't anticipated my experience or desire to end the fight as quickly as possible. And the time it took him to adjust to our restricted surroundings proved to be his undoing.

The Grand General drops, his armor clanging against the brick wall as he gasps and sputters, quickly falling silent. Aldus stares at me, stunned, while I pick up the Grand General's sword. A far superior blade to the one I had.

"You've been lying to me from the moment I met you," I grit out, my muscles burning with hatred. "I thought you were a good man, Aldus."

"I am," he says defiantly, standing strong. "I swear it. I give you my word."

"Your word means nothing." I step over the Grand General's body and Aldus backs away, but he has nowhere to go. There is a tall wall at the far end of the alley. The sounds of battle and chaos echo around us, though it feels like we are in our own secluded world.

"Thanek's power," I say. "It is the same power that flows through Galene." It's becoming clear now, the more I think about it. "The Dark King wields black magic while hers is gold. Pure. Untainted."

Aldus scowls at me, his dark eyes flashing. "You are insane. You make connections where there are none."

"I heard you speaking with the Grand General," I say. "You wanted to bring Galene here. That's what this is all about, isn't it?" I regard him with a frown. "You know, one thing hasn't sat right with me. The messengers from The Kingdom. The plea for help that had led to us coming here. There was no plea for help, was there? The Grand General sent a messenger for you to make up your story."

A grim smile shifts Aldus's beard. It makes him look predatory, like a cold killer. Something I'd missed within him this whole time. "You are good. Yes, the messenger was a ruse. Not that it makes any difference now. We are here, with Thanek and his army. And nothing can stop him."

"You mean for him to rule," I say in horror as it dawns on me. "You wanted this to happen. And you needed Galene here."

I search his eyes for the truth. "Galene shares his blood. His power. You... Your family."

"I underestimated you, my boy," Aldus says. "Yes. My family is descended from Thanek. The heroine who had defeated the Dark King all those years ago, Irina Dashna, was not an opposing soldier. She was Thanek's wife. She killed her husband and posed as a hero. Her magic passed down through the generations, staying pure with the females, and has now ended with my daughter, Galene. It's a shame she never had a daughter of her own. That would be an even easier sacrifice."

I raise my sword sharply, making Aldus flinch. "You're a monster," I grit through my teeth. My mind races with everything that's happened lately, trying to put the pieces together.

"The behemoth attack," I say. "It had come for Galene."

"It was meant to take her to Thanek, yes," Aldus says. "But you had to stick your nose into our affairs, like you've done this entire time. A new plan had to be made, to get Galene to Thanek. And as the Dark King was intent on taking over The Kingdom, I had to bring her here. It was surprisingly easy to manipulate the thoro-seer to make people see what I wanted, and to encourage our pathetic Shanti army to come to The Kingdom's rescue. I still can't believe any of you thought you would make it out of here alive."

"They are good people. You wouldn't know what it means to have a good heart."

An explosion shakes the nearby buildings. I need to get back out there. We can't give Thanek more time to wreak his devastation.

The attack on Galene's mother. My father must have known of their family's lineage. That's why he had slain Galene's mother. He must not have realized that she'd already had children by then. He had been trying to break Thanek's family line. To cut his power and stop him from returning some day.

Once magic had been restored to the world, Thanek could return because his power was still in his bloodline. I have to wonder if anyone else in the Oathlands knew of Thanek's lineage.

"You said Thanek needed Galene here," I say. "He needs to connect to his bloodline. That means he has not yet risen to full power. He needs Galene. He needs you. You maintain his power in your blood."

"That's enough, Rourk," Aldus cuts me off. "I've allowed you to meddle in our affairs for far too long."

That freezes me. He said my name. He must read the shock on my face as he grins and nods.

"Yes, I've known of your identity this entire time. Rourk Bearon. General Commander of the Oathlands Military."

He knew of me, and he still chose to keep me alive and befriend me? None of this makes sense.

"Why?" I ask. "Why would you want the world to fall? Why wish for the murder of your daughter?"

"You know nothing of me. Everything I've done has been for my family. For the future generations. We will all rule with Thanek. His rise was inevitable. Only a few of us in this world could foresee it. This has always been the way."

He sounds like a cultist. Like a madman. "I really thought you were a good man. I've never been more wrong about anyone."

A great wave of dark energy crashes through the alley, throwing us both off our feet. I land by the Grand General's body, my head spinning and exhaustion gripping me. Thanek must be nearby. It feels like he is on a nearby rooftop. His power is almost palpable, like an invisible hand holding me down. The screams of many people ringing in the air, and the blasts of explosions, urge me to get up.

Aldus has recovered and is facing me as I stand. He must have more resilience to Thanek's power, seeing as that same power courses through his blood. There's no way I'm going to let him get by me.

"You wanted to learn all about us," Aldus says. "But there's still a lot you do not know."

I prepare to block him when he tries to escape. I won't let him get away to go free after what he's done. He needs to be held accountable for his actions.

"You can't beat me, Aldus," I say.

A smug, knowing look appears on his face. He stands tall.

The ground shifts and trembles. At first, I think it's an earthquake, but then I see that the crumbling ground is directed at my feet. Deep cracks shift and my boots become swallowed up by the rising stone that surrounds me, fastening around my shins. I try to move, but there's no use. I'm stuck in place.

Aldus pushes past me before I realize he's begun moving. He barges past me before I can I swing my sword at him, and runs around the corner. That leaves me firmly held by the rocky earth around my shins.

I groan, hating how much time this is going to cost me. I have to get back out there. I'm not used to dealing with all this magic.

I slam the butt of the sword hilt into the concrete, which does little to break my imprisonment. I strike again and again, chipping away.

So, Aldus had been the person with the ability to manipulate the earth. I hadn't figured out who the Shanti villager had been with that power. He had kept that to himself to keep the advantage over others.

That doesn't matter anymore. What matters is that I get out of this damn stone. I strike with the blade and the hilt over and over until the earth cracks and I'm able to pull some chunks away. A few minutes later, I've managed to break enough to free my legs. Sweat drips from me as I push myself out of the rubble, taking a moment to catch my breath.

As I gather my strength, I look up at the sliver of sky between the two buildings. Window sills and outcrops litter the walls, giving me a way up. I don't have the time to run around and look for a staircase.

I hook the sword hilt to my belt to free up both hands, and spring up to reach a window sill. I push off to the next wall and work my way up, ignoring the burning in my legs and finding purchase where I can. A crack in the wall becomes a handhold. It's an arduous process, but I finally make my way up to the roof.

Panting and catching my breath, I see Thanek is two rooftops away. The curved spikes of his helmet, like branching antlers, give him a demonic form. He is throwing down blasts of black magic into the Kingdom Guards below. Shanti People are among them, being thrown about and falling under the debris crashing around them.

This is my chance to face Thanek. To face The Dark King of Old. A horror from the old world. Not only does he want to rule the world, but he means to find Galene and kill her. He must be stopped immediately.

I know I'm going to my death, but I have no other choice. I have to try, even if it's the last thing I do.

Chapter Twenty-Eight

ROURK

I know I'm going to my doom as I run across the rooftop, about to battle a legendary enemy of the world.

When I reach the edge of the roof, I leap the short distance to the next roof and keep running. I catch sight of Galene's white blouse in the small crowd on the street below. Her eyes are wide and fearful as she sees me heading for Thanek, but I have no time to speak to her. No time for anything but to keep heading to my doom. The Grand General's hefty broadsword gives me little comfort.

There is a wider gap to the next building, where Thanek is battling Kingdom Guards. I pump my legs and leap out into the open air, spreading my arms out, and fall. I manage to reach the outer stairwell of the next house and slam into the metal railing, my breath bursting from me. I have to throw the broadsword through the railing to rest on the stairs while I hoist myself up and over the railing. My chest and side burns where I'd crashed into the railing, and my muscles flare with pain, but I retrieve the sword and rush up the stairs to the roof.

I think I hear someone, possibly Galene, calling to me, but I don't dare stop and look back. My target is above me.

I reach the roof, panting heavily and desperately trying to catch my breath, to see Thanek dispatching the last of the Kingdom Guards. Several bodies in white armor are strewn about the roof.

Thanek's spiked helmet turns to me and he pauses. He is an incredibly imposing figure and feels more like an otherworldly demon than anything resembling a person. I see no face within the dark depths of his helmet visor. Darkness swells around him, consuming the light. His bulging black armor makes him appear taller and bigger than any man I've ever seen. The overly large broadsword he carries in one gauntleted hand is etched with blood-red engravings, and is easily four times the size of my blade. His arms become engulfed in black flames as he takes a step toward me.

"You are foolish to face me," says a voice through the darkness within his helmet. His haunting, gravelly voice feels like grinding rocks, and sounds like it's coming from a distance and from many directions.

"I've never been very bright," I respond as I ready my sword and begin slowly circling him as I approach, careful to step over the fallen bodies.

I must look like a strange sight to him. No armor, and no comrades. Just a man with a sword.

"All will surrender," Thanek bellows, and throws an arm out.

A torrent of inky black energy shoots out at me. I dive away and the magic explodes on the roof, cracking the bricks. The thrumming heat of the magic rattles my bones, but I try to ignore it as I close in on him.

I unleash a combination of sword strikes, but each one is blocked or dodged. For a powerful figure, Thanek is surprisingly fast and agile, and he wields his massive sword as easily with one hand as he does with both. He swings a backhand, which I duck under, and a wave of vibrating black magic passes over me. The power of the magic burns in the air and seeps into my bones, weakening and disorienting me. Sweat flies from my brow as I strike at him.

Thanek swings his sword down at me. I intercept with my sword, but the force is too powerful and I'm knocked several feet through the air. I hit the roof and roll to a heap, my muscles jarred and my head spinning.

He is beyond any foe I have ever faced. I know if I keep attacking, he will land a strike that will end me.

But I realize that it is all I need to do. Keep fighting him. Keep him distracted while the others take down his forces and help the civilians. If I buy the world enough time, the combined efforts of the Kingdom Guards and the Shanti People could defeat Thanek together, if they manage to weaken the rest of his army enough.

I have to fight for as long as I can.

Thanek throws out spheres of black magic which I have to run and duck under to avoid. They crash into the roof and break through, leaving smoking holes. When the magic strikes the fallen Guards, their bodies disintegrate and char like wood on a pyre. The stench of their burning bodies fills the smoky, tortured air.

I get close enough to swing at the Dark King, one blow scraping against his thick armor, but he blocks and avoids my attacks with ease. Even when I land a blow, I can do minor damage to him. And the longer I stay close to him, the more I feel myself weakening from the thrumming energy surrounding him.

Our swords meet with a powerful swing, and my blade cracks into pieces. The force throws me onto my back, causing me to slide several feet. I feel stunned and dazed as I realize my weapon is gone. So much for the ornamented blade of the Grand General.

When another blast of magic comes for me, I throw myself to the side and leap to my feet, snatching a spear from a downed guard as I go. The crashing sounds of battle, and of bestial cries, echo around us.

I realize this is my true purpose. Why I had been taken to the Shanti People. Why I'm still alive. It was my destiny to face the Dark King of Old. Perhaps I am meant to die at his hands to help others defeat his undead forces.

Thanek steps toward me. "I should know of you." There's something curious in his deep voice, and perhaps a hint of being impressed.

"You might, if you got the chance to get to know me," I spin the spear in my hands. I take any chance I get to catch my breath and fight through the burning pain in my muscles.

Thanek regards me—at least, I think he does—within the darkness of his helm. "You are insignificant. My forces will spread through this land like fire. Nothing can stop me."

I ready my next attack as we draw closer. "Let's not get ahead of ourselves now."

A fierce roar bursts from Thanek, and he charges at me. Our weapons clash in quick succession before he steps back and leaps into the air. He brings the sword down as I dive and roll away, leaving the blade to crack into the roof. The strike sends concussive waves through the air that hit me and push me back. I stumble to the edge of the roof and catch myself before I teeter over.

Thanek approaches me, a ball of black fire growing in his hand. A flash of white comes from behind him. My eyes bulge at the sight of Galene, coming up to the roof from the staircase. Her arms glow with a golden light as she takes a wide stance.

"Hey!" she calls out.

Thanek stops and slowly turns to her.

No, I don't want him to face her. He needs to stay focused on me if I'm going to keep Galene safe. I need to protect her.

It suddenly dawns on me, like a great weight hitting me.

This was all part of Aldus's plan. He had wanted Galene and I to fall in love. That's the real reason he had saved my life and brought me to the Shanti Village. He had Tasked Galene to tend to my health, and for the two of us to spend enough time together to develop feelings for each other. He wanted Galene to have a protector, to keep her bloodline safe. That's why Aldus wanted the Grand General of the Oathlands Military to befriend their tribe. He wanted a guardian for his youngest daughter. He'd been waiting for us to care for each other this entire time.

Thanek flares with black flames as he approaches Galene.

Chapter Twenty-Nine

GALENE

What have I done? I came up here to help Rourk, but hadn't been anticipating running into the Dark King like this. Fear grips me and holds me in place as I take in the vast darkness swelling about him, and the jarring thrumming sensation washing over me.

"There you are," Thanek says, his grinding voice hitting me from several places, like he's all around.

I straighten.

Rourk calls out, "Galene, get away from here!"

"Galene," Thanek draws out my name like a heavy sigh. "Come to me."

It strikes me then that Thanek has been searching for me. He wanted me here. I can feel it. But what does it mean?

The towering Dark King reaches out to me, his arm glowing with inky black light. I flinch and dart away with a flash of golden light that snaps his hand back.

"Insolent child," Thanek growls like an avalanche of rocks coming for me.

Rourk strikes out from behind as Thanek throws a wave of magic at me. I block the darkness with a shield of golden light and get pushed back, my boots scraping across the roof. My mind blurs and swells, as though I had just lost consciousness for a second. I blink back my focus to see Thanek swinging his sword at Rourk.

I rush forward and channel a sphere of light in my hand. The light cuts through the air and crashes into Thanek's back, causing him to stumble and catch himself. Something heavy thuds into my mind, making me dizzy with nausea.

It's my magic connecting with him. And his magic connecting with me. It slams into me each time. But there is something different with my magic. It feels fuller. More vibrant. More powerful. Whatever is happening to me in Thanek's presence, it's connecting me to my magic more than I've ever felt before.

Thanek knocks Rourk back with a heavy sword strike and he spins to me, thrusting a gauntleted hand out. Black vines spiral out from his hand and encircle me, meaning to pin my arms to my side. But I cry out and slash at the vines with a sword of light that blinks into existence. I hadn't even known I could do that.

Thanek darts back and forth as Rourk and I try to land blows, circling him and looking for an opening. I have to fight through the immense fear coursing through me and battle on as best I can, knowing any second may be my last. I just have to trust in my magic, and in Rourk. My arms swell with blinding golden light as I throw out magical blasts and block the black magic coming at me.

When Thanek's enormous sword swings at me, I leap up and push off a step of light to jump away from the blade. As I fall, I throw out a golden spike which plunges into Thanek's chest. The light disperses in a flash, leaving no visible damage, but it was enough to knock him back and give Rourk an opening. Rourk ducks low and stabs his spear into Thanek's side, but the blade bounces off the armor. Thanek throws out a backhand and sends Rourk spiraling through the air. A fear-filled scream bursts from me as Rourk hits the roof and rolls to a stop.

The Dark King turns to me and slowly approaches, forcing me to step back.

"You should not be fighting me," Thanek says. "You are meant to be here, with me. By my side."

A heavy chill shivers my shoulders. "W-what do you mean?"

"You already know." He holds out his hand.

Dark fear roils with the adrenaline coursing through me. But my mind becomes clear, like a flame igniting to reveal something hidden.

This power. His power. It is the same as mine. I can almost see his thoughts drifting to me through the air. Flashes of the truth. I have the same magical power as Thanek, because I come from the same family line.

I am... descended from him.

My face twists into a tortured grimace. "No!" I yell, shivering, on the verge of tears. "No. This is not..."

"It is," Thanek says, his deep voice low and almost soothing. "Galene." He draws out my name like a long echo. "Come to me."

He reaches out again, his gauntleted hand swirling with ebbing darkness. I feel myself falling into that deeply welcoming darkness. Like reaching home after a long journey.

No.

I snap out of the trance and a dome of golden light bursts over me. Thanek jerks back, and I can feel the torrent of anger rising through him.

"Stay away!" I yell and throw a golden spear at him.

He knocks it away with his sword. Behind him, Rourk is struggling to get to his feet, his shirt stained with blood.

Thanek comes for me again with a grasping hand. I leap over the body of a Kingdom Guard and clear the distance between us.

He's trying to get to me. He means to take my power. To take... me.

Yes, it's clearer now. Thanek wants to take me and use me as a vessel for his new life. Waves of feelings and images hit me as I throw out my magic to keep him back. I think the more I connect to my magic, and the more my power connects with his, the clearer everything becomes.

I am the last female of Irina Dashna's lineage and power. And my father has been plotting to sacrifice me to the Dark King, to restore him to full power. It's all suddenly in my mind, in an instant. My father faking the letter from the Kingdom. Forcing Rourk into my life. Arranging to have me here, in the Kingdom, on this night. To be here with Thanek at this time.

There was no stopping this moment from happening.

His power is fueled by mine, as mine is by his. That's why I'm stronger now in his presence.

I keep Thanek back with spears of light while I try to get closer to Rourk. He's on his feet now and has picked up a new sword from a fallen guard.

"Rourk!" I call out to him. "He needs me alive. He needs his family alive. To return to power. Without those of us with light power, he is helpless."

None of this feels real. I am the last magic source of the Dark King's bloodline. The last with light magic. Without me, he won't be able to grow to full power. My family's existence has allowed him to return to this world.

Once he has combined with my power as he had once tried to with his queen, he will be unstoppable. I can't let that happen.

Rourk engages Thanek in combat, their swords clashing and spirals of black magic shooting out. A blast of magic strikes Rourk's shoulder and sends him spinning to the ground. He gasps and collapses, his shoulder blackened and scarred. Thanek raises his sword to strike a killing blow.

I cry out as I summon an explosion of light between them that pushes Thanek back. The exertion forces me to my knees. I stay there, panting, sweat dripping from me.

Beside me is a fallen dagger. It calls to me.

"Enough!" I scream, with tears flooding my eyes. All of this pain, all of this turmoil, it has all led to this moment.

Thanek turns to me.

"I know what I have to do," I say, my lips quivering. Rourk looks up at me with fierce intensity. "I'm sorry,

Rourk. I need to cut off his light magic at the source. When he is weakened... finish him. For me."

Horror dawns on Rourk. "Galene! No!"

"I'm sorry." Tears stream down my cheeks. "I love you."

I grip the knife and thrust the blade into my stomach. White-hot pain burns through me, taking my breath. I make sure the last thing I do is force the blade firmly in. A killing blow.

I drop to the roof and cough blood. Darkness takes over. The last thing I hear is Rourk calling out to me. My Rourk.

Chapter Thirty

ROURK

A guttural cry bursts from me as Galene falls.

Blood seeps from her stomach and stains her clothes. Horror and rage fuel me. I charge at Thanek with a sword in one hand and a spear in another. I can't think about losing Galene. I channel the anger and lash out, striking with my sword and swinging the spear.

Thanek blocks or avoids my attacks, and the ones that land on him do no damage at all. But that thrumming sensation is no longer jarring me. I realize, as I duck under his sword, that something has changed. Galene has done something to him.

Thanek strikes out and the sword gets knocked from my hand, so I spin the spear in a flourish and bring it down into his boot. The spear tip pierces the boot and causes Thanek to jerk and reel back.

Relief floods me as I side step a swing of his sword while he staggers away. He *has* been weakened. His attacks have slowed slightly, as well. Galene harming herself has removed some of his power.

That's it. Thanek's bloodline. It needs to go. Removing his family will weaken him and allow us to defeat him. That's what Aldus had implied, and what Galene was trying to tell me in her last moments.

But Thanek is enraged and I know he's still too powerful of a foe. He slams his sword down, and I jump away in time to feel the rush of air and the shockwave behind me as the blade strikes the roof.

I spare a glance at Galene's fallen body and my blood runs cold. Did she just move? I can't be certain. I need to stay focused on my enemy. Tears sting my eyes as I fight.

It's then that I see someone is watching us from a nearby roof. Across the street, on a lower building, is Aldus. Nearby flames on the street highlight him in a blood-red light. He's been watching us this whole time. Waiting for Thanek to consume Galene's power. The man is a monster. The sight of him churns my stomach and floods me with dark anger. I can tell he's proud of himself for getting the better of me with his earth manipulation magic. He thinks he's better than everyone.

I duck and roll under Thanek's next sword strike, and as I come up, I run to the edge of the roof. I let my spear fly with a heavy grunt. Aldus has a second to register the trajectory before the spear pierces his chest and pins him to the roof.

Weaken the bloodline. Weaken the enemy. So be it.

Thanek growls with anger as he comes to me. I snatch up a sword and then roll to collect a second sword as a wave of black magic passes by me. He is weakened. I can feel it. His magic and presence no longer jar me.

"Insolent wretch!" he yells as he swings at me.

I meet him in a flourish of strikes. He is furious and relentless, and my left arm has begun to numb and weaken. Twisting away from his sword swings, I lash out and manage to slice through his shoulder armor. A pauldron drops to the roof with a heavy thud. Despite my bruises, the blood seeping from several places, and the numbness in my arm, I fight on, fueled with renewed energy. I can no longer feel myself. I just know I have to do everything I can to send this demon back to hell.

While I duck and sidestep two sword strikes, I unleash a quick succession of attacks with both swords to slice through Thanek's thighs and shins. That will slow him down even more. One of my swords gets stuck in his leg and I lose my grip on it.

A wave of black energy crashes down on me, but I twist to the side and drop to the ground, letting it crack through the roof. I come across a spear on the ground. Now's my moment. I throw the sword at Thanek's face, causing him to deflect it with his broadsword. As he does so, I spring up with the spear. He moves faster than I expected and a torrent of burning black light erupts like a rupture of water from the roof. It knocks me into the air and breaks the spear in two. Crippling pain grips me as I'm thrown upward amid the gushing black flames, my bones trembling and muscles burning.

I fall back toward Thanek with the two pieces of spear on either side of me. Before the tumultuous agony overwhelms me and I pass out, I snatch the spear tip from the air and slam it down into the flesh of his neck. A beam of black energy shoots out from the puncture and throws me off him. I hit the roof hard and look up to see Thanek staggering back, his steps faltering. He drops his enormous broadsword and falls to his knees, the spear tip still in his neck.

Thanek reaches a weak hand up to the spear tip, but he is too wounded to grasp it. His helmet is cracked and, as I push myself to my feet, the helmet begins to snap and break apart. It falls in three heavy chunks and thuds onto the roof. A bone-white face is revealed with matted hair the color of straw. He is just a man, who looks no older than me. His face is hardened with pain, gasping for breath with blood sputtering from his mouth. Other than his height, he could be any man I walk by in the streets. Hardly what I expected the Dark King of Old to look like.

Waves of nausea crash through me as his power disperses. He's down. His power is leaving him. But it's not over yet. Life is still in him.

I push myself to my feet and pick up Thanek's broadsword with great effort, managing to get it up and resting on my shoulder. The dark, thrumming energy from it rattles me, but I ignore it as I stand over him. On his knees, he reaches my height. There is a dull melancholy on his smooth face, as if he is waiting for me to strike the final blow. Accepting it. Thankful for it. His lips move as if he's trying to tell me something, but no sound comes out.

Thanek sways in place for a moment, before I bring the broadsword down with a heavy grunt to slice into his torso. The blade slices through his shoulder and almost cleaves off his arm.

A torrent of black energy detonates from him, throwing me off my feet. The power dissolves into the air and vanishes in the night sky. The Dark King becomes a corpse once again.

I lay on my back, gasping for breath and fighting through the pain searing through me. Now the fight is over, my injuries are hitting me at once. But I have enough left in me to push myself up, and I stumble over to Galene's body.

Chapter Thirty-One

ROURK

She looks dead.

But relief floods me and gives me new life when I see Galene is still breathing. She's alive, but barely. I kneel beside her and gather her in my arms, holding her close. I can feel the life fading from her and it poisons my heart.

"No, no, no," I mutter incoherently as I look upon her smooth features, not knowing what to do. The knife is embedded firmly in her stomach. Her blouse is stained with so much blood that it looks entirely red. "Why did you do that?"

Galene sputters and gasps quietly. "I... had to." She swallows, needing a moment to continue. "Is it... over?"

"Yes, yes." I wipe her hair from her face and stroke her cheek. My hands are dirty and bloodied and I leave marks on her face. "It's over. Now you can stay with me. You don't have to go."

Her eyes glaze over for a second. Her lips are dry and cracked, but she tries to grin. "Too late. I think."

I pull her closer to me, not wanting to let her go. Fear and anger roil within me, but they are no match for the grief consuming me. I well up with tears as I take in the depths of her blue eyes.

"Rourk," she breathes. "I love you."

The words hit me hard, like they have cracked open my very being and tugged at my core. Tears fall. My soul feels pained and tortured as I flood with emotion.

"I love you, too." Chills wash through me and shiver my shoulders.

"You are the... The greatest man I have ever known."

I lean down and kiss her brow. "No, no. Galene. Stay with me. Please. Please. I can't lose you."

I'm overwhelmed with grief as I hold her, seeing the life draining from her. All I can do is stroke her cheek and stay with her until the end.

An explosion lights the night sky across the city. The rooftop trembles and the rest of Thanek's army continues to devastate The Kingdom. The sounds of battle ring out all around, coming to me muted and dull, like a distant dream. There are still too many of Thanek's forces. The battle is not over. The city has not been saved.

I should go out there to keep fighting, but I can't let go of Galene. All hope drains from me and weights down my shoulders. We are all going to die. Thanek may be defeated, but his forces are still strong. I can feel the tide of battle swaying in their favor, and the diminishing defenses.

I just want to be with Galene in her final moments. In our final moments. That's all I want.

Galene reaches a weak hand up to touch my cheek. But her shaky hand moves beyond me, and I realize she is pointing into the sky. The first red glow of daylight has blended into the fading night sky. We've fought through the night. I look up to see a blue light in the darkness, like a star falling toward us. My mind is in so much turmoil, I'm not even sure of what I'm seeing.

The blue star grows bigger as it plummets toward the city, leaving a faint trail of light. I watch it shoot down and crash into the city center, throwing out an explosion of blue-white light.

I squeeze my eyes shut and blink back my focus to see tendrils of light billowing out from the impact point. The vibrant tendrils strike into the undead horde and detonate their bodies, exploding them in a bloody, gruesome mess. Hope begins to swell within me.

More stars fall and land throughout the city, blue spheres expanding from their impact points. My eyes adjust as the light around the stars fades, and I see they are not falling stars, but giant birds with sharp beaks and long tails. People are riding these birds. No, not birds. Griffins. Bird-like horse creatures, like from the storybooks. A hundred or so of these people have flown here on these griffins. The riders swoop around the city, throwing down blasts of magic at the undead army. It takes me a long moment to believe what I'm seeing.

Many of the griffin riders are throwing down spears. Somehow, they seem to have an endless supply of spears to throw. And these people are wearing the armor and uniforms of the Oathlands Military. The Oathlands have come. And not a moment too soon. I don't even try to understand how all this is possible.

The battle still rages on as Thanek's forces put up a good fight, but I can see they are on the losing side now.

I smile down at Galene, and she gives me a weak, hopeful smile in return. Her eyes look heavy and distant, telling me she is losing strength.

On a far-off rooftop, the writhing tendrils withdraw into the orb of blue-white light as it begins to fade. A figure is revealed as the light vanishes. It's a red-haired woman in a glowing silver gown. She looks radiant and otherworldly. It's too far to see her clearly, but I know who I'm looking at. Clio De'Kalo. The newly appointed Fae Queen of the Oathlands. That means, I hope, my brother will be near.

Clio calls down to the nearest groups of Shanti People and Kingdom Guards. Though I don't hear her words, her voice sounds soothing and commanding. A part of me had thought I'd never see her again, or anyone from the Oathlands.

Overhead, someone leaps off a griffin and drops to the city. The figure shifts into a larger form before it falls from view. I perk up. I know what that was. *Who* that was.

The crashes of ravenous slaughter echo through the street below. A familiar bestial growl accompanies the monstrous cries and whimpers. That brings a smile to my face.

Something large leaps up and lands on the roof before me. It's a tall bear-like beast, huffing and grunting, its claws dripping with blood. Its wolf-like snout has sharp teeth bared, its golden eyes gleaming. The large form shifts and withdraws, taking the shape of a heavily built man in regal armor and a flowing maroon cape. He is just as

I remember, with his short beard and heavy, brooding brows.

A joyful gasp escapes me. "Brother."

Arthur Bearon comes to us, his steps hurried when his eyes fall upon Galene in my arms.

"You are saved, brother." Arthur's familiar deep voice is a welcome sound. "We are retaking the city."

I swell with relief, feeling the tension seeping from my bones. There is no way the Shanti messenger had reached the Oathlands so soon. "How did you...?"

"We sensed the power surges here," Arthur says. "Well, Clio did. She's proving to be quite resourceful."

"I bet," I say, looking over the griffin riders darting through the sky and the flashes of magic across the city. I hold Galene up. "She needs help. She's dying."

Arthur frowns deeply, but he gives a short, hopeful nod. "We will do what we can. I promise." He looks over at Thanek's downed body and regards me. "You did well, brother. It's a miracle you still live."

I sniff, fighting back the welling of tears. "I don't care about any of that. Please. You have to help her."

Galene sighs quietly, fighting to keep breathing.

Something in my tone gives me away. Understanding dawns in Arthur's eyes. He knows how much I care for this woman. The bond we have.

He darts away and leaps off the building in search of help. No more words needed.

I hold Galene close and caress her face, helpless, as I watch her strength fading. She closes her eyes.

Chapter Thirty-Two

GALENE

I drift out of the darkness and gradually shift into consciousness. I blink against the harsh light. I take several long moments to find my bearings and realize where I am, or what has happened. A pounding in my head dulls my thoughts, and when I try to move, my breath leaves me sharply and pain flares all over.

I'm on my bed, in my family's tent. How did I get here? Someone stirs, and I notice a man sitting on a stool beside me. Rourk is there, with his left arm in a sling. Scratches and bruises cover most of his face and arms, and his flesh is charred and blackened around his left shoulder, showing beneath his shirt.

"There you are." Rourk's voice is deeply familiar and comforting. "Steady. Go slow."

I clear my throat, finding my voice hoarse. "What... happened?"

Rourk gives me a crooked smile that tells me everything is going to be okay, though there is pain in his eyes.

"You're going to be okay. We won. The threat is gone."

My senses come back to me, as does a rising panic. "Leila. Jonah, Milo."

"They're safe. They're out right now, but they're going to be happy to see you awake. The healers told me you should wake up soon. I wanted to be here."

I look around, as best I can without drawing fresh pain through my ribs. A bandage is firmly wrapped around my torso, beneath a floral-decorated blouse. My dress is also fresh and new. Rourk must see the questions on my face.

"You've been out for two days," he says. "We got back early this morning. We lost... ten people. And many more are recovering from injuries. But the world is no longer in danger. We did it."

"I thought I was dying," I wince as I struggle to sit up. "Why am I not dead?"

Rourk helps me gently to sit up against the stack of pillows. "Because you're too stubborn to die. And the Oathland healers got to you just in time. A minute later, and it might've been too late. It appears that healing magic is back in the world. But you need to take it easy. It will be some time before you're back to full strength."

That would explain why my strength has already begun to return. The weariness is gradually drifting from my mind. I gingerly feel the bandage on my stomach. Healed by magic. I'm not sure how to feel about that, but I'm relieved to be alive.

"The Oathlands turned out to be more powerful than we knew," Rourk says. "A combination of griffins and magic helped them reach The Kingdom in time. Clio, the

Fae Queen, led the rescue with my brother Arthur. They would be happy to meet you."

"They are here?" I ask.

"They're with the villagers outside. Do you want to try to stand? See how you feel?"

"I do. But, Rourk," I say, touching his arm. "A moment. I... We said some things before I passed out. I want you to know I meant everything I said. I..."

His smile warms my heart. "I love you, too," he says, and leans down to kiss me.

The taste of him fills me with renewed strength as I hold his head and pull him closer. We both laugh in relief. I've never felt so relaxed and happy before. Nothing on this level of joy.

Rourk gives me a firm look and says he has something he needs to tell me.

"Your father. Aldus." He gives me a serious look. "I'm sorry to tell you. He was killed." He swallows and tenses. "By my hand."

Dark terror grips me. A chill washes over me, numbing everything.

"What happened?" My voice feels miles away.

"I had to weaken Thanek's bloodline. Enough to defeat him," he says. "And I... I had to do it, Galene. I had to kill your father. And he was trying to help Thanek return to power."

Tears well in my eyes, but I don't let them fall.

"I needed your sacrifice to be worth it," Rourk continues, his voice hoarse. "I couldn't lose you for nothing. And I know that you will never be able to look at me the same again. My bloodline has been nothing but poison to yours. And I—"

"That's not true," I whisper harshly, cutting him off. "You did not choose my father's actions."

"I chose mine."

"And your decision was the right one."

"He was still your father," Rourk says. "I know he loved you, with all his heart. Even if he was misguided."

I nod, feeling another chill. "I don't hate you. Just so you know."

A dark look passes over him, making me wonder what he isn't saying.

"Leila knows he died," Rourk says. "I have not given her any of the details, though. I wasn't sure what you wanted to tell her."

"I'll talk to her later. Thank you."

I live in a world without parents. I feel numb and lost, but the compassionate look from Rourk gives me a dull sense of hope.

Rourk helps me to stand with his one good arm. It takes me a while to support myself under my own weight, my body feeling fragile. I manage to walk, careful not to go too fast and bring on a bout of dizziness.

"So this is what it feels like, huh?" Rourk says as he helps me through the tent. "Just like old times."

I grin at him, trying my best to look unimpressed. "Just like old times. It was more fun being the uninjured one, though."

"I would make you some berrybush tea," he grins. "But you'll likely just throw it at me."

"Hey, I threw it at the wall, not at you."

As we make our way through the tent to the bright daylight streaming in through the gaps of the entrance flaps, Rourk tells me how Clio and Arthur have stayed in the Shanti village as honored guests while the rest of the Oathlands soldiers returned home.

I stop him before we exit the tent and turn to face him, pressing myself against him. He wraps his arms around me. We take a moment to just stare into each other's eyes, observing our faces and having an unspoken conversation. We smile at each other, and then kiss.

I want to stay in his arms and be with him forever. There's nothing I've ever wanted more. I wince when a wave of pain hits me. Rourk looks at me with concern. "You need to take it easy, my love." He kisses me on the forehead lovingly. "We need to get you back to bed."

I pull away, but grab his hand. "Just a few minutes. I want to see a few people first."

The warmth of familiarity and comfort overwhelms me when we step out into the village. It almost looks like the world hasn't almost come to an end. But there is a heavy tension in the air that speaks of grieving and loss, mixing with the joy of victory.

I smile and give a small wave at the familiar faces who stop to look at me. It's good to be back.

Rourk's brother Arthur is a very large, muscular man with a short salt-and-pepper beard and intense eyes. He has the look of a king about him in his regal uniform and long cape. I see that haunting good looks run in the family.

"It's a pleasure to meet you," Arthur tells me, gently shaking my hand. "And a relief to see you up and about."

His searching eyes remind me of Rourk, as do his heavy brows. "It is a pleasure to meet the King of the Oathlands," I say. "Thank you for saving us."

Arthur gives a wry grin. "Well, I am not actually a King. It is complicated. But close enough."

"Well, whoever you are," I smile back, "It is good to meet you."

Arthur chuckles. "I like her," he says to Rourk. He has that playful, mischievous gleam in his dark and brooding eyes, like Rourk.

Someone calls my name. Leila and the boys are rushing up to me. My heart swells at the sight of them. They swoop me up in their arms and we bounce with joy, holding each other. I fight through the electrifying pain shooting through me so I can keep holding them and enjoy the moment.

"Go easy," Leila scolds the boys for squeezing me too tight. She presses a hand on my hand and thanks Arthur and Rourk for bringing me back.

A look of pained torture constricts Leila's features, though she attempts a small smile. I know the look. Mourning for our father. I wonder what exactly she's been told. Can I ever tell her the truth about our father?

I crouch and ruffle Milo's hair, pulling Jonah closer. "Oh, it's so good to see you all."

"We were so worried about you," Johan whispers in my ear, before kissing my cheek.

I notice Rourk stepping closer to his brother and overhear their discussion.

"I thought my eyes were playing tricks on me," Rourk says. "But I was sure it was Tabetha. She is still missing, right?"

"You saw correctly," Arthur says. "Tabetha was indeed in The Kingdom. Clio told me all about it. We were thinking of a way to go and get her without starting another war. But we found her before we left the city this morning, and she has been returned home. She was with a good family. She was cared for and treated well."

Rourk shakes his head in bewilderment. "That's a relief. How did she end up in The Kingdom?"

Arthur places a hand on Rourk's good shoulder. "A story for another time."

I notice the withdrawn, heavy expressions of the villagers around me. A tense sadness is in the air. We mourn our dead while we celebrate the survival of our world. I'm still acclimatizing to everything and want to ask who we've lost, but I don't think my fragile mind can take that information right now. I still have to accept that my father is no longer with us.

Magdalena and Colm walk over to us, accompanied by a red-haired woman I have not seen before. This newcomer has a petite frame, but she carries herself with a commanding, regal presence, her oval face pale and smooth. Her silver and white corseted gown speaks of royal palaces and grand balls, making her stand out among the rest of us.

The graceful woman steps up to Arthur with a smile. "We have been invited to a celebration festival tonight in the village."

"We will mourn our dead and bless the land, as is our custom," Magdalena says.

"A celebration is in order," Arthur agrees. "The resilience and spirit of the Shanti People is admirable."

Something flashes in my mind. A glimpse of Rourk's thoughts. I hadn't realized I had become so connected to him, or that my ability has developed to this level of ease. What I sense, however, stuns me.

Rourk knows that Magdalena and Colm are the true elders who lead us. Along with Yovin, Abby, and... my father. The elders we know are merely the faces of the true people who have been governing and advising us. I feel like the ground has shifted and I need to collect myself.

Rourk has no intention of revealing what he knows. He sees it as not his business.

My mind races with jumbled thoughts. Our elders have been puppets to the true leaders hiding among us. My father kept so much from me I don't think I ever really knew the man he was. I wonder if my magic has become clearer and stronger after the battle, and if that had a hand in my recovery, accounting for how I've been healing so fast. Have I also become more connected to Rourk? There is a great deal I need to explore once my head stops spinning.

"We hope you can join us," Colm says to Arthur and Clio. "It would be our honor to host you."

"I'm afraid we must be going," Arthur says. "We have a very challenging time ahead and lots to take care of."

"We are in talks with The Kingdom," Clio's voice is smooth. "We may have a chance for a peace treaty. The first of its kind."

Rourk straightens beside me. "Peace between The Oathlands and The Kingdom? Is such a thing possible?" The tension in his voice tells me he doesn't fully support the idea.

"The Kingdom is open to discussion," Arthur says. "The last few days have changed everything. The Oathlands and The Shanti People coming to their aid. This could be the dawn of a new era of peace."

Rourk raises his brows, bewildered. "The world keeps changing."

"It is time for us to return home," Arthur says, turning towards the griffins that are grazing in the field, waiting for them. Curious children watch and play with them.

It suddenly dawns on me that Rourk will be leaving. My throat catches and my chest tightens. Rourk keeps his arm around me.

"It would be a shame to leave before the celebrations," Rourk tells them.

Arthur grins at him. "You have also changed, brother."

"The world is a new place," Rourk says. "We should all get used to change."

Clio is watching us closely with a small smile. "We could stay for some of that stew that smells delicious." She nods to the cauldron over the central campfire, where sister wives are preparing a meal.

I wonder if she suggested staying for the stew because she sensed Rourk's apprehension about leaving.

Magdalena and Colm are happy to host them for a short while before they return home. Jonah asks if Clio could show them a magic trick, which makes them laugh.

A wave of nausea hits me when pain flares in my stomach. Rourk supports me with his good arm.

"I'll join you in a bit," he says to the others. "Galene should rest now."

"I can take her," Leila says.

Rourk gives her a small, reassuring nod. "I've got her."

Leila straightens, her eyebrows rising. She gives us a look that says, *Oh you do, do you?*

Rourk nods to Arthur and Clio. "It really is good to see you both."

Clio gives Rourk a knowing smile. There seems to be a lot of unspoken words between her and Rourk.

"We are glad we could help," Clio says. "Now we know of the Shanti People here, we would be happy to build a trade route and share resources, to help each other."

"Actually," Rourk says. "The Shanti People pride themselves on their independence and prefer to stay out of the affairs of the rest of the world. It's their way."

"Well," Madgalena says. "My mother is an elder, and she was telling us how they have been looking to make some changes. I believe they would be very happy to open channels between us and The Oathlands."

"Please, let us discuss this more over some stew," Colm says. "I will bring the elders. They will be happy to meet you."

Rourk looks stunned. "I guess the world really is changing," he mutters.

He helps me back to my family tent, where we can be alone.

Chapter Thirty-Three

GALENE

Rourk changes the bandages on my abdomen with a small smile on his face.

"That's creepy," I say to him.

He raises an eyebrow at me, but doesn't take his eyes off my torso as he spreads a salve over the wound. "What is?"

"That weird grin you've got going on," I say. "Like you're getting some sick sort of pleasure out of this."

Rourk laughs and shakes his head at me as he gently arches my back for me so he can wrap a fresh bandage around me. His hands are gentle—not the sort of thing you'd expect from a soldier of any position, though the callouses that scrape carefully against my soft skin are no surprise at all. It sends a wave of heat down my spine and my core tightens as I remember the other places those fingers have been. He says, "Not pleasure. I'm just recalling a time when it was me getting salve rubbed in my injuries."

I can't help my smile. "Yes, well, I'm a far better patient than you were."

Rourk is grinning now. "You're just saying that because you couldn't stand the sight of me then."

"You say that as if I can stand the sight of you *now*," I tease.

He grins and gently squeezes my sides. "You haven't stopped staring at me since I lifted your shirt to change your bandage. I'd say you like *more* than just the sight of me, Galene."

"You're the one who saved my life," I retort, though my voice isn't as strong as I'd like it to be. "I'd say that means you like me far more than I like you."

"Oh, I wholeheartedly agree," Rourk replies. "But that wasn't the argument." He winks and stands up, backing away. "You should rest."

I'm protesting before I can stop myself. "Rourk."

He pauses. "Yeah?"

I shake my head. "I don't need rest. And—" I stop the words before they leave my mouth.

But his mouth quirks up, as if he has a good enough idea of what I was about to say. "And what?"

"Nothing."

"Say it," he urges. "Or I'm walking out that door."

I lift my chin, even as I fight the blood that rises to my cheeks. "And I don't want you to leave."

He's smiling again as he strides toward me. Sits down on the edge of the bed. "What *do* you want, Galene?"

The words are heavy in my throat, but they tumble from my lips like stones. With those depthless eyes boring into mine and the potent scent of him washing over me, I can't bring myself to lie, or even tease with him a moment longer. "You."

Those eyes flicker with surprise, as if he didn't expect such a truthful, simple answer. "Galene."

"You've been saying my name a lot," I murmur as I sit up, slowly sliding into his lap. "I can't help but wonder if that means you want me, too."

His words come out rough like gravel. Desire lights my blood. "Of course I want you. I always want you." His hands bracket my waist as he stares up into my eyes. "But you're wounded. I can't—we can't."

I nod slowly. "Yes, we can. I know my limits, Rourk, and I know you'll be gentle with me."

I rake my hands through his hair as he buries his face in my neck and groans. I can feel his hardness growing beneath me. "We shouldn't."

"Of course we should."

"It's going to make things... far more complicated between us."

"Impossible," I murmur, tugging at the handful of strands between my fingers. I start to rock my hips slowly, creating just enough friction.

He sucks in a breath. "You're a terrible influence."

"I disagree. But we can talk about that later," I whisper in his ear, pressing a kiss just beneath the lobe. I'm still rolling my hips as I tilt my mouth upward and say, voice sultry, "Please, Rourk. I want you to peel my clothes off layer by layer. I want you to lay me back and spread my legs and—"

"Fuck," he groans, and then his mouth is on mine.

Rourk doesn't waste a moment before slipping his tongue between my lips, tasting me, gliding his tongue against mine.

He pulls back just long enough to growl, "If I hurt you, you fucking say so." Then his lips are pressed against mine once more, and one of his hands slides under my clothes and up against my core. I gasp when he pushes my underwear aside and slides his fingers through my folds, groaning against my lips at the wetness he finds there. "How long has your pussy been begging for me like this?"

Our mouths tear apart when my head falls back as his index finger finds my clit. "Since you first walked in," I confide. I'd give him any truth he asked for if it meant he'd keep touching me like this.

He laughs roughly against my skin as he kisses and nips at the base of my neck. "Never say you hate me again, Galene. We'll both know you're lying."

He rotates his hand so that he can slowly stretch at my entrance, and my hips are helping him with it, unable to keep from grinding down against his fingers. The hand that isn't pressed against my most sensitive part slides under my shirt and lifts it off my body with little help from me. A noise leaves the back of Rourk's throat when he sees that my bare breasts were the only thing beneath it.

Slowly, his mouth trails sucking, biting kisses down to my breasts. While that free hand takes my right breast and kneads it, flicks and pinches the nipple, his mouth descends on the other, leaving wet kisses on it. He blows cool air from between his lips that instantly hardens it even further, almost painfully so, before he goes back to his gentle licks and kisses.

Rourk thumbs my clit once before finally sinking a finger inside of me. I let out a high-pitched sigh, unable to keep the noise from escaping. He rolls his own hips to pitch us at a different angle and create friction between our bodies. I gasp, then, as the hot electricity that spears through me gets my hips moving again. I balance my arms on his shoulders, wrapping his hair in my hands again as I move my hips, gasping breaths falling from my lips.

"That's it," Rourk murmurs against my breast. "Take what you need, Galene. Use me to make yourself come."

"Rourk," I whimper, my movements becoming faster, shakier.

"What do you need, love?" he asks, and I look down to see him peering up at me from beneath his lashes, a look of pure desire in his eyes. He gives my breast a tender, open-mouthed kiss. "Tell me."

"A second finger." My breath hitches as I keep rolling my hips. "Please."

Rourk bucks his hips once more, and I slide off his finger for just a moment before sinking back down. I instantly feel that he's indeed added a second finger. "Yes," I gasp.

I start pulling his shirt off through the haze of my pleasure and Rourk helps me, pulling away from my breasts just long enough to get it off and toss it on the floor before he's descended again. And this time, when he bucks his hips, I sink back down just in time to feel him curl and angle his fingers deeper. Right against that spot that, as my walls clench and he flicks my clit, has my orgasm barreling through me, so heavy and full and deep that it feels never-ending, feels like I'll never stop crying his name and writhing on his fingers as his teeth scrape my nipple and he lays me back against the bed.

Rourk slides his hand out from my underwear and licks his fingers while I watch, then slowly lays me back on the bed while I shake with the aftershocks of my climax. He tenderly peels the rest of my clothes off before removing his own.

Rourk lowers his mouth to mine as he hovers over me. I taste myself on his tongue when he slips it into my mouth once more. Then, against my lips, he whispers, "You can't possibly understand how much you mean to me, Galene." Then he's kissing me again as he slowly guides himself inside of me.

I think I understand, as he slowly rolls his hips, arms flexing with his restraint as he does everything he can to not do something that will hurt me and my wound. As he groans with pleasure at even that slight movement.

I arch my hips and angle him inside of me deeper. My hands latch around the back of his neck and I watch as he pulls out and slides back in, listening to the delicate sighs that fall from me, waiting to hear an ounce of pain but slowly beginning to thrust harder and faster when he doesn't hear it.

I meet his hips with mine, rolling and pushing and pulling as we find a rhythm between the two of us. Rourk slips his hand between our bodies and finds my clit, giving it lazy, teasing flicks each time he presses himself into the hilt. I gasp each time we meet and fight the urge to beg when we pull apart, feeling the release building within me once more.

And when he suddenly changes the angle and I clench on him, I find it, just as he does, too. We come together, limbs shaking, groans coming from him and whimpers from me.

When we're both still, when Rourk pulls out of me and drops onto the bed beside me, immediately wrapping me in his arms and pressing a kiss to my sweat-slicked shoulder, he whispers, "I can't leave you again, Galene."

"You hardly left before," I whisper.

"I know," he says. "That was difficult enough."

The words are almost a plea. "Then don't leave me."

Another gentle kiss. "I can't. I won't."

Chapter Thirty-Four

ROURK

I lead Galene back to her tent, where she can rest. Strained thoughts wrack my mind, as I know these will be my last moments in the village. "Will you tell me about your daughter?" she asks.

I blink away my surprise. "You really want to know?"

She smiles. "Of course I do."

My chest tightens at her expression, at the earnest honesty in her voice. So I say, "Her name is May. She... she doesn't know I'm still alive yet. Arthur wants to be the one to break the news. The thought of her, my beautiful, caring, kind girl, devastated because of me is... unbearable." I swallow thickly and continue, "Not a day would go by that she wouldn't smile. She has a very big heart. Cares far more for others than she does herself, which worries me, but... she gets it from her mother. Same as the stubbornness." I can't help the smile that forms.

"She sounds lovely."

"She is." I throw an arm around Galene's body, fighting back a wince. She sees it anyway.

"Are you okay? How's your arm?"

I sigh, tempted to lie but knowing that there's no use in it. She'd just poke and prod until I gave her the truth. "Still hurts. But it's bearable. I'm fine, really."

"Are our healing salves helping?"

I nod. "Very much." I pause, then add, "But a little whiskey from the Oathlands would help even more." I give her a teasing smile.

She smiles back, but there's something else in her expression that I can't quite decipher. "Are you looking forward to being back home?" Galene asks as we sit by the dinner table, the sounds of the village fading within the tent. I sit myself on the same side of the table as her, so that our knees are close together. It's so easy to be close and comfortable with her now, like all of our barriers are down.

"I am," I say. "And I'm not."

Her eyes are filled with unspoken words. I can feel how hard this is for us.

"I will miss the ways of your people," I continue. "And the simpler life. But I was always going to go home. I can't stay here."

She perks up, her face hardening. "Who asked you to stay?"

I grin at her. "No one. I'm not assuming anything. I didn't mean to-"

She chuckles. "You are cute when you're unsure of your words."

"And you are just cute," I reply, grinning down at her.

We hold each other's gaze for a long moment. I realize how much I'm going to miss her. And I realize there's no way I can let her go.

But before we go on, I have to reveal the truth to her. Even if I know it's going to make her hate me. She has to know the truth.

"I have something I need to tell you," I say, my heavy voice telling her this is going to be serious. "About your mother."

She grows tense.

"I told you before I had heard the name of the Oathlander, but did not know the man. Which is true, in a sense. There is a lot that I don't know about my father."

Galene freezes. "Your... father?"

I nod, squeezing my hands into fists to keep them from shaking. "Delton Alacante." The last name feels foreign on my tongue. Arthur and I hardly ever speak it. "Alacante was my last name, before my brother and I disbanded from the royal line and took our mother's maiden name instead."

She inhales deeply, but says nothing.

"I know I should have told you sooner. Immediately, even. But you had just started looking at me as if I was more than an enemy, and I... I didn't want to go back. I couldn't risk ruining what was between us."

She holds a hand in the air. "Hold on a moment, Rourk," she murmurs. "I need to think."

I nod and fall silent, though words pile up on my tongue. Apologies. Explanations. Excuses. I force them all back down my throat before I can blurt them out.

Galene is silent and reserved for a long moment, not showing any anger. Which unnerves me even more. A dark, withdrawn aura surrounds her.

Eventually, she says, "The sins of our parents should not govern us. I know there is a lot about my family I did not know about. Same for you and yours. I... I'm tired of hating your people, Rourk. I'm tired of feeling so much hate and anger. It eats away at me. It consumed me for so long. I'd forgotten what it was like to be happy until I grew closer to you. Until you reminded me what being safe and comfortable and happy felt like. I want..."

She clears her throat when her voice falters. "I want to be happy. But I don't know if I can. I don't know how to be happy anymore. To be honest, I don't even know who I am anymore. I've been living in lies my entire life."

I take her hand on the table and grip it gently. She squeezes back.

"I don't hate you, Rourk. I wouldn't want anyone to hate me for the actions of my father."

"You are a remarkable woman," I say. "I can... I mean, I could try to help you figure things out. I could stay. Well, I want to stay. But I know I can't." I shake my head. "I don't know what I'm saying."

"I know," she says quietly, watching me carefully. Our eyes are glued to each other.

"Do you think your daughter would like me?" she asks, breaking the silence.

My heart jolts. "She would love you."

My pulse rises as we stare at each other, having our own unspoken conversation. Is she saying what I think she's saying?

"It occurs to me that you Oathlanders may like to have a representative of The Shanti People, to help build the relationship between our people." Galene has an overly innocent look on her face.

The corners of my mouth rise. I lean closer to her. "I think that's a good idea."

"Purely for the sake of our people, you understand. I could be an Advisor for the Shanti People."

"Chief Advisor."

She cocks an eyebrow.

I shrug. "It sounds better."

"How about General Commander Advisor?" she suggests with a wicked grin.

That makes me laugh. "We'll work on that."

We've been inching closer to each other for some time. Our faces draw close enough for me to feel the pull of her, and how much we desire each other. How much we need each other. There is no way we're going to part.

"What about Leila?" I ask. "And the boys?"

"I know," she says, her brows creasing. "I will miss them. But I'm sure I will be visiting here as often as I can. They'll understand. There is nothing else for me here."

"You would move to the Oathlands?" I ask.

Her deep blue eyes draw me in. "I would."

A wide grin spreads across my face. I'm going to be returning home with the woman I love.

"The world certainly has changed," I say, my voice lowering.

"And it keeps on changing," she whispers as we draw close enough to feel each other's breaths.

"One day I'm going to stop being so surprised," I say.

"Not today," Galene mutters.

Our lips meet, and we kiss passionately and hungrily. She straddles my lap and I hold her close as we kiss. I stir at the feel of her. She gently presses herself against me as our passions rise.

She caresses my face as we stare at each other, connecting on a greater level than I've ever experienced.

This really is the start of a new world. And I've finally learned the true purpose of my being brought to the Shanti Village. To find my love.

EPILOGUE

Galene

Two Years Later

Clio and I watch as Rourk and Arthur spar in the courtyard. May watches on the sidelines with her young cousin, each of them cheering on their fathers. Amil, Clio's son, is a quick-witted two-year-old who seems to know too much about everything. May adores him and dotes on him.

Rourk and I are grateful to know she'll feel the same about the child I carry now. We haven't told her yet—we're waiting until after her birthday, so she can have one final year to herself.

Clio grins at me. "Arthur cannot wait to be an uncle, you know."

"Oh?" I ask.

She nods, laughter dancing in her eyes as she glances at me, then at my stomach, before turning back to her husband. Love glows in her eyes. "Yes. He plans to teach your young one every cuss word he can think of just to piss Rourk off."

"Can't wait," I reply, joking.

Clio grins. "Rourk did the same with Amil. It's only fair."

"I suppose you and I just get caught in the crossfire."

"And we wouldn't have it any other way, would we?"

I shake my head. No, we wouldn't. This life, though far different from the one I thought I would lead, the one where I imagined myself spending every day until my death in the Shanti Tribe, is the one I was destined for. I feel it in my bones. I was meant to be here, with Rourk and May and Clio and Arthur. We were meant to start this new generation of family, to bring peace between our people and make this world far greater than it has been in centuries.

But most of all, we were meant to love.

Rourk and I were meant to find each other. We were meant to fall in love, to marry each other beneath the sunset tucked within the branches of a willow tree with nobody but our family surrounding us. I was meant to meet May, to hear her call me Ma for the first time and to carry her sibling in my belly a year later. I was meant to find a profound friendship with Clio and a brotherly sort of fondness for her husband.

Love comes in so many different forms. But it is always powerful.

And it will always be what saves us in the end.

WHAT'S NEXT

Thank you for reading *The Lost Guard's Healer!*
Did this book give you all the feels?
Reviews are the high-fives of the literary world, and you'd be my hero by leaving one. Only a small percentage of readers take the time to leave reviews—you could be among that exceptional group who helps others discover the magic within these pages.
Plus, they make my day. So, please share your thoughts! Or even just taking a few seconds to drop a star rating is hugely appreciated! You should see one right about this point in the book....
- Alexa

Also, if you started this duet with this book and want to learn about Arthur and Clio's journey, you can read it all in The Bandit Lord's Captive!

Did you enjoy this book? Want to see more of my books? Then you'll LOVE **The Forbidden Royal Mates Series**, a completed series of 4 a full-length enemies-to-lovers, fake fiancé romance books.

Here's a sneak peek of the first book, *Bargain with the Witch Prince*—

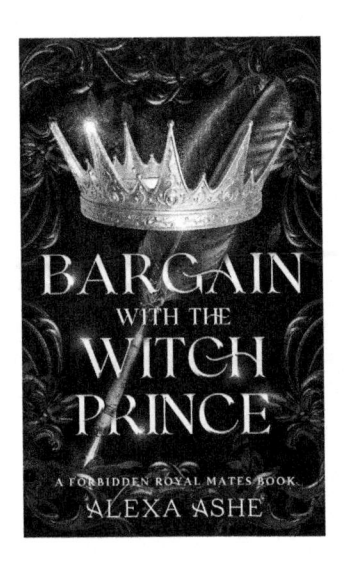

"Unbutton your shirt," she demands.

I grin at her. "I do like a woman who knows what she wants."

She glares at me as I undo the buttons and then pulls my arm out of the black sleeve. Joula's warm fingers lightly glide over my skin, feeling for any injury. I hiss when her fingers skate over the back of my bicep, and she frowns as she twists my arm and her head to get a better angle. I angle my face toward my back too, trying to catch a glimpse.

I see dried blood, but that's it.

"This is a pretty big gash," she mutters. "You've probably lost a lot of blood." Her eyes flick down to the couch and the new bloodstain that goes with the grossly out-of-style orange cushion.

"You didn't see it before?"

"There was a lot more wrong with you, and your shirt was black. How would I have noticed?"

"... Fair point."

Slowly, I feel my skin wind back together; the pain dissipating with the wound.

I stare at her, eyes wide. "It really was you. How'd you do it? How are you healing me?"

Joula rolls her eyes and backs away. "If you've got nothing else I need to fix, you can leave. Just head east for a mile or so and you'll be back in the city. Goodbye, Prince Kell," and she disappears down a dark hallway before I have the chance to answer her.

Read more in Bargain with the Witch Prince – Book One in the Forbidden Royal Mates series today!

ALSO BY

Did you like this book? Love Romantasy too? Then you'll want to grab *Cursed in Love.* It is a story of enemies to lovers and forbidden love, with a curse, a prince and the witch who caused it all.

You can get your FREE copy by signing up at: http://author.alexaashe.com/freebook

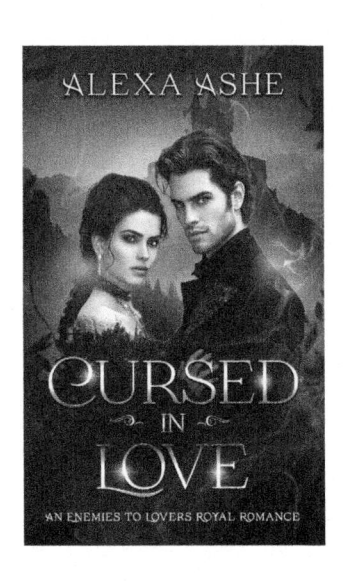

Witch Elara Nightshade has been in hiding her whole life in an anti-witch kingdom. When she's tricked into cursing Crown Prince Darius, binding their souls, she's forced into his world.

Their initial clash, fueled by years of mistrust and betrayal, slowly morphs into a magnetic pull, drawing them closer. And with every moment spent together, the intensity of their forbidden connection grows.

The witch, marked by magic and mistrust, finds in him an enemy who becomes her only ally.

The Prince, trained to despise the witch, discovers in her a soul that mirrors his own.

Together, they must navigate a curse that draws them irresistibly together and challenges their beliefs, but can they survive a love that seems destined by fate?

Cursed in Love is a steamy forbidden love fantasy romance novella, recommended for ages 18+ due to language and sexual content. It's a full-length standalone book with a happily ever after and a lead-in to the next couple's book.

ABOUT AUTHOR

I've always been fascinated by the magical worlds that exist only in the imagination. In fact, I once tried to cast a spell on my math teacher to make him forget about homework - it didn't work, but it did inspire me to start writing my own stories.

When I'm not busy creating new characters and stories, I'm usually snuggled up with a good book and a hot cup of tea (or a glass of wine, depending on the time of day). Just don't disturb me while I'm in the middle of a particularly juicy chapter - I probably won't even hear you anyway.

I'm inspired by so many things - nature, history, mythology, and the human experience, just to name a few. I pour my heart into every story I write, and I'm always humbled by the positive feedback I receive from readers.

If you've ever read one of my books, thank you from the bottom of my heart - it means more to me than you'll ever know!

Alexa Ashe

https://www.facebook.com/authoralexaashe

Printed in Great Britain
by Amazon